TERRANE

By

Philip Newton

Published by Unsolicited Press
www.unsolicitedpress.com
info@unsolicitedpress.com

Unsolicited Press Books are distributed by Ingram. Printed in the United States of America.

Attention schools and businesses: for discounted copies on large orders, please contact the publisher directly.

Editor: S.R. Stewart
Editor: Sarah Keen
Cover design: Erin B. Lillis

ISBN: 978-1-947021-45-7

To Cindy, who inspires me.

TABLE OF CONTENTS

Chapter One

The highway smoked, shrouded in mountain fog, rising from the pavement in torn sheets and ribbons. Allen Wrangell walked along the highway's edge, footsteps muffled in the still air. There was no traffic and there were no other travelers. He gripped the leather handle of a large, tan suitcase which he shifted periodically from one hand to the other without varying his step, right foot scraping into the gravel drifts at the highway's edge, left foot hitting solid roadway, stepping squarely on the yellow fog line with a numb leather thump. Allen had been walking like this for hours, although it was still early morning. At first, he had stumbled in the darkness but as the light grew he found his way by the fog line. After a while he could see the ghosts of trees and after that, through the thinning mist, the sharp profiles of ridgetops against a lightening sky and the beginnings of pale hues in earth and leaves. Now he walked past narrow meadows, through narrower creek gullies shaded by dripping pine, spruce, and fir. In the wider, flatter places, Allen and the old road passed pin oaks warming their leaves wherever Indian summer broke through. He didn't stop to warm with them. He was already warm, sweating with his efforts, although his deepest marrow remained chilled.

Allen Wrangell was dying. Something in his cells had gone all wrong, so that he could no longer trust them or the work they did. One day he found his body cinched into knots, then leaping up, flapping and trembling, eyelids blinking, jaws clenched and hands shaking, wringing the empty air. Words failed and eyes blurred. Then a torrent of wild strength, the desire to run, keen and ferocious; then exhaustion, days of rest and a slow surfacing into an otherwise unremarkable world. This had been going on for some time: some days worse, some days better, but no good day quite as good as the last.

He didn't know how long it would all take. The day would come when he would not see it. There would be no Next Thing. Now he walked the empty highway, as steady and humorless as a drum major, and his thoughts were not on anything but on the regular machine of feet, hot muscle, legs, lungs, hips, knees, arms, heart, buttocks, nerves, hamstrings, bones, jarring his frame, pitiless but not yet failing him.

As morning deepened the highway mists cleared completely, revealing a pale sky and a sun that poured into the turning leaves of the creekside maple and birch. This was high foothill country, where the season changed early. Allen paid no attention to the scenery at all until, cresting a hill, he passed through a road cut and slowed his pace. He looked to his right, peering at the tumbled rock mélange, then stopped, dropped his suitcase and stepped off the road, into the pebbly ditch. Raising his eyes, he searched the road cut, crevice, and knob.

"Cretaceous, metasedimentary." He walked along the road cut. "The islands out there in the Pacific moved east and our great stone island moved west. Then we smashed into each other and here we are. Still moving, everything always moving."

As he ran his hands along the glossy green stone, the crumbling marine edges and sharp, twisted bands of shale, Allen recalled another morning, back in the Bay Area, when he had encountered a shopping cart wraith outside his apartment building, one of the countless ragged mumblers prowling the city sidewalks as if forever running late for an important engagement. This man had stopped, though, and looked at Allen from under his hood with shaded eyes, bearded mouth moving soundlessly. Then he pointed at him, grimy finger extended and steady. In a voice Allen found unexpectedly pleasant the man said, "The now that we are is already was. The will be is just going by."

Allen continued to rub and scratch the rock face, picking out fragments of mica and wafers of schist, the words of the homeless revenant echoing in his mind. They made sense to him now when he laid his hands on this slice of planet, able to touch in a handbreadth eras separated by millions of years and laid down or thrust up in mountains, bays and rivers long gone, on continents and seas that had flickered and faded in a relative instant of time.

He stopped and wiped his face. It was warm here, and the road cut reflected back heat mingled with an odor both rich and bitter, a familiar ocean scent, as if these jumbled stones had just risen from the deep.

Scrambling out of the ditch, Allen resumed his march. Downhill, crossing a faded green girder bridge that spanned a deep, granite-choked riverbed where ice jade waters hissed. A few cars now passed, and big, dirty log trucks, grumbling. Allen didn't notice them or look down into the river gully. Aiming straight ahead, he pounded up the grade from the bridge, passing a sign that said *Forester 10 Miles.* He kept moving.

Allen had wrecked his car, plowing the ordinary brown sedan sharp right into a steep embankment and not, fortunately, going left and down an equally steep drop. He didn't know how it happened. The road took a turn one way and Allen went the other, hitting the mossy wall at an oblique angle. Just before he'd lost control, however, he recalled struggling with the wheel. More than that: he had fought with his own left hand, which seemed determined to wrench the car to its own will, and he lost the contest.

It occurred to Allen that when a car is crashing and one is inside it, the moment passes so quickly that it slows to a practical stop. Gravity and friction are suspended as car and driver hurtle unrestrained and silent serenity prevails, a clear drop of moment ripped from past and future, eternal in speed; one hangs there in the hush and that's all that there has ever been.

That was how Allen remembered it, right up to the moment that the car struck the embankment and the silence exploded in a muffled shriek and boom of sheet metal and shattered glass. His vision flashed white as he was punched pack by the blunt pop of the airbag. All suspended physical laws resumed in full, demanding instant compliance. Tossed between object and spent force, coming to rest in the driver's seat, he'd sat listening to broken steam whistle of the radiator and the tick and clang of decompressing car frame. Cold air mingled with the fog of maple sweet engine coolant poured through the ruptured windshield, snapping him back into an early morning smashed-up roadside world, lit by one headlight.

Then he'd started walking. His suitcase nudged his leg as he went, trying to stay on the road. There was blood in his mouth. He knew he'd be sore, but he was all right, not seriously injured and moving along as quickly as he was able.

And now as he crested the last ridge he stopped and dropped the suitcase, breathing in the resinous mountain warmth. The balsam rose in his head and he felt drugged, but full of quick energy. He stood a long moment on the ridgetop, letting the sun dry his sweat. Once again, the car crash replayed itself in his mind. He looked down at his hands, at his left hand in particular, and not for the first time asked himself, had this hand acted on its own volition? And if so, had it pulled the wheel toward safety or tried to steer the car into a wreck?

It was afternoon when Allen began the switchback descent into a mountain prairie, flat, round and golden-gray, except for a lush band that marked the course of a river that curved through the grasses. Coming around a bend in the highway, he saw, still some distance away, a town straddling both sides the river and running up onto the hills that bounded the left side of the prairie. From this distance it looked alien, opposed to the land around it, smudged, with windows glittering dully here and there.

As the road dropped, pine and fir gave way to alder, willow, and cottonwood. Granite receded, and ochre, tame soils rose around him. Allen looked ahead at the town, growing larger and more in-focus with each footstep. He saw now that it was one of a series of failed timber and gold mining propositions, fading unnoticed in the high valleys. The buildings were old, and some had been grand but were no longer. Wood, stone, brick, and galvanized metal prevailed. No one had thought it worthwhile to build a burger franchise or a chain store here. There was a noticeable absence of plastic signs and the old neon ones were subdued, humbled by many winters, and now dimmed by the autumn sun. Stolid poverty drifted around the corners as Allen entered Forester from the south, his pace unwavering.

As with most other foothill towns, the highway was Forester's main street, and Allen walked it north, taking the sidewalk between plate glass storefronts and diagonally-parked cars and trucks. He ignored the restaurants, hardware store, bars, and nail parlors, and all the people going in and out of them. Once only he allowed his gaze to wander, darting quickly to a small office across the street with gold lettering on the glass announcing, *Liz Terry, Attorney.*

Allen looked quickly away, observing now the street signs as they approached. He walked several blocks until he saw one that said Jefferson. Rounding left, past a sandstone bank, Allen left the highway for the first time and took the steadily-rising street as it passed into a neighborhood of small houses. Here the trees were old and large, thick with yellow, crimson and silver, the leaves beginning to loosen, painting the sidewalks, streets, and tired housetops with sharp daubs.

After some blocks, the houses on the right gave way to a steep bluff overlooking the river. The street, still climbing, followed the river for a few blocks until, veering left and sharply uphill, it doubled back across the face of the slope.

At the edge of town, where the houses were fewer, the yards larger and the tawny fall fields encroached, Allen stopped in front of a large two-story home surrounded by an old wire fence. The leaves were even more vivid here. They stood out crisp in vermillion and lemon against the house's faded chalky paint. They fell thickly on the porch roof that ran the entire front of the place. Allen could see comfortable chairs perched behind the front railing, and large French doors reflected the blaze of the leaves in the yard. Over the door, a wooden sign said, *Maria's*.

He opened the complaining gate and went in.

"Your room is upstairs, all the way down the main hall, on the left."

"Thank you."

Maria stood by the stair railing in the hall, outside the old-fashioned front sitting room. She had a bucket in her hand, with rags and spray bottles spilling out. Behind her, the house rambled into dim spaces punctured by warm sunlight: a buttery kitchen, a second, larger living room, more halls, more doors, with brass oval handles gleaming dully.

"There's still some lunch, if you like."

"Oh, I'm good, thank you."

Allen thought she was about forty years old, but she could have been older or younger. She didn't look like her name. Her hair was black, and her face was pale and sharp-boned, but her eyes were round and jet, like two stones set there. She was slender. She looked right at him with those round eyes, and that didn't bother him as much as it might have. It didn't bother him at all. She stood, holding her green plastic cleaning bucket with the rags and gloves and bottles spilling out and she watched him, as if waiting for something. He tried to think what it was she had waited for, and for how long. He felt he should have brought a gift. In the silence he heard a patter of leaves, blown onto the roof by a passing breeze.

"You have your own back door. In your room, I mean."

He stirred and shifted his suitcase. He looked around as if waking up. He looked at Maria. She made him think of the Andes, of Peru, the eastern slope going down into the warm endless tangle of the Amazon, but she, still standing in the high places, looking down from there, waiting for something. He wanted to tell her that, that he saw her looking down from the stone towers of the Andes and he laughed inside, thinking how she might reply. He resisted saying anything, except to thank her.

"It goes out to the deck, this door, and there are stairs down. Your key works on this door, also."

"Oh, good. Sorry I'm a little late. Car trouble."

"Oh, no problem. Is your car back in town?"

Allen looked away. "No. It's—no, it's not."

"It's not."

"No."

Maria moved slightly away. Allen saw it. She no longer looked at him. Her eyes reflected the panes of the French doors, each one ignited with leaf glow. "Is it a long way—"

"I left the Bay Area early. I was going to check out some of the BLM roads, so I left myself a lot of time." He shifted his tan suitcase again, to the opposite hand.

Maria relaxed. A slight movement, or none at all. A minuscule change of expression, but Allen noticed. She smiled slightly, and she no longer looked forty. The smile released something young in her high bones. "Oh, well then. Will you need someone to go get it?"

"No. No, I'm here, it's good."

"But your car."

Allen's shoulder ached and stung. There was a space behind and below his ears where his skull joined the neck that pulsed hollow like an electric drum: a nasty, snapping, acid reverberation that dizzied and dulled him. He tried to think about what could be causing this. He could not. He saw shattering glass. He heard the crunch and shrieking twist of metal and there was a stinking hot hiss.

He said, "The car might not be worth worrying about."

"I see. Well."

Allen looked up the stairs to where sunlight lit the long hall. "I'll just go up then. To my room."

Maria straightened. "Yes, yes, make yourself at home. The bath has everything you need. There's coffee in your room. Please." She gestured toward the stairs with her free hand. "Just give me a ring if you need anything."

"I will. I will, thank you"

Allen's room was large and open, with windows and a glass-paned door that looked west. He placed his suitcase on the bed and pulled the curtains aside. Beyond Maria's back yard small farms and ranches occupied the slope to the foot of the western mountains, which were already casting a shadow over the grazed flats and blackberry hedges. He stood a long time, leaning on the desk that sat under the window, then sighing, he turned and opened his suitcase.

There was not enough room in the tiny bathroom cabinet for Allen's pill bottles, so he put them in the desk side drawer, standing them up in orderly rows. He finished unpacking and lay on the bed, watching the shadows lengthen over the land. The room grew brighter as the sun looked in. Allen noticed that all the pictures on the wall were Gauguin reproductions: brown women resting, reclining, eating tropical fruit;

Gauguin himself, anxious, alert, and world-weary. He wondered if Maria chose the pictures, and why. He thought he might ask her. In the warm light, their tropical lushness grew and made him drowsy. His eyes closed, and he heard his own voice, speaking in the odd echoes of dream.

"Hell, if one believes Jesus, is simply outer darkness. There will be wailing and gnashing of teeth. Jesus said this more than once. He might have wanted us to be sure. But the customary view of hell has a lot of flash and bang. This current vision has fluorescent lighting. It has desks, mail slots, a soda machine. It has old magazines with the names and addresses of the subscriber blotted out. It has an all-night chicken drive-through. It's aggravating. But it wouldn't be so bad to stumble around a placid sort of hell; a single street lamp, out on its own, for no reason whatsoever, a lonesome light, lighting nothing. It would not be so bad to hear wailing and gnashing of teeth on some empty highway, by some razor-wire maintenance station where the gate is always locked and the machines are melting into the ground. It would be tolerable to have a hell that was easy on the eyes, even if it meant barking your shins now and then. There is nothing written that says hell can't be restful."

The room was utterly featureless when Allen opened his eyes. It was a moment before he knew his eyes were open and a moment longer before he could remember where he was. Remembering didn't help very much. He was lost, alone, naked to the unseeing, silent eyes. Every muscle ached, and he knew he had missed his evening meds. He sat up slowly and gingerly swung his legs over, grunting without meaning to. He stood, adjusting to the strange space, waiting for it to quit spinning. Stepping over to the desk, he switched on the little green-shaded brass lamp and opened his pill drawer.

The hall outside his room was empty. Allen couldn't see downstairs, but he heard no voices, no sounds at all. The house was softly lit, and he thought of that lonesome light, revealing nothing to no one. He wondered if Maria had other guests. Returning to his room, he shut and locked the hall door, then put on his old trench coat and stepped out onto the deck, locking the outside door behind him.

He was instantly struck by the crowded cold, when everything he had just left inside was warm, glowing, and empty. It was not empty out here. The night was full of living voices, hunting things, their language not less cowing, stern or urgent because it wasn't human, but more so—insistently so—smelled, heard, felt hard against his awake skin. He breathed the language of the things around him, expecting at any minute that they would strike him down, claw his yielding middle, drag him to some place, to those western mountains with their roots sunk into long-cold plutons. It didn't seem like a bad way to go.

Allen had to pass the kitchen on his way around the house to the front gate. He kept well away from it, but could see inside. Maria stood in there, washing something in the sink. He paused in the shadows and watched her. It was as if she swam in tropical water, in some other land. She might be on one of those bright, hard stars up there, so icy and blue, but with mild pools for bathing, full of silent brown Gauguin women. She might be washing dishes in some other century, the last one or the one before that, patiently washing and waiting for what the world and the heavens might bring. He wished again that he had brought her some gift. He wanted to go around to the front door and pretend he was coming in, not going out. He wanted to see if it was she who had chosen those paintings for his room, and why. He wanted to stay and watch her, to be as she was, belonging in that night kitchen. Instead, his feet started up again, taking him past the kitchen, past the old-fashioned front room with no one in it, past the porch light, up the old cement walk and out through the ancient wire gate, swinging open with its low complaint, then closing with a snap and hum behind him.

The sidewalk in front of the house was lit by streetlamps which, although few, drove back the night voices and maintained a grudging silence. As the street descended back into town, the lights became regular and ordered, filling up the air as if wild mountain night didn't press in from all sides and there was no such thing as the howling wolf odor and medicine leaf moan rising from the roots of trees and crack of stone. The house comfort he passed made him more and more a ghost. Each warm bungalow seemed to turn away from his approach and he haunted them, more with every step.

They made each other lonely, the cream-colored windows and the tall, thin man in a long coat. The rhythm of his long highway walk resumed, beating a wan march. By the time he reached that sandstone corner bank, Allen guessed, he would be invisible.

This is the going away, he thought, in time with his march. *This is how we walk out of the world.* He looked ahead and saw an approaching storefront, the first business on Jefferson before it intersected with Main Street. He wondered if he would see himself if he looked in the window. He began to believe that he might not.

It was a saloon, one of the many faded neon places he'd seen on the way in. He hadn't noticed this one, however, wedged between the stone bank and the first houses on Jefferson, an unlit alley on its right keeping it a little apart from the neighborhood. The neon over the door stuttered *Pete's Place* but the smoky letters on the plate glass said *Joe's*. As he passed the window, Allen looked to see if he might not be seen. But he was there, wrapped in black linen, too thin and not yet old, hair like straw, sharp eyes peering back at him from the depths of Joe's, or Pete's, or whatever the place was.

And looking out from behind his own translucent face, just inside the glass, the real face of a bartender was turned toward him. He was wiping a glass, one elbow leaning against the long bar, which ran straight back from the street. Other than the bartender, Allen saw only empty tables and deserted barstools. No one crouched over a drink. No couples leaned against each other in boozy waltzes. It was twilit, a place which invited things to remain still a moment—that collected such moments, storing them, hiding them in the back with the bottles. The dark-eyed bartender looked neither old nor young. Like Maria, he might have been doing his chores in another century. Allen wanted to go in, but he knew that it was not possible, no more than it would be to go to that night kitchen on the star where Maria washed her dishes.

Ghost-glass Allen and the ageless bartender traded eyes a moment, then Allen turned and walked on, rounding onto Main at the stone bank and heading south, back the way he'd come that afternoon, if that afternoon it had been. There were only a few cars and trucks in the diagonal parking spaces. No one except Allen walked the street, and he had an immediate sense that, in this moment, the town was his own, something he had inherited and did not want. Backtracking a few blocks, he stopped across from the darkened office belonging to *Liz Terry, Attorney*. He crossed his arms and stood a long time. Then he crossed the street.

It wasn't much of an office: a small reception desk, a couple of comfortable seats, shelves of law books that had likely never been read. There were photos on the wall, sepia, depicting downtown Forester as it had once been—almost exactly as it was now, except the cars and log trucks in the pictures were older. Behind and to the left of the reception desk, partially blocked by a partition, a frosted glass door glowed dimly, washing the office in thin backlight. Allen wondered if Liz Terry, Attorney, was in there, doing late-night lawyer things. He watched and listened a long time for any sign or sound of activity, but there was none. He scanned every inch of the office, from the bland Berber carpet and somber-paneled walls to the acoustic tile drop-ceiling. There was nothing there at all to hint at who Liz Terry, Attorney, really was.

Allen's nose was cold. He realized that it was pressed against the glass and his own gray eyes staring back startled him. He took a step back and looked around. Nothing and no one moved in downtown Forester. The town belonged to him still.

The walk back to Maria's was colder. The sky had deepened into rich mercury, each star standing out, declaring glory. Joe's or Pete's place was closed, nothing but a lamp on the back bar shining now. Allen hurried by, head down, pushing up the hill. Off to his right, down in its cold bed, the river muttered, speaking always of rock, willow, and water. Allen let his footsteps find their voice with the clattering water. He hurried up the last block to Maria's, edged past the lighted porch, past the now-dark kitchen window, up the stairs to the back deck. He listened, but the night voices were silent now. Only the stars pulsed, ripe, ready to fall, each one a world, or many worlds, their regular throbbing beating against the back of his eyes, exactly opposite the hammer of his heart.

It was cold, colder than he'd ever remembered cold being. He unlocked the door and went in.

There had been a dining room at Maria's, off the kitchen, at the back of the house, but it was now a study and Maria served meals at an oak table in a nook of the big kitchen, overlooking the side yard. Allen sat there now, drinking coffee as Maria cooked oatmeal on the big gas stove across from the sink.

She turned and looked at him. He tried to smile. "You have other guests?" he asked.

"It's the end of the season." He wondered what season could visit here, besides the regular four. "Now it's hunting, and those guys aren't much into bed and breakfast." There was that. Hunting season. But it passed Maria's by.

"No boarders or anything?"

"Yeah, an older couple, but they go to San Diego this time of year. I hold their room."

"That's nice of you."

"Oh, they pay a little to hold it. They insist on that. But other than that, the place doesn't earn much after summer. So, this winter I might waitress downtown, get out of the house, you know. I usually work from home, but that's gotten kind of old. But it pays the bills, and DJ does odd jobs." She responded to his inquiring look. "My boyfriend." He nodded. Maria brought the oatmeal. "And what about you, Allen? You and the rocks, huh? That's why you're here."

Allen ate and said nothing for a moment. He didn't look at her. "Rocks."

"Yes. The geology. The rocks."

"How did you know about this."

"You, when you booked the room. You mentioned the—you said you were interested in the rocks here."

Allen stopped eating, spoon hanging in his hand. "Did I." He said nothing else.

Maria stood a moment, until the moment grew awkward, then started to turn away. "Sorry, I—"

"No, that's okay. Yeah, I have an interest in this area, this region. Rocks. Yes. I guess I did tell you that on the phone. It's geologically interesting around here, yes. Unusual. I'm not a geologist. Just like that sort of thing."

Maria stayed by the table. "What's so interesting about this place?"

Allen put his spoon down. "It's not just the rocks themselves, which are always worth looking at. It's how they got here."

She sat. "I didn't think they'd been anywhere but here."

"They've been lots of places. More than most people, some of them. And the places they've been, those places have been places." Allen leaned forward. He held his hands out flat, lapping one over the other. He lowered his voice. "So, the West Coast here, for instance, it's moving. It's moving farther west, a little bit more each year." He slid his right hand over his left. "The continents are on enormous plates, floating on this hot, mushy ball. They're floating around, moving all the time. And the plate we're on is moving west while out there in the ocean the Pacific Plate is moving north and east."

"But they can't both be moving in opposite directions, unless—"

"Yes, something has to give. In this case"—Allen pushed his left hand down with his right—"the Pacific Plate does. As we go riding west, we run over the top of it, and it pushes down, down, down, this huge conveyor belt of rock, down into the world under us." Allen slid his left hand sharply down. "Then the pressure and the friction, the trapped radiation, they heat all that rock up, so much so that big chunks melt and pop back up, through the plate we're riding on. Volcanoes, you know." He pushed the fingers of his left hand through the fingers of his right, waggling them. "And this is where we are. These wiggly fingers poking up here, these are the mountains where you live."

Maria nodded. "All the granite."

"Yes. The volcanoes, the basalt and granite, they came from down there. But they rode in first from the west, on that conveyor belt. And now that belt is also pulling these giant rafts of the Pacific Plate north, along the West Coast. Sometimes the belt gets stuck, or the cracks, the faults, hang up against each other and we get those earthquakes when they let go."

"It came a long way, this land."

"It did." Allen drew close to her. "It did. But there's more rock than that moving around."

Maria's smile faded, and she drew back. Allen turned. A man in a dingy, paint-stained truckers' cap leaned in the doorway between the sitting room and the kitchen. Maria's smile returned, thinner, and she stood.

"DJ. This is our guest, Allen."

DJ walked past the table to the coffee pot by the stove. A rooster walk. "Hey."

Allen's fingers, still conjoined, knit into a ball. "Hello."

Maria went to the stove. "Oatmeal?"

"Nah, I'm going downtown." He swallowed his coffee noisily. "Be back later." He turned and left.

As if from miles away the front door slammed. Maria blinked. That was all, but Allen saw it.

"Off to work, then."

"Hmm? Oh, I guess. Someone needed something moved, he said."

"Ah." Allen stood and brought Maria his coffee cup and bowl. "Thanks for breakfast."

"You didn't eat much. Is that all you really want? Just oatmeal?"

"Yeah, that was great. Thank you. Woke me up."

She put the dishes in the sink. He wanted to stay and watch her, but he edged away, toward the hallway door.

She wiped her hands on her navy shirt. They left damp palms and streaky fingers. "You get lunch. Really, if you like, you can have dinner also."

"That's not in the agreement."

"It's my place." Maria smiled and again looked young, a girl. "I make the rules."

"Okay. I might take you up on it."

It seemed a very long walk back to his room, back through years of himself, through several skins, many nights awake and staring at a merciless ceiling and regular, dull mornings sealing new coral layers across his eyes. With each numb step he thought of Maria, cleaning up her kitchen, heavy oatmeal pot tolling, smelling of earth and cast iron, the warm porcelain bowls, and her fingerprints invisible on them, nestling on Maria's clean shelves. Something stung as he thought of her arms moving, lifting those bowls up, shutting the cupboard door. She would wipe her hands again, and smooth stray hairs back. Then she would right-about and move on to the next thing.

By the time he reached the door to his room Allen no longer wanted to go in. Inside were drugs, a bed, another ceiling. Behind the door was a hermitage, hauled on his back from the Bay to the mountains, grown over with decades of aversion and meals alone. Below him was kitchen life. Down through the floorboards and the cobwebbed joists and yet another ceiling was motion alive. He would rather roost like a gray bird and watch that life moving about. But he didn't go back. There were other places to go today. He reached his hand in his pocket for the key.

Chapter Two

Jefferson Street in the morning bore no resemblance at all to its night self. Allen walked down the left side so that he could see the river, olivine shot with silver, sweeping north and west, catching and magnifying the morning sun until the houses obscured it. Continuing down, he passed Pete's and Joe's Place, retiring into its little spot across the street, closed and anonymous. There might have been someone inside, in the back, but he could not be sure. Reaching Main, he hesitated, realizing with a start that this street, too, was not the same one he'd owned last night. Where he had traveled alone humans now walked, parked cars in the old-fashioned parking places, waved to each other, went into and out of stores, chatted outside restaurants. The day life of the town in this small button of a valley shouted down the greater, wider, more numerous but more subtle mountain voices of canyon and root and fur, feather and scale. Babble smothered forest hymn as macadam suffocated soil.

He couldn't stand there gawping. It was imperative that he begin to be busy or appear to be on his way to be busy or at the very least find some place where no one noticed that he was not doing anything. Something worse than panic rose against his breastbone. It was, he knew, the sneaky crazy that crawled along with the stalking death; the sneering weak-kneed exhausted nuts despair grinning from the bedpost, scuttling in the storm drains as he passed, chewing at his organs as he lay sleepless and dreamless. Now it walked with him under the sun and invited him to run up to that bridge crossing the river on the north edge of town there and take a flying leap. He could see the bridge from the corner where he stood. It would only take a couple of minutes. There would be a rush of frigid air, a shock of hard water. Then nothing.

Looking back over his shoulder, he saw the sign in the window of Pete's and Joe's flipped by an invisible hand from Closed to Open. It was tempting to walk back there, to go in and let the day forget itself in bar light and hot coffee, but something still restrained him. Knotting his fists in his trench coat pockets, he crossed Main and entered the babble.

It was still shady on this side of Main, and it comforted him as he walked south to go where morning hadn't yet arrived. Now that he had plunged in, what had seemed a throng was really only a few uninterested souls, what passed for a crowd here. If he looked hard at them, these people would fade. He would see through them, read signs through their ribs, watch the sky growing daylight through the tops of their skulls.

As he came to *Liz Terry, Attorney's* office his feet slowed. Now that it was awake, under the living sun, he wanted to turn away, not go past it, as one avoided walking under a ladder, or over a grave. The office awake was a different place than the office asleep. It was not a thing to be trusted at any time, but now it was full of peering danger. His breastbone pulsed with crazy terror once more and he had to pause, to breathe, to stop being dizzy.

He didn't know how long he stood there. It couldn't have been very long—the sun hadn't moved perceptibly—but it felt like a very long time, indeed, so long that he worried about drawing attention to himself. There was nothing to do but walk.

"Hey." A hand on his shoulder. He turned. DJ's stained-cap face near his own. "Lost?"

"No."

"That's good. Because if you can get lost in this town, you should probably just stay indoors."

DJ laughed. Passing Allen, he walked up a few doors and, grinning, disappeared into a bar.

"Easily amused."

Allen stood a moment longer, then retreated north on Main, moving toward the river and the bridge. After a few blocks he stopped, shook his head, crossed back over Main and resumed walking south again.

He crossed Jefferson, going faster now, on the naked, sunny side of the street. Soon the office was in view again and Allen slowed as it came broadside.

She was in there. Greeting a client. Shaking hands. Liz Terry, Attorney, still blonde, still an inch taller than short, but closer to fifty than seventeen, a grownup, business casual. But it was Liz. Even from here he could see how her mouth pulled crooked when she smiled and, instead of nodding up and down, her head described oval circles of agreement. She guided the client back to the inner office, followed by a plump girl carrying a large black book. The frosted glass door closed behind them and that was it.

No. That wasn't it. Just before the girl with the book closed the door, Liz turned and looked at him. It was the same look she always had: the look of someone who has just asked an interesting question and is expecting a fascinating response; a completely engaged, sincere, full-of-attention gaze. Still, after decades, across the highway, still Liz, waiting for her answer. Then the door had closed, and she was gone.

It was safe to keep moving. It didn't matter where. Allen rolled along Main for a while, then let random streets pick him. He adopted a business-like gait and a sober expression, a going-places facemask, designed to ward off inquiry. It worked. No one came from a house or a school or a gas station to question him or engage him in conversation. He slid along, sly, impervious, and slippery as a tomato seed in a sink. Slowly the gut-rocking spying mission walked its way out of his blood and he calmed enough to notice he was drifting south, approaching the grade he had first taken down into the valley.

The town stopped abruptly at a berm of bar run cobble and Allen looked down onto a wide expanse of fall meadow running all the way to the long curve of the river. Deer were grazing far off where the mountains began. In the granite shade some of the trees kept their leaves, so that a leaf gradient from cool to blazing autumn ran from mountain to river. It was mild and drowsy here, lazy forgetfulness reaching up from moist roots.

Allen slid down the loose stone slope and wound up in the meadow. He didn't think about it or decide to do it, but after a few steps he lay in the grass, soaking in the heat radiating off the berm behind him. The yielding field buoyed his aching muscles and Allen lay, looking up at the mountain sky.

Aside from certainty, dying held few pleasures. Certainty was nonetheless a singular boon and Allen relished its bland guarantees. There was an edge to it, a stopping place. It was not unlike standing at land's end, by the soothing ocean, its muted, drowning sounds, bird cries, decay and birth commingled, murmuring "sleep, sleep," until his eyes closed and warm sands pulled him under. Allen knew that under the waves rude continental shoulders shoved against each other and soundless, sightless sparks radiated heats and poisons which nothing that walked or flew or hopped or swam or crawled could endure. But that didn't matter, while he breathed. It wouldn't matter when he had stopped breathing, and until then the ocean pressed her cheek against the shore and the shore was drowsy under the sun and there it was: the edge of it. The place where one stopped running. One could turn and face what had been, but there would be no other place to go unless one took a voyage.

And now, as he had all his life, Allen clung to the edge of things, not wanting to fall into that endless middle—that Kansas of the soul, bowed down by the prairie's endless gravity, choking on the dust of a dry land. Allen kept his back always to it, facing west, never far from his ocean home from which he had come and to which he would return.

A certain muted joy. Aside from this, there was little to recommend disease. It hurt. It was tiring. One hesitated to get interested in anything that required long-term considerations. Space and time were squashed and there was to be no dawdling. The very forward motion of Allen's life carried him down the last stretch of road left to him, leaving his fleshy bits behind until there was nothing to arrive at the nowhere which awaited. This reality did, however, reveal another modest benefit, and Allen was reminded of it when he considered his upcoming voyage. As the thing that ate him chewed on his moorings, Allen found that with practically no effort he could cast himself adrift, floating on the cool currents, forward and backward, up, down, and sideways. There was less to hold him down, and so away he went, to almost any place he desired.

As he lay now in the grass, Allen traveled to the lost continents, territories long submerged but somehow left intact in his mind's eye. Here were ledges and rifts and mountains of memories, become more solid and alive as what had been Allen Wrangell thinned out.

This day under the sun he recalled many funerals: first his father, then a sister, a brother, then his mother. Another sister. There were a few aunts, uncles, and cousins in the cortege as well. Some co-workers also requested his attendance—he had carried one or two as a courtesy—but not one friend joined the ceremonies. There were no friends, not one to bury or be buried. Allen went, then, when he was summoned to the last dance of people dimly-remembered, of slight acquaintance, attended by living others of equally distant and faint intimacy. As time passed, the departed became even less familiar, the mourners with few exceptions complete strangers. But he went, and carried when asked, and ate the starchy casseroles and salty funeral meats, nibbled the pastries, and drank the sour coffee as one or another widow bereft or consoling sibling extolled and exalted the memory of the barely-recalled decedent. Before long, his feet would swell, his belt and tie would become uncomfortably tight and he'd want to nap.

On occasion during these solemnities he also wished for sex and knew without question that there were others there who wished for it, also. The desire was fleeting, but undeniable, and he had little doubt that there were those who acted on it, after a short decorum. There was more than one widow whose embrace was humid with something more than grief. Allen supposed that life desired life and would not be denied.

Of all the partings and passings, one in particular surfaced in Allen's memory and he let himself drift across the country to revisit the scene. The decedent had been a co-worker, a postal clerk like Allen. They had sorted mail side by side for long years. Allen remembered him because there was so little about him to remember, a remarkable absence of anything remarkable. This thoroughgoing blandness intrigued him. It practically compelled Allen to discover depths beneath the featureless surface, but try as he might, in lunch room conversations and occasional walks, he found nothing interesting about the man at all. He was, if anything, more insular than Allen, and as far as he knew Allen was the only person with whom the man spoke regularly.

Eventually the man retired and moved back east, to New Jersey. Allen stayed in touch with him by mail (as postal brethren were bound to do) and occasional phone calls. When the man became disabled and needed a caregiver, Allen got acquainted with her as well, having tacitly assumed the obligation to attend to minor affairs and to see his absent comrade safely off when the time came.

Within a year or two, this happened. Allen and the caregiver made arrangements with the Veterans Administration for burial and, still under that tacit obligation, he agreed to travel to the funeral.

The night before his flight east, the military chaplain called him to ask a few details of the decedent's life. Allen supplied what little he knew and gave the chaplain the caregiver's phone number. Then, on a sharp October day, so much like spring except for the fallen and falling leaves, Allen and the caregiver met at the VA cemetery. She was a kindly, thin-faced woman and he liked her. They were the sole mourners, in the front row of two dozen metal chairs lined in neat ranks under the small shelter on a barren knoll in New Jersey, his co-worker's gray casket behind the podium, where stood the chaplain. At a respectful distance the cemetery manager stood by a shedding tree and only once glanced at his watch.

The chaplain delivered his eulogy. It was short and consisted entirely of what thin data he had gleaned from Allen and the caregiver. They sat and nodded as their words they had spoken the night before were read back to them from the podium, the chaplain dutifully giving proper attribution: ("Allen tells me that [name forgotten] enjoyed walks by the post office and was a fast and able sorter, while [name also forgotten] remarked on his generosity to pizza delivery boys.")

When it was over, Allen and the caregiver stood. The cemetery manager caused pre-recorded Taps to issue from unseen speakers and the assembly dismissed. As he escorted the caregiver to her car, Allen looked back once at the casket. He tried to remember one thing about his former co-worker's face and was unable to do so.

The caregiver had wanted to have sex.

Allen had scheduled a return flight back to California, leaving early the following evening. The caregiver drove him to the airport and bade him farewell with a kiss from her thin, friendly lips.

After receiving instructions from the flight attendant, including the admonition to put on his oxygen mask before helping others and, in the unlikely event of a water landing, to use his seat cushion as a flotation device, Allen closed his eyes.

He opened them again as the plane dashed down the tarmac and broke contact with the ground. Soon they rose above the clouds and the sun slanting across their billowed tops gave them the appearance of old chrome. When the sky below cleared Allen looked down at the passing terrain: cities fragmenting into towns, farms and woodlots, rivers great and small, draining south and east across the stable platform, the craton of America. The land began to darken beneath their wings as they crossed the Mississippi, and by the time they reached the Missouri the cities and towns were sprays of light, strung together by webs that faded in the middle. Some settlements were glowing spangles, galaxies that answered those appearing in the night sky to the east; some looked like kites, strings grasped by phantoms. The cities along the Western rivers, the thin veins of the continent, were sharp, sodium vapor shards, backed up to scraggy voids, slicing into waters. In parking lots and factory spaces, earthbound angels glowed, considering the prayers of lonesome waitresses, the supplication of slaughterhouse workers, saying the rosary. In countless shelters down in those lights people drank, made love, excreted, wept, studied, schemed, argued, and laughed. The pipes of featureless apartments and circumspect brick ramblers rang with their night calls, the streets thrummed with fugitive dreams.

Allen watched it all pass beneath him and it seemed he heard one sigh—it might have been his own—and he looked away from the passing night nation, looked up and saw the long-escaping sunset, the one they had chased from New Jersey, pulling slowly and steadily away from them.

The plane was fast. Its westward progress delayed the inevitable, but the sky before them went from orange and searing blue to the faintest crimson curve capped with a dome of night. As they crossed desert places where no lights showed below, the horizon thinned to a hazy yellow line separating earth from firmament. By the time the lights of California appeared, nosing the ship-spattered Pacific, nothing at all distinguished earth from sky.

In that intermingling of sea and star Allen had fallen at last into a brief, dreamless sleep. When he woke up on landing, he became aware of a dizzy throbbing, a rodent sort of skittering and a kind of chewing just inside his skull, as if clawed things were trying to peel his brain and nest there. These were the first symptoms of the illness that was growing inside him, a tiny army marching through his fiber and already wearing him away. As he walked through the airport pulling his rolling suitcase he tried to shake the warm, sour acid stiffness from his joints. He was never fully-able to do so. The tiny army bivouacked in his interstices, filling his inner streams with their filth.

Allen attended no more funerals after this. They appeared to be bad for his health.

Afternoon shadow stretching from the berm reached him and that former source of heat now cooled him. He rolled away from it, farther into the meadow and so woke up. Instantly he sat up and looked around. There was no mystery, no terror here of blank amnesia, but his exposed position in the broad light of afternoon was almost as disturbing. He wanted to dig down in the earth of the meadow and pull the hole in after.

Getting up, he brushed himself off and looked back to town. Its frayed sameness was reassuring. Nothing new was there, under this sun. Somewhere near the middle of it, DJ was moving beer under his paint-stained trucker's cap at a dollar a glass. The bank was taking money from people and charging people to get the money back again. Gas was pumped, letters learned, songs sung. Liz Terry was nodding in her ovals and making her crooked mouth beneath severely interested eyes while her plump clerk notarized a long string of signatures, the wake of names on a never-ending paper tide. All the while the river spoke its stony speech and the mountains whispered a prelude to the night song that would triumph over all, daunting all light and noise and heat that humans could devise. It was only a matter of time.

Allen continued into the meadow until he reached the river, then he followed its broad sweeping course south, towards the peaks where the river had its headwaters. As his legs woke up, they seemed to enjoy being taken for a walk. The river was wide and shallow here, with frog water eddies and boggy spots full of cattails. The water's talk was all murmuring and innuendo. The river talked as if it was saying something not especially nice about someone. Allen preferred it when the talk was loud and the water rapid, where things were going on. A bored river was trouble. It was not to be trusted. Its damp declivities led to parasites, stagnation, blindness, beavers, and feverish desires that were bad for the digestion. Farther south and west he could see where the water ran steeply down from the slopes to the valley, but he didn't have the strength to walk that far in the warm afternoon. He decided to circle back.

It wasn't far to the highway. Allen caught it and took it right through town, squinting in honey light. He liked how the clipped afternoon shadows dressed the place up. The long sleep wore off and he felt easy in his stride, walking free. He didn't try to avoid Liz's office; for the moment it had no power over him, the glass glare of the westering sun almost obscuring the interior, except for a brief glimpse of the plump clerk, typing at her terminal. It could have been any office, and in fact it was any office, one of millions just like it, with clerks, gray chairs and windows washed once a week.

The rest of the Main Street journey was almost enjoyable. The same honey warmth that fed Allen's contentment was running in everyone's blood. Eyes flirted, mouth lines smoothed, hair bounced, hands touched hands. The act of getting groceries filled the grocery-getter with unfathomable joy. There was no better thing to be doing, and one could gather carrots, milk, and cans of beans, then die happy, if it came to that.

Looking to his right, Allen saw DJ rooster-walking on the other side of Main, beer shift over, stained cap pulled over his eyes, headed back home. He would cross Main at Jefferson. Allen didn't want to see him or listen to his rooster talk all the way back to Maria's. He increased his pace, beat DJ to the corner, slipped past the bank and without pausing to think, entered Pete/Joe's Place, closing the door behind him.

DJ went by the window and continued up Jefferson. Allen let out his breath and turned, fully aware for the first time that he was actually in the bar and wondering if he'd been standing there, peering out, for long. An inexplicable chagrin blew his afternoon contentment to tatters and he was once more on guard. He was wary, a stranger in a strange land. His eyes adjusted to the place and he saw that he was alone. Relief mingled with new apprehension, magnified by something which he could not identify, or something missing which he could not recall.

Besides the lamp on the back bar, the only other light came from a single yellowed globe under an ancient ceiling fan that rotated slowly under the pressed-tin ceiling of smoky arabesques, a sepia heaven that infused its own umber light into the long, narrow space. Allen could see the door leading into the back room was slightly open. He was wondering if he should call out when the door opened wide and the same bartender he had noticed on his walk the night before backed out, pulling a hand truck loaded with cases of beer bottles.

"Hello," Allen said, not too loudly. He sat at the bar, near the register.

The bartender looked over his shoulder. "Hi." He turned and pulled the hand truck behind him. "How are you?" There was a familiarity in the question, a manner of greeting a long-lost acquaintance.

"Joe or Pete?" Allen asked, as the bartender set the beer cases carefully down near him.

"Come again?"

"The sign says Pete's Place. The window says Joe's"

"I'm neither." The bartender turned and began loading bottles into the cooler under the back bar. "But you can call me either, if you like."

Allen was still trying to figure out what was missing in the place. "You the owner?"

The bartender stood and looked a moment at him. "The present occupant."

"Oh."

The bartender held out a hand. "Ted."

Allen shook it. "Allen."

"Want something?"

"Um, yeah." Allen pointed around the bar. "What's missing?"

"Missing? Nothing, as far as I know. Got a bar. Got drinks. Want one?"

"How about a coke?"

Ted got a bottle, opened it, and handed it to him. Allen paid him, feeling the examining weight of his look. He didn't like it. After a moment, Ted resumed stoking the cooler. Allen sipped the coke. Neither man said anything for some time.

At last Allen asked, "How's business?"

Ted finished his job and stood, wiping his hands on a towel. "Business is consistent with the locale."

"I know a guy who'd improve your till. He walked by just now."

"He's not welcome."

"He's not? How'd you—um, you know, you don't really talk like a bartender."

Ted arched an eyebrow. "How are we supposed to talk?"

"I don't know. Can't you throw in a colorful phrase or a bad joke now and then?"

"Why the long face. So, I bit him. Boy are my arms tired. All swole up like a poisoned pup."

"Thank you."

"No problem."

Ted hit the old-fashioned cash register and dropped Allen's money in it. He rolled the drawer shut with a percussive thud. "DJ walks by here around the same time every day. He used to stop in on the way home. Now he doesn't."

"That's good."

"Yes, it is."

Allen stood. "Thanks for renting the safe spot. Appreciate it." He turned to go and, still puzzling, looked around once more. "Something. I don't—so, anyway, what is this place called, really? Couldn't you call it Ted's Bar or something?"

"That's a nice name."

"But what is the name, really?"

Ted looked out the window, *Joe's Place* casting a faint, reverse shadow on the glass. "That depends," he answered, "entirely on the time."

*

This time when he woke up in his blind room, Allen knew where he was. He remembered the day with absolute clarity, from the morning talk with Maria to the visit with Ted, then walking back, avoiding Maria and DJ, coming here to his room, taking his pills, and passing out. He hadn't eaten anything. He hadn't wanted to. He had only wanted oblivion. That had come readily, easily, full of diffident mercy.

Now night crowded in again, disturbing the little passing- away. "The night life ain't no good life." He lay, wishing for the nothing to return. Instead, the mountain voices began again, louder than before. Mingled with them were human shouts, cries, and mutterings.

That was what woke him: the shouting. It didn't come from outside, but from inside the house. Downstairs. He sat up, listening. It was DJ's voice. Yammering, threatening, growling. And below it, answering, Maria's. He couldn't make out the words and didn't need to. The alcohol inflection was unmistakable, Maria's responses cool, low, and unafraid.

He got up and turned on the light. Still dressed in the day's clothes, he only had to put on his shoes and he was out the door, into the hall. Here the voices' volume increased six-fold and he could make out echoing words:

...drive if I fucking want to...you have no business even walking...did have a job, ended early, when are you

The front door slammed as Allen reached the top of the stairs. He hesitated. The house was silent now, and in the silence the mountain voices rose, keening, summoning. He ignored them. There were footsteps, Maria, returning to her kitchen. There was a clatter, a glittering clink. She was picking up the mess. He listened a little longer and then returned to his room.

He lay in the dark, listening to the mountains howl. It was this way more and more: he was closer now to the voiceless voice. Already his feet walked dim paths, where no one else could follow and where the invisible took off the mask to display its many phantom faces. The part of him that would have gone to Maria, to give solace, listen, offer help, this part—never strong—was weakening further. Here in the blind room that waking daylight self would answer no call.

When the physician judge and jury pronounced his sentence, what tenuous connection Allen had with other people dissipated. Having been informed of his disposition he was allowed to quit sorting mail and go home forever. There he watched the ceiling for signs and portents. Finding none, he returned to digging in the soil, the roots of things, where signs and portents abounded.

Nothing he found gave him hope. Nothing he discovered in the strata of worlds long lost provided Allen with a reason to go on looking, and so he stopped doing it. He went back to his apartment and ceased. Museums, funerals, movies, sunlight, voices in shops and offices all stopped. Dry hours calcified seasons. Hollow and stiff, he waited with folded hands for the weeks to bury him. Restless, Allen's husk sought escape and wandered in the dry places alone. One morning, with nothing else to do but breathe, Allen followed his ghost and it led him here. He watched, divorced as ever from human concerns, for what his ghost would show him.

"You didn't come back until late, huh?" Maria sat with Allen as he ate oatmeal. "Missed a pretty good lunch and dinner." Her words were thick with distance. She might have been in another room, another house, on her ripe, sparkling star.

Allen swallowed with difficulty. "No, that's right. I got in pretty late."

"Well I hope you got something to eat."

"Oh, no problem, yeah, got it taken care of." He didn't like lying. "I'll be missing lunch again today. Looks like there might be some good road cuts north of town and I'm going to head that way today."

"I'm not sure exactly what you're looking for, but I'm guessing the best place for rocks is in the canyon, and that's north, yes, a few miles out of town."

"A few miles. Oh well, the walk will be good."

"Why don't you take one of the bikes? We have, like, four of them."

"Yeah? Huh. Okay, thanks, if you're sure you don't mind."

Maria poured a cup of coffee from the table carafe. "They're in the shed out back. We can look at them whenever." She shot Allen a look. "Did you sleep okay?"

"Uh, yeah, pretty much, yeah."

"You didn't get woken up?"

Allen almost touched her hand. "I never sleep that well."

Maria looked away, then got up and went to the stove. She grabbed the oatmeal pot, went to the sink, and started scrubbing. "DJ stayed in town. His brother's."

"Yeah, I heard him leave." He wished he hadn't almost touched her hand. Whether he regretted almost touching her or whether he regretted not having touched her, Allen didn't know. He suspected it was both.

Maria concentrated on the pot. "Some people shouldn't drink." She said it as if to herself.

Allen sipped his coffee. "True." Hesitating, he added, "But would that make much difference?"

"I don't know."

Allen finished his coffee and stood. He watched Maria's back, her arms and shoulders moving in rapid, short rhythms, scrubbing the pot, placing the pot in the dish rack. Her head was bent. Her neck was strong. Her jet hair was up, one tuft vibrating with her efforts.

"Have you ever thought of—" He shook his head.

She bent around just enough to look sideways at him. "Have I ever thought of what?"

He walked over to the sink and began drying the oatmeal pot. Something in the earlier night's shouting had shaken loose a small piece of daring. He thought of his empty apartment back in the Bay Area, paneled, carpeted, stainless and vacant. His being there had made no difference and his leaving had made no difference. Now he was here and that made no difference, either. This couple, Maria and her rooster, they would live, eat, quarrel, have sex. They would not be happy. It would end badly. And he, Allen Wrangell, would pass like a draft through their lives and have no effect on the outcome at all. The knowledge made him a little crazy. It made him bold.

He said, "Sometimes I look at those old pictures. Some old city or town. I look at the old signs, the people in their sort of uncomfortable clothes, you know?" He took a bowl from Maria and wiped it dry. "All those years ago. The cars some guys made in some factory, on some shift that ended eighty years ago. And in the picture this lady is driving one of those cars down a street."

Maria handed him another bowl. "Any special street?"

Allen dried the bowl and set it in the rack. "Yes. No. Maybe, I don't know."

Maria smiled. "That about covers it."

Allen smiled back. "Yes."

Maria said, "She's going to work. Getting her kids at school."

Allen said, "That sounds right." He handed Maria the towel and she dried her hands. They stood now, with nothing to do. He turned slightly towards her and she turned slightly towards him.

Allen said, "Or she's going grocery shopping. Or she might be leaving town."

Maria nodded. "Never coming back."

He looked at her. "Where would she go?"

She shook her head. "It doesn't matter."

"It doesn't matter because why? Because she can just go anywhere?"

"That might be. It just doesn't matter."

"Because," Allen said, "she isn't going anywhere."

Maria's mouth straightened into a firm dash, but he noticed the muscles at the corners twitch. She looped the towel through the rack by the sink. "She is doing all she can to stay in one place. That's more than enough, don't you think?"

Allen looked out at the clear fall morning. "It's always the same woman. The same guy at the gas station. The same couple walking along the sidewalk. They never left." He looked over at her. "They never left. They never went anywhere. The world rolled past them and a new world rolled up to them, right up that street. Rolled up to them, through them and past them again and left them just where they were." He placed a hand on her shoulder—yes, he did it, this thing, and he could both regret and not regret doing it, but he would at any rate regret and not regret doing something—and he said, "They're still here."

Maria stared into the empty sink. "Want to look at those bicycles?"

After two days of walking, riding the bicycle was like flying.

Allen flew down Jefferson and pedaled up Main, to the bridge. Stopping there, he looked down into the mouth of a willow-choked gorge that compressed and amplified the river's voice. Looking back and to his left, he could see Jefferson Street climb the slope to Maria's, hidden back behind other houses and fall-torched trees.

She would be there now. She never left the house. Maybe she never would. DJ would be slinking home sometime. There would be firm resistance. There would threats and pleading. They would stand in the hallway as the day outside burned away. Someone should take a picture.

Car tires squeezed deep bass notes from bridge steel. The road music rumbled in Allen's feet and he suddenly wanted to laugh. It was that way sometimes. He mounted up and headed the rest of the way across the span, then took the highway north, the sun on his right cheek and the cool river following him on the left.

He flew down the canyon, loud waters getting louder, cool day becoming frigid in the deeps of the canyonland. Pulling off the highway at a road cut, Allen ran over to the sheered-off wall on the right, touching, tapping, muttering low, telegraphic strings of joy: *Contact...this is part...the fault right here, look look, the syncline begins here, now here, rolled like a Bundt cake, oh here is the place where the land never dies, here is the place where some portion was saved from pressure, heat and fire, anticline running here, look, look.*

He tapped and mumbled for an hour, squinting at fragments through a small magnifying glass, then sat abruptly against the road cut, eyes closed as the sun rose to noon and bored straight down into the canyon.

When he woke up, the roadside was in shadow again. The sun had moved behind a western mountain shoulder. It was bone-gripping cold. He was weak. He wanted water. Crossing the highway, he scrambled down over huge, rounded blocks of granite to the icy river. Shooting in a natural flume through the canyon, the current sang in various frequencies and Allen listened as he drank and splashed his face. It was a grindstone underwater rumble, a tenor spume pulling at the birch branches, their leaves still green, a dominant midrange, Gregorian, echo upon infinite echo, overwhelming the stone-walled chorus. The water and the music revived him.

Climbing back out, Allen wondered how long it would take him to get back up the canyon to town. The bicycle waited, no longer ready to fly. It was now a burden that he, lacking the strength to ride it much up the steep highway grade, must push for miles. But he began, and it wasn't too hard. The army that marched inside him hadn't pillaged everything yet. On some days, in certain circumstances, he found he now had a manic will, a final burst of crazy vitality leeched from his marrow. He consumed the last of himself in this way.

He was able to mount and ride near the top of the grade and took the remainder of the more-gentle part to the bridge on wheels. He regained the last of the sunlight here, before it slipped over the edge of the world, and once again the town was bathed in humble glory, cheering and welcoming in the afternoon, much warmer here than in the canyon. From the bridge he coasted into town, exhausted, sweat-soaked, spent and satisfied. He passed Jefferson Street (Pete and Joe's Place was open) and kept going.

Across Main, DJ strutted north, Rooster Reborn. He saw Allen and stopped. Even from a distance and moving at a good clip, Allen felt the malignance of DJ's stare: a sort of spastic, gibbering fury suddenly fixed on him, a blind, stupid rage with no roots in anything except beer, and...something else. It had no reason. It didn't need one. Allen was there and it found a place in him to ground to earth, that was all.

Allen ignored DJ's stare and rolled along Main with the traffic. Slowing across from Liz Terry's office, he saw no one at the front desk. He kept going, looking for a place to stop and eat. It was the first time in many days he could remember being hungry.

Near the south end of town there was a corner diner that appeared safely deserted. He stopped and leaned the bike against the glass by the door, where he could keep an eye on it. He patted the seat and went in.

Liz was at the cash register, just inside the door.

She was talking to the waitress, nodding her head in the oval-fashion, smiling in the crooked way, her lip pulled down and to the side. He heard nothing of what she said, but took her in: almost as slim as she'd been thirty some years ago, but now her blonde hair was cut shorter, stylish, where before it had been long and straight. She retained her manner of looking intently at the speaker, in this case the bewildered-looking townie girl whose utterances included references to pies and television shows. Liz was a great listener. He wished suddenly that he'd had more to say those many years ago. He wished he could say something now.

Sliding past Liz and her undivided attention, Allen sat near the back at a Formica and vinyl booth. There were only a couple of other patrons and no one had taken much notice of him, certainly not the townie waitress, still monopolizing Liz's amazing ability to listen. He imagined she made a lot of money, even in this isolated town. No one listened like Liz, and she could now charge by the quarter hour. Every time she nodded, her hair just touched the shoulders of her business casual jacket, sweeping from left to right. Allen thought of Maria, scrubbing the pot with her strong arms, her tuft of hair vibrating with the force of her action. Liz's hair didn't vibrate. It stroked her shoulders like a soothing hand.

The waitress handed Liz a slip of paper and she signed it. Allen saw that she had her arm through the loops of a plastic bag. Late lunch, dinner, maybe. Working late at the office. Now she handed back paper and pen. Now she turned to go.

Turned back.

Looked at Allen.

Looked away and walked briskly from the restaurant, waving at the waitress.

Chapter Three

Ted wiped the bar in the patient manner mastered by all bartenders. Allen, seated at the bar near him, drank a coke. There was no one else in the place.

"In the Old West," Allen said, "miners often paid for their drinks with gold dust."

"Makes sense."

"The bartender kept a little scale. He'd pinch some of the gold dust, weigh out the price of a drink, hand back the bag. But he'd often spill just a speck or two. He was always wiping the bar, you know. He'd wipe up enough gold dust that way to ring out a tidy sum at the end of the night. A pretty generous tip."

"Cleaned up on them, as it were."

"Yeah. As it were." Allen cocked an eye at Ted. "That's why I will not pay you with gold dust. I don't trust a clean bartender."

"Cash is just fine. Want another?"

"Sure." Allen handed the empty back to Ted along with some bills. "I took that bike up north of town, looking at road cuts and river bottoms."

Ted handed Allen a fresh coke. "Any special reason?"

"Yes. To look at what was likely a deep slice of the Orogenic Belt."

"Excuse me?"

"This valley, this town, it sits on a fault, a suture where two completely different kinds of rock, from two totally different places, have crashed into each other. That's what I was looking at, I think. The place where you crashed into that other pile of rock."

"No kidding. All that going on right here. Go figure"

Allen eyed Ted. "Are you making fun of me?"

Ted let go of his towel and raised his hands. "Not me."

"Well, it's like I was telling someone yesterday, see, the whole West Coast is moving, a little bit each year, riding west, up and over the Pacific Plate. It's like an ice floe, pushing another ice floe under it. But sometimes not all of that other ice floe goes under."

"No? What happens to it?"

"It gets stuck. It sticks on to our continent as the rest of that raft it was riding on goes under, goes right under us and is melted away. But this piece that gets stuck on us, it stays with us, millions and millions of years after the raft it was on got destroyed. So instead, then, it stitches itself right on to our raft and goes riding west with us." Allen swallowed more coke, surprised by his own exposition. "And as the mountains rise here in the West, sometimes it rises with them. But it isn't one of them."

Ted leaned forward confidentially. "It's a stranger in a strange land."

Allen put his bottle down. "Yes. That's it." He also leaned forward. "This chunk of surviving raft, it has a name. It's called a terrane. T-E-R-R-A-N-E. A big piece of someplace else, some other time, right here, now, with us. Still alive."

"And we have one right here in our little town."

"It is your little town."

"You think?"

Allen looked at Ted, to see any signs of mockery, but there were none. "You know what I mean. This town, Forester, it's on the terrane."

"We're on the someplace else."

"Right on it. I can see the places where you're stitched together, under the earth, all the way down, sometimes miles, where it gets pretty spicy. Or I can guess where these places are, what they're like. The clues are in the rocks, their shape, what they're made of, what other rocks and soils are with them, where they dive down and from where they rise up."

"So," Ted said, pouring himself a glass of water, "Where did we come from?"

"I have no idea."

"None?"

"Not really. You came from out there." Allen gestured west. "Hundreds, probably thousands of miles. You were an island, in the middle of the ocean. You were a chunk of continent, or even a small island continent, all by yourself, like Australia. As the plates we're all riding on shift and move and push each other around, you moved slowly east as our own continent pushed west, drowning the raft you floated on, until that raft got pushed under."

"And we didn't."

"That's right."

"So here we are."

"Yes." Allen looked quickly at Ted, then away. He was suddenly reluctant to talk about this: the smashing and shearing of these great plates, the drift of stone and drowned continents. Some private shame oozed through the cracks and fractures, old and sulfurous. He couldn't look at Ted. He studied his own hands. "Here we are."

"And here," Ted said, lifting Allen's coke off the bar and swiping under it, "you are."

Allen picked the bottle up. It was the old-fashioned kind, a watery beryl. He drank from it. "Here I am." He set it back on the bar. "For now."

Ted sipped his water. "You know something?"

"No, not much."

"You're not alone."

"I'm not?"

"No." Ted spun the damp bar towel. It opened like a kite, then spiraled into a knot and seemed to hide under his sleeve. He shook it out again and, holding it by two corners with each hand, he gave it a snap and it disappeared under the bar.

Allen watched, smiling. "And you?"

Ted looked out the window a moment. In profile, a blotch of afternoon light across his face, he looked old, older than Allen. But that impression faded when he turned to look at him. "You're here." He leaned in, lowering his voice. "Aren't you?"

"As I said, I'm here for now."

"All anyone can ask for." Ted smiled and his face was again young, but sad, Allen thought. It was a face acquainted with sorrow, many stories, a parade of lives going by the mahogany bar, stopping to drink before moving on, their shoes polishing the nickel rail into blurred bronze, leaving their shavings of clay on the floor to be patiently blotted out. Allen had a brief vision of Ted, in the still hours of the early morning, sweeping away the lost footprints of departed customers. "Anyway," Ted continued, "We miss a lot. There's a lot going on and we just catch a little bit now and then. You know, what we can see—all that's visible to our eyes, out of everything that is—it amounts to about three percent."

Allen nodded. "I have heard something like that."

"Three percent of everything. The rest is either just void or dark matter, and we can't see that and we don't know what it is."

Allen finished his coke and declined another. "I know what it is. Dark matter. I know what it is."

Ted looked at him, his expression inscrutable. "You do."

"I listen to it. At night."

"And what does it say?"

"It says 'the time is short.'" Allen looked around the bar. He turned back to Ted. "There is definitely something missing in here."

"What would that be?"

"I don't know. It's not here." Allen picked up the empty coke bottle. "They haven't made these in years."

Ted took the bottle and looked at it. "No?"

"No."

"Well," Ted said tossing the bottle in a tub where it made a hollow sound, "business has been slow."

The wire gate snapped shut behind him and Allen wheeled the bike up the old concrete walk to Maria's. As he neared the big front porch he stopped. Something was wrong. The porch light was off. There were no lights on in the kitchen, living room or sitting room. The house was sinking into twilight under the fading leaves.

Allen shook his head and started around the side, towards his room in the back. He stopped again. Off to the left, in the deeper shade, someone stood, watching him. He recognized the profile of the cap and the rooster stance, at once puffed out and slouched over.

"Hello, DJ."

DJ approached, side-walking in his rooster way. He stood in front of Allen, smelling of beer—and something else. Cocking his head this way and that, he tapped the bike's handlebars.

"Enjoy your ride?"

"Yep."

"Like riding my bike?'

"Yes. Thanks for lending it to me."

"I didn't. Maria did."

Allen appraised him: drunk, but keeping his words straight, a pro. He wasn't as tall as Allen, but was clearly much stronger. His neck muscles clenched and unclenched, his hands worked, vibrating into the bike frame.

Something else. A cat piss odor. That was it.

"That was nice of her. To lend it to me."

The bike was between them. DJ gave the handlebars a shake. "You fucking her?"

Allen shook his head.

"You banging my girlfriend?"

"No."

DJ let go of the handlebars and stepped back, eyes skewed up at him. "You're some kinda egghead." He laughed, hard and flat. "Some kinda egghead. Like a scientist or something."

"No." Allen shook his head. "No, I'm not."

"Naw? Then what are you? Besides some guy who walks into town. Takes my bike. Fucks my girlfriend."

"I'm a postal clerk."

"A wha—a postal clerk?"

"Yeah. Is that a problem for you?"

DJ looked at him, apparently trying to determine if this was a challenge. He laughed again and abruptly pushed past Allen, headed for the gate. "No, man," he called over his shoulder. "No, that's no problem." He opened the gate and it slammed behind him with a sound like hammered piano wire. "You're no problem at all."

Allen watched DJ until he disappeared down the hill, a strutting shadow cartoon under the streetlight. He turned and continued up the walk, and as he neared the side door by the kitchen, it opened.

Maria stood there, barely visible in the hushed light coming from some distant room.

"Hi."

Allen stopped. "Did you hear that?"

"Some of it."

"What are you doing with him?" He burned cold. He shook and hoped Maria didn't see it.

"It's complicated."

"It can't be that complicated. The guy's on tweak, Maria."

He saw her head turn. She said nothing for a long moment. Then, "Will you come in?"

"I have to go to my room."

"And then?"

"And then I'll come down."

The night song wailed outside his window. As quickly as he could, Allen dispensed his medication, washed down with tap water. As he swallowed the pills—each one a capsule granting a little more time, or a little less pain, or slightly less distorted perceptions—he tried to make out voices in the music that poured out of the mountains, screamed through the fields, and roared around Maria's in a bacchanal. There were no voices. The song remained anti-voice, anti-thought, anti-light. It snarled with hidden muscle stronger than anything he could imagine. It was implacable, injured, out for revenge, but Allen didn't fear it. There was nothing the night could do to him. He would soon be singing with it. He would soon be in the song.

It was dark on the stairs, but he could see a comfortable butter glow pouring into the downstairs hall from Maria's kitchen. He went in. She sat at the table, hands wrapped around a teacup.

She looked up, face drained, pulled tight with anxiety. "Hi."

Allen walked over to her, but didn't sit. "You okay?"

She nodded. "Tea?"

"No." He sat. "No thanks, I've had a lot of soda."

She smiled, but there was no smile in it. She sipped. "You had a good ride, then?"

"Yeah, oh yeah. Great, thank you for that bike. It's back in the shed."

"You're welcome."

"Is it really DJ's bike?"

She shook her head. "No."

Allen laughed. "Well, then." He wanted to say more, but he held back.

Maria didn't laugh. She looked at him over her cup. Then she looked away, at the reflection of the kitchen in the window over the sink, her head shaking almost imperceptibly.

Allen looked away, too. "I found what I was looking for."

"Did you? And what was that."

"A story. The story of what's under you here. How it got here. I'm finding pieces of it."

"And what will you do with all the pieces?"

"Hmm? Oh, nothing. I won't do anything with them. I'm just interested in them, because. Just because." He felt again the urge to say more, but he resisted. There was something decadent in his geology, something secret and crafty and forbidden there, an indulgence. He was sorry he'd ever let Maria know about it.

"Are you really a postal clerk?"

"Yes. I was. Now I'm not."

"Not a scientist."

"No. I'm a nobody. I'm a former nobody. Soon I'll be a—" he stopped, looking back at her.

"A what?"

"Nothing. A nothing."

"Did your car really break down?"

Allen rubbed his temples. "Yes." He looked up, into her round black eyes. "Yes. But I—I helped it. I helped it break down." He shook his head. "I'm not, you know—"

"Crazy?" She blinked in the tea steam. "Does that really matter?"

Allen shook his head. "The car is crashed into a road cut back there." He waved vaguely south. "It's crashed."

"Did you crash it on purpose?"

"No. Yes. I—I don't know if I did or not." He went back to rubbing his temples. "Air bags are a really terrific invention."

"If you want to live, yes."

"Yes."

They sat a long time, not talking. Allen could hear her take sips of tea as he sat, staring at the table top, his head suspended between his fingers. It was good to sit here like this, listening to her small inrushes of breath as she sipped. He liked the sound and motion of his own breathing, too, and he took in a little of the tea cloud, and some of her scent: soap and lemon. A pine fragrance.

After a while Maria asked, "Was that the only reason you came? Those rocks?"

Allen shook his head. "No." He dropped his hands and folded them together. "That's not the reason I'm here at all."

"The rocks."

"I look at rocks wherever I go." He heard the impatient sound of his voice and he regretted it. He took a breath. "It's just an interest. Like how some people collect stamps, or, like, how some people like to read up on sports. I like the history of rocks, and how they move. I especially like the exotics, the places where different kingdoms of rock go crashing into each other."

"Kingdoms of rock?"

"Yeah." He wanted to stand up and walk around, but he stayed seated. "Places where, say, rock from an ocean bed will collide with rock from a continent. This whole part of your mountains here is one of those exotic terranes." He wanted to change the subject. "It's all around you. It's all right here." He saw Maria's expression slip into blank puzzlement. A sudden itchy panic made him sweat. He might have been speaking in tongues. "It's all not very interesting," he said quickly. "And really that's not why I'm here."

There was a long silence. They didn't look at each other. Under the sound of their breathing he heard the night song. It was different now. It called and tugged; it asked for him by name. Allen wanted the song to stop. He wanted to break the silence. He wanted to tell Maria things about himself: that his life had been spent sorting mail; that he had never had children, had never gone to a wedding; that no one in his apartment building knew his name; that only rocks had been important to him; that he'd always had a dental plan; that the crashed car was no accident (but she knew that) and that in any case he would soon be leaving the land of rocks and sun. But there would be no reason to go into all that. It would be pointless to give this information to someone he hardly knew, who might forget his name when he was gone. But he couldn't escape the desire to entrust some secret to Maria, something only she would know and remember. There were many people named Allen. Each had a face and a story. He wanted Maria, when she heard that name, to think of him.

The urge passed. He started to stand up and found he could not. She saw this and looked closely at him.

"Are you sick?" she asked.

"Oh, I did more than usual today." He knew that was not the answer to her question. "I'm fine." Raising his head, he found her face was near his. "I'm fine." Her breath was warm, and there was mint in it. He thought of the mountain streams where he loved to walk, full of herb, branch and clear ice noise.

She looked at him sternly. "You didn't eat again."

"No, no, I did. I really did." He placed a hand on her arm to stop her from rising. "I did."

She looked doubtful, but sat back down.

Allen said, "DJ and you fought again."

She nodded.

"He thinks there's something going on," Allen said. "With you and me."

"DJ doesn't think. He just reacts. And much of the time he is—he's just, I don't know—reacting to whatever it is that's going on in his head."

"What's going on in his head is tweak."

"How do you know that, for sure?"

"I didn't live in the nicest neighborhood. I know tweak. It's either that or maybe he likes a nice cat piss and drain cleaner cocktail at night."

Maria pressed her fingertips against her forehead. She rubbed. "If it is this drug, he just started."

"Have there been changes?"

"Yes. Yes, I think so. I don't know. I can't read him."

"I wouldn't bother." That might have gone a little far. He watched her, but she showed no expression under the lattice of her fingers.

At last she said, "He has changed, I guess."

"Does he often just go threatening innocent retired postal clerks for imaginary indiscretions?"

Maria almost smiled. "I don't know that he has ever met any allegedly indiscreet retired postal clerks."

"Have you known each other long?"

Maria hesitated. "For some time, yes." Her voice was guarded.

"I don't mean to pry."

"You're not prying." She looked up at him sharply, then she looked off, peering at something far away that he couldn't see, her mouth pressed thin. "It's been a few years. Yes, a few. We met down in the Valley, at a place where we both worked. It was a little factory, you know, where we met. I did the invoices, some of the accounts, shipping. He, DJ, he did maintenance."

"And you liked him."

"I don't know." She smiled. "He could have been the one who fell for me, you know."

"But you liked him."

"I liked him okay. He kind of stuck at it. He just—"

"Didn't take no for an answer."

"I don't know that I ever said no." She looked down at the table and ran a finger along the grain of the oak. "He had a pretty nice smile."

Allen didn't want to think about DJ's smile. He said, "How'd you wind up here?"

"How? I don't know, this is where he's from. We both got tired of the factory, so we came up here and I started this place. Things just worked out." Her voice was flat, as if she were reciting a lesson.

Allen tapped the tips of his fingers together. There were things he wanted to ask, but didn't. He said, "DJ must have been different, before, when you first met."

"Yes. He smiled more. He was happier. I think sometimes that I don't really, you know, make him happy."

"Does he make you happy?" He waited, but she said nothing. "I mean, is it up to you to make him happy?"

"You want someone to be happy with you," Maria replied. Her voice was soft, almost a whisper. "Everyone wants that, I think."

"But does he make you happy? Is he, at least, not making you sad?"

"Happy. Sad." Maria looked at him. "Do you know what those words even mean?"

Allen thought. It was a simple question, but he decided he couldn't answer it. He shook his head.

"Then," Maria said, "any answer I give you won't mean anything."

"Come on," Allen insisted. "I told you some truth. Tell me some truth."

She brushed a wisp of hair back from her forehead. "We've been together some time. You get used to someone."

"That isn't all."

Maria's eyes flashed. "Did you tell me all?"

The silence that followed had an edge. Then Allen laughed. "No. No, I did not."

Maria's face softened. "Then I don't have to tell you all, either."

They both smiled, then Allen said, "You never leave your house, do you?"

Maria looked down. "Not, um"—she looked him squarely in the face—"not very often, no. No, I do not."

"You're not going to waitress this winter are you?"

She shook her head. "No."

"Do you really need him? I mean, you can get groceries delivered."

"I don't need him. As I said, you get used to people. I know that's stupid, but that's the truth." Her hands fluttered by her teacup and landed flat on the table, ending the subject.

They said nothing for a long time. The silence was slightly bruised, Allen thought, but it was comfortable. They could be two pebbles, with pebbly thoughts that went back through epochs. They could be two cats, sitting for hours, listening to the cat symphony of scent, chirp, tongue and fur, thinking of mice, warm fires, night walks along fence-tops, laughing at the world.

When he was a boy in the city, he would wake up around this time of night. He'd dress and go out, past his sleeping brothers and sisters, into the streets, running. The moonlight vibrated around him and he thought it shone out of his pale skin. He'd run into parks, past alleys, under bridges, laughing. He snarled and shouted, running faster than anything else in that midnight world. He knew he was invisible and couldn't be caught. He snapped his fingers at the witches and red dwarves and tree shades that would have terrified him in the ordinary hours. But these were not ordinary hours. In these hours he, Allen Wrangell, was king of the night.

And the night was full of cats. They were the only living things that could see him. They winked from gate posts, arched in greeting as he flew past, padded invisibly past and around him. They were in on the secret. Those wild city runs took him through and past himself, past all that he had been taught this place was, into the howling, hidden realm where he and the cats roamed free, lords until morning.

Allen came back to the kitchen, aware that Maria was looking at him. He was a little dazed, now careful and shy. But still, she was a safe place. There would be no harm done here. It would be all right to stay awhile, sitting with Maria.

"What are you thinking about?" Maria asked.

"I'm thinking about cats."

"And rocks?"

He looked back at her and smiled. "Not at this moment."

She got up and heated the tea water. He watched her and he knew she knew he watched her. That was all right. Her movements were shy, because of the watching, and the shyness made the movements charming. He could see the thought in her arms, the small of her back as she reached for the tea tin, the nervous awareness of her legs, every motion considered. He could not recall watching anyone like this before, and the little pleasure of it warmed away everything else. There was no sting this night, only Maria in her kitchen, in his eyes.

"Tea now?"

"Yes. I'd like some tea."

The kitchen became dream, and dream became a song which Allen heard in his sinew. His bones resonated to dream, all motion, gesture, expression. And if the song was mute, his eyes heard, and knew with greater certainty every passage of their exchange: the rise and fall, the walking to and fro, the leaning together and the pulling back, the sitting still. Night became morning and the dream murmured between them until it was time for her to go.

"I still have things to do tonight," she said, frowning a little.

"Hmm? Oh, yeah. Well, don't let me get in the way."

"It's just easier to work at night, on the computer."

"Well yeah, yeah." He looked at the wall clock. "It's not night anymore."

"No." She shook her head. "No, it's not."

"So, yeah. All right." He tried to stand and was surprised that he could. He held the edge of the table, a little unsteady, and waited for his balance to return. "You have a home business, you said?"

"I do medical billing."

"Ah." Medical billing. There was an awfulness to the term. It landed, cold, dispelling dream.

"Are you okay?" Her gaze narrowed.

"A little dizzy. I'm okay."

"You are very thin. You need to eat more."

He winked and took a step to leave. "I'll try."

"Allen." She stood, hands at her side.

He didn't turn around but waited by the hall door. "Yes."

"Um, thanks."

He closed his eyes. Opened them. "Thank you, Maria."

The downstairs hall, the stairs, the upstairs hall, all were dimmer than before. Allen could hardly see the door to his room and was glad to get in. He lay down immediately. He slept, but the dream did not return.

Chapter Four

When he opened his eyes, Allen had no memory of how he came to be lying on a bed in a room in his clothes with the light on. For some time he also did not know who he was. For a moment, he had merely kidnapped himself, for what purpose and to what end he did not know, and did not feel he had the right to know. It was hidden knowledge. Who, how and why he was, it was none of his business. But the hands folded across his chest had familiar hard places and moving parts in them. The close-fitting leather boots lay just so. There was the long torso, concave belly, skinny legs. The aftershave was familiar. It was all right. He remembered now that this happened frequently now. The night and Maria, the good dream, all returned to him.

The clock on the nightstand read three-thirty. Allen sat up and knew he must leave, right now. Standing, he fought the dizziness, went to the desk and fumbled through his medications. Clutching a handful, he got a glass of water from the bathroom sink and swallowed them all at once. It was easier that way. He splashed his face, wetted his hair, put on his trench coat, opened the door and walked out.

Only silence greeted him. The mountains slept. Nothing peeped from tree boles or holes in the earth. The night was ice-rimed cold and Allen buttoned his coat to the neck, peering around in the blue-black world as he descended the slippery back steps. The kitchen was dark, but the smaller windows of Maria's office were awake. He couldn't see in, but she was there, attaching dollars to X-rays, intubation, medicines and excised lesions. It seemed he could hear the tapping of computer keys and pity welled up in him.

From the top of Jefferson Street the town dozed before dawn, steady lights bereft but brave under agitated constellations. Allen hurried down, his footfalls the only living sound, punching against the ghost drone high-up buzz from wires and filaments, the phantom electric shadow of an echo that found out obscure alleys, worked into the walls and pooled iodine beryl in the bottles of Ted's silent bar. Allen hurried past it, onto Main, his aloneness as assured as if he'd been lost in the deepest canyons of the most desolate forest of the farthest mountain of the most distant range in America. But this time he did not own the desolation. It owned him and there was no redemption. He could no longer crawl out of that world he crawled into as a boy. He was no longer king. He was not even a servant. He had no name and his passing went unmarked.

Liz's office was just ahead. Allen crossed Main and approached it warily. Something was wrong with it. He tried to figure out exactly what as he neared the front door, and just as he reached it he saw two things: firstly, the place was not lighted, its interior barely visible in the street light.

Then Allen saw the sign: *For Lease*. White on red. A phone number for a local realtor was written in the white space at the bottom. He memorized it. Looking in, he saw only a partition. The plump clerk's desk, the chairs, pictures, law books, everything else was gone. Liz's inner office door was closed and lightless. Allen saw himself inside, unable to get out, stuck for all time in the tomb husk of a memory hole. If he stood there much longer he might indeed ooze through the glass, fall with an echoless thud on the bland Berber carpet. He would become an exhibit: The Man Who Could Never Leave. Except no one would see him. They would only feel the cold whisper of him as they rushed by. Soon, they would avoid going near the place. That's how these things worked.

He turned and walked slowly back up Main. The first dull hint of dawn troubled the east, erasing him with every step. By the time he reached Jefferson he had all but disappeared.

Behind him, in Liz's office, the opaque glass of her inner door began to glow dully, illuminating the empty space with a fossil light.

Chapter Five

Ceilings had for a long time been screens on which Allen watched and reviewed the course of events. He didn't own a television, and found it impossible to be around one for long. Radios and even ringtones interfered with his inside hum. Melodies and images clashed with his own pictures and songs.

The ceiling in Allen's room at Maria's suited him far better than the one in his old apartment. In that place he had been aware, as he lay on his bed looking up, that other lives were playing out above him. There he could hear their footsteps, the scrape of chair legs, the unwelcome pipe music of pressurized water. There was none of that here at Maria's and Allen's vision wandered undisturbed on the ceiling.

He was eight years old. There was a filthy tennis shoe in his face. He didn't want it there, but there it was. It pushed down, bent his nose, shoved it sideways until his sinuses hurt with a cool chlorine sting, like when swimming pool water got in. The shoe's dirty rubber slid down until it deformed his mouth, pressing lips into teeth, forcing Allen to bite himself, and he hated doing that. The shoe ground around, almost delicately, opening up holes that bled down his throat until everything was a stench and taste of blood and old shoe. He was gurgling. Pink liquid ran from the corner of his mouth and the shoe slipped in it, punishing his chin and sliding to his throat, closing the airway. Allen knew with a certain calm clarity that he'd stopped breathing and that he was going away.

Then it stopped. Air rushed in with a gob of spit and blood and the shoe left his face, letting him turn his head to the side, cough and vomit. The knees which had pinned his arms into the grass and dirt of the family back yard now released him and Allen realized that his own sneakered feet had been kicking impotently the whole time. His body, now free and still kicking, flopped and bounced in the dirt, raising some dust, jarring his tailbone numb. Noises came from him.

When the dust settled there was someone standing over him. Not the brother whose sneaker he had been smelling. Another brother. The one with the dirty tennis shoe had already left, with the neighborhood friend whose knees had pinned Allen down.

The new brother looked at Allen for a moment, then he too walked away. Allen watched him go into the house. It was a summer day. The windows were open and the radio was playing. It said, "Hey shout, summertime blues/Jump up and down in my blue suede shoes/Hey, kid, rock n' roll, rock on."

The vomit and blood didn't bother him. They were already a memory, running into the dirt. His throat was bruised and numb, but he didn't think about it. Something else pushed it all aside: a blank face, somewhere above the grinding shoe. The face had an amoebic disinterest. Behind the flat eyes the machine sent intelligent strength into the foot that wore the shoe that ground his own face, but that other face, although it resembled his, did not occupy the same backyard summer day. He was utterly alone with the tarry rubber stink that had bloodied him.

Then this face was pushed aside by the second face, the one belonging to the other brother, whose arrival had evidently put a stop to the choking. That face, too, had nothing in it and it was this particular nothing that sank in, deeply and forever: it denied the smallest reflection of kinship, affirming that there was nothing between the boy in the dirt and anything above him. It had stopped the proceedings for the sake of self-interest—to minimize the evidence and the likelihood of punishment.

Allen was ashamed for wanting anything from those faces above him. As he lay in the dry summer adobe the sour odor filled his sinuses. It had a blood metal scent of its own and it mingled with his. He felt the earth turning and groaning beneath him and he wanted to sink down into it. He wondered for the first time what it was that lay below, whose skin he walked on. For the first time he knew that the earth was alive and moving and here was where his kinship was buried. He remained in the back yard for hours while the sun burned him.

On the evening of this same summer day, when their father came home from the post office and saw Allen's face, there was no doubt as to how the afternoon had been spent. The intervention had not come in time to conceal the evidence, and justice was swift and thorough. Allen was spared the blows, but not the view.

It was the sparing of the blows that could never be forgiven. Blows eventually led to more blows, and these in turn led to more until there was no more strength to strike.

Later, awakened by shouts as his father patrolled the eternal nighttime war jungle with his ghost platoon, Allen crept out, for the first time, into the street with the midnight cats.

Allen's hands were cold. It took some moments, after coming to himself, to realize that he was not an eight year old boy, but was a man, past middle age, dreaming dreams. He sat in a cushioned wicker chair on Maria's front porch, staring into the morning sun, extracting warmth through the orbits of his eyes. He rubbed his hands together, tendons and bone working against thin skin, knuckles surfacing like messages in a Magic 8-Ball. *Better not to tell you now.* His joints ached and in spite of the cold he was on fire with itchy nettles.

The French door creaked and Maria came out. She handed Allen a cup of coffee. "Aren't you cold?"

Allen accepted the coffee. "*Signs point to yes.*"

Maria stepped back and looked at him. "Okay. Would you like a blanket or something?"

"*My sources say no.*"

She smiled. "And will you be staying for lunch?"

"*Ask again later.*"

Maria waved her hands and walked away, laughing. "Okay, 8-Ball. I hope you snap out of it."

The French door opened and closed. Allen still stared straight ahead. "*Outlook not so good.*"

They ate lunch in the little sitting room off the kitchen, where the sun, low on the horizon, peeped in. Allen balanced his plate on his knees, picking at macaroni and salad, trying to appear hungry.

Maria sat across from him in an easy chair. "How's the macaroni? And no 8-Ball answer."

"It's good," Allen replied. "*You may rely on—*" He ducked his head at her look. "Really good."

"Good." She dabbed at her salad. "And, um."

Allen put his fork down. "Yes?"

"Any luck finding what it was you were looking for?"

"Looking for?"

"This morning. Early. When you went out."

Allen didn't reply. He picked up his fork, but didn't even pretend to eat. "You don't miss much."

"I know the sounds of this house."

"Like, the back steps."

"Like that, yes."

"I'm not crazy, or dangerous, you know."

"I know."

"I, uh." He put his folk down again. "I did go out. I went to town."

"Not many rocks there."

"No. Um, you ever go to a lawyer in this town?"

"A lawyer. No, why?"

"I was just wondering."

"Are you in some sort of legal trouble?"

"I wish," Allen mumbled.

"What?"

"No. I'm not in any legal trouble. I don't have the guts to get into trouble."

Maria looked out the window, her face in the golden light like those Tahitian women in the paintings on Allen's wall. She looked back at him. "It doesn't take guts to get into trouble."

"But sometimes it takes imagination. And I don't have that either."

"It just takes stupidity. And that you also don't have."

"Speaking of which, is—"

"No. No one else is here, Allen."

A long silence settled between them, more comfortable than ever. Allen wanted it to go on. He had never known such a thing, had never imagined that it could be. He watched Maria, looking out the window again. "Did you pick out the paintings for my room?"

"Yes."

"I love them."

"Thank you." Her voice was suddenly heavy.

"Something wrong?"

She smiled. "*Better not tell you now.*"

Allen looked at her, somber. "*Reply hazy, try again.*"

Maria was still smiling, but her eyes glistened in the sideways sun. "You are kind of crazy."

"But not dangerous." He put his plate aside. "I can't eat any more, I'm sorry."

She stood and took his plate, shaking her head. When she was out of the room, Allen pulled a cellphone from his trench coat pocket and hit redial.

The number you have dialed has been disconnected or is no longer—

Maria returned to the sitting room with more coffee. "You're living on this, huh?"

"You make great coffee."

"Oh, stop it. You're just making up for insulting my macaroni."

"It was great, too."

She sat again, pulling her feet up under her. "Did you find them?"

"Find who?"

"Whoever you were trying to reach."

Allen didn't know how to answer, or if he wanted to. No, he did not want to. There was no way to honestly answer her. It lay too far down and away, that answer, down too many twisting stairs, across too many miles and far too many deserted roads. It might not exist at all. He didn't feel he had to answer her, but he wanted to say something.

"I think she's gone," he said at last.

"Was she here?"

"I don't know." The stinging nettles returned, scorching out from his joints, burning the inside of his skin. He grasped at something to distract him from the fire. "That moving job downtown? The one DJ had? Do you think he ever did it?"

"Hmm? Oh, don't know, I doubt he ever had it, but possibly, why?"

"I don't know."

"He doesn't do most of the stuff he says he's gonna do."

"I get that." He sat up. "Listen, how long have I been here, at your house?"

"How long? This is your third day."

Allen closed his eyes. "Well, it's not, possible—not unless he—no, forget it."

Maria looked at him. "You need to sleep."

Allen opened his eyes and tried to smile. "Maybe."

"If you want to rest awhile, I'll tell you when dinner's ready. Or I could take it up to you."

"That is very nice of you, Maria." He got out of the chair, trying to hide his dizziness. "But you know, I think I want to head west."

"Head west. What do you mean, head west?"

"Just up into the mountains behind your place, across the fields there."

"Oh. Are you—do you think you should try that, really?"

"I really want to get up there."

Maria looked at him, her expression troubled. "You can take the bike."

"Thanks. Thanks, Maria. I will. Thanks for lunch."

"Lunch that you didn't eat."

Her gentle scolding was a balm, cooling away the nettle fire. "It was more than enough."

Allen swung left out of Maria's yard and took the narrow country lane that ran northwest, following the canyon of the river, now far below. The road rose steadily and gradually turned straight west, heading directly for the higher peaks. Pausing at a viewpoint, Allen looked back and could see the road cut, miles away, where he had explored and slept. Now he could see the broader picture, written across the canyonside, and it told him of eras beyond his ability to grasp. To the west high meadowlands, cut with fins and ribs of granite and basalt, sloped more steeply upward to the cordon of ridges. They were nearly treeless, argent and etched with deep afternoon shadows. He mounted the bike and pedaled slowly up toward them.

It was good to go up. Good to go away from that town, where blue spirits wandered, ate echoes, muttered in the wires. Here was living rock, stabbed straight through the flesh of the continent, new and ancient, howling on the edge of the world. Here the cold streams ran, drawing Allen to them, where he could soothe his boiling blood. The story was told here that he knew and could never know, all the more reassuring because of it. "Higher up! Higher up!" He pedaled into cold mountain shade.

The country lane ended, became gravel Forest Service road, and still Allen pedaled, breathing hard, past pools of meadow where herbs grew, past somber streams singing in their own carved vales. Now his blood was up, there was no illness and he couldn't remember what weariness was. Some few remembrances of the Boy King lived on. He had to get off the bike, pushing it along under drooping boughs of fir and yew, but his speed didn't slacken. He maintained a steady pace, breathing in the sharp tang of mountain tree air. The road burrowed up and in, dug into brittle hill flesh. At last, bending north across the face of the ridge, it crested on a lower reach of the mountains, doubling back south across the ridgetop and reaching ever-greater heights. Allen stopped, here looking down into a tiny moraine where a boulder-studded greensward descended to a sable pool notched into a crack of the mountains. This crack in turn rose behind and high above it to the deep, late afternoon sky. It was like a hearth, but not for fire; a water hearth, cool wet flames licking the ice dark shore. Still pushing the bike, he took the trail down to it.

The bike dropped into the grass with a discordant clang of spokes, gears and chain. Allen left it where it fell and stumbled to the edge of the pool. Holding on to a cedar branch, he peered into the water, at first seeing nothing but his reflected face and the evening sky above it. But slowly the water changed. There were trout and crayfish, worms wriggling down for winter hibernation. Bits of water weed waved and summoned. Death was there. It was a glad death in which his face floated, staring back at him, content. There was no pain. The things that never were and never would be were there now, calling. He drifted down until he, too, rested on cool mud, gray weeds folding over him, caressing his forehead, kissing his mouth. He no longer needed to be jealous of those who went before him.

Then she came to him, down through the water. Her eyes were blue, or the sky shone through them, in which case they were nothing. Her hair was blonde, or else it was some captured sun, forced into currents of water, drifting above him. But when she lay by him, her smile was Sunday morning in the fields of long ago. The crook of her arm was just-so. If they had drowned, no matter. Her hand found its way over his shrunken belly, and they, both of them, slipped with skin made unguent into the lost space of each other. That's when he no longer cared: something of the night-roaming ferocity found its way into his limbs and he wrapped about her and she wrapped about him, disturbing the silt floor of the pond, roiling the waters and spilling fruit and pearls into the wilding deep. She spoke, he spoke, but only a crying and a thin ring shivered between them, from them, finding the hidden nooks, telling them of the secret things that lay in the drowning pool. Locked together they spun and spiraled and wriggled still deeper in, where gushing springs poured from cold fissures in the heart of the mountain. Here they remained, what had been them, what was left, autumn castaways lost forever to the living world.

He called her name, and she was gone.

When Allen's eyes opened the world still whirled around him. The sky through water was dense with weeds, drifting and blowing. It was not a surface sky, but a deep place, like the pool, freezing and infinite, starting where vision started, but stretching, if he wished to follow, out to where all senses ended and the Everything began. But if he were to enter in to the sky, there would be no squeezing down into ooze. He clawed up, pushing away the weeds, flapping wildly against the water weight. With a force of will he sat up, water, worms, weeds and mud slaking off him. He shook his head, flinging bits off his matted hair and still the world spun and he could no longer tell where land met sky, because land and sky no longer met.

He remembered his lungs and made them work, sucking in stabbing breaths. Instantly the world quit spinning and, wrapping his arms around himself, Allen discovered he was on dry land, a dry man, sitting at the edge of the evening pool. He looked around. Here in the lee of the stone bowl it was almost night, but on the surrounding peaks the memory of daylight lingered. The sky had resumed its impermeable surface, and a new moon began its traveling arc across it. Seeing the moon, Allen came fully-awake and jumped up, holding on to the cedar tree as the world resumed its spinning around. He knew he must travel too, and quickly, if he didn't want to be caught in the mountains when the night song began.

As soon as the dizziness eased, he got the bike and pushed it back up the trail to the gravel road. It was lighter here and Allen had no trouble seeing, even without a headlamp. It was far quicker going downhill than up and he was soon at the paved road, moving with even greater speed. Even so, it was full night when he neared the outskirts of town. The new moon closed its delicate, glowing jaws over a mouthful of earthshine. He paused to gaze at her, reluctant, now that he had reached it, to go back to the town on its broken bit of lost terrane.

"This town is not to be trusted," he said to the moon. "It lives on traveling lands. They smashed into us from who knows where. We can never know in what latitude they were born, or in what island arc they first appeared, breaking the ocean, or from what busted up continent they escaped."

How many pressed bones and carapaces did this rolling stone scrape up, dragging its cherty mess up against the continental shore? What chalcedony mingled with the gold? He laughed. The whole place should have gone under, pushed down deep, made food for the granite teeth back there. This lump should have fed the batholiths.

Still laughing, he got on the bike and flew.

As he rode, he thought about Ted, down there in his bar. He wondered what Ted would have seen if he had been standing by that mountain pool. Would he have seen a man drowning in the water, or just a mumbling wreck, passed out in the grass as night crept in? Would Ted have seen the worms and weeds and the girl with ice eyes, wrapped in Allen and Allen wrapped in her? Or would he have seen someone shivering and demented, sitting under an old cedar, lost and alarming? Would he then have shaken his head and walked away?

Ted had seen stranger things than that, Allen guessed. Older things, and things more painful than any inconvenience he might suffer now. Stored in the back of Ted's bar with the bottles, the mops and the oil soap were the broken bits: lost dreams and stolen glances, recorded in yellowed ledgers. Wanderers lodged with Ted, and told him their stories. He listened, offered cool drinks and remembered them all, saying little, but keeping track of the words, the tears and the hours. And if did speak he could tell them not to worry. He kept their secrets safe and they could read them all back later, when their stories were over.

Ted, Allen decided, was someone who could be trusted.

The remainder of the ride home was leisurely, down the country lane and into Maria's neighborhood again. It seemed to him that Allen had survived a great danger, the exact nature of which he couldn't be sure. But as the lights of Maria's came into view, he knew that the menace had arrived there before him.

Chapter Six

It was completely quiet as Allen climbed the back steps. The hills slept, or lay listening. The house said nothing except creaking talk in its boards and in the treads under his boots. The kitchen and living room lights were on, but he'd seen no one as he came in. Still, as he opened the door to his room, he knew that the house was aware of him. He closed the door and turned on the light. Something was wrong with the room, but he couldn't tell what it was. He'd asked Maria not to clean unless he requested it, and everything appeared as he'd left it that afternoon. Still there was something not right about it. Allen stood, looking around. The bed covers were still thrown back; the bathroom door ajar, towel hanging from the curtain rod over the tub, dresser drawers closed and the suitcase on top, half-zippered, all as he'd left it. But.

The smell. There was a different smell in the room. A hint of rank must.

DJ. He'd been in here.

Allen's gaze fell on the desk. There, that was it. The drawer where he kept his medicines was just slightly open. He yanked it all the way out and looked closely at every bottle. Sitting at the desk, he counted the pills, bottle by bottle. None seemed to be missing, but nonetheless he knew they'd been gone through. He always placed the prescription labels facing forward, and he'd found them pointing in all directions.

"You little fuck."

After taking his night pills, he sat on the bed. The dizziness was returning and he was weak again. He needed to think. It wouldn't do to have DJ pawing his medicine. It might no longer be a good idea to remain here at all, but he didn't want to leave. In the few days he'd spent at Maria's, Allen felt more at home than he ever had in the anonymous East Bay apartment he'd lived in for half his life. Now that apartment was empty, waiting to be occupied by some other nameless soul, and everything he owned was in that tan suitcase, on his back, in the bank or in the desk drawer. This was home. He would not leave. There was nowhere else to go.

Allen got up. Having made up his mind, he went quickly from his room, down the hall and to the top of the stairs. He thought he could hear the quiet tapping of Maria's keyboard in the study, back down the lower hall, entering billing codes. But there was another sound, jagged and obscene, that rattled down the halls. From the front living room uttered the inane chatter and fake laughter of some television show. That, he knew, was where DJ was.

The television's chemical glow jittered through the living room door and spilled out into the hallway, its noise and glare pushing against him as Allen approached. A solid rage moved him forward. It filled him, fuming and anesthetizing, making his lungs feel dense and square, jutting against the inside of his ribs. It fueled his forward march, obscured all but a pencil lead focus to his immediate front. A pneumatic hammer beat on the inside of his skull. The television was no longer heard in the way one ordinarily hears a television; instead the yakking and the laugh tracks imprinted directly on Allen's brain, indwelling and stultifying, electronic barking polluting nerve, artery, and lobe. He wanted to smash the screen emitting it, rupture its circuit voice. In his last steps to the living room, Allen resolved to do this. He swung in, ready to break and beat.

There was DJ, sprawled across the couch, a beer on the floor, just below his inert hand. His mouth was open and he breathed deeply inside his skewed trucker's cap. Under the T shirt and stained jeans, DJ's muscles were retreating before beer bloat. Allen saw what was left of his stupid bulk, a plague of brainstem indulgence that would leave nothing to rot, ossify or rust away. The absolute absence of anything under that clown hat made Allen instantly ashamed and nauseated. It was impossible to believe that a thing that breathed could be so dead. The illusion of something that was DJ melted away before him, not even leaving an impression on the mission oak couch tapestry.

Allen shook his head. He had no more desire to smash the television. His veins felt hollow, contracted, frozen. The fire went out and only crawling loneliness remained. This was what inherited the earth. This was what walked around on it after he was gone. It got its greasy fingers into the cracks, pried open the drawers, rummaged around in the accounts of the departed, looking for something sweet. It sucked out the lukewarm marrow, squatted and shat on the carpet, wiped its ass on the winding sheet, winked and chuckled, fouled the water. It was stupid, mouth-breathing. It was blind and it never went away.

He started to leave, but was stopped by DJ's narrow eyes, staring up at him from under his cap.

"Hey," DJ said.

Allen returned the stare but said nothing.

"You don't look so good. Come down for some a Maria's home cooking?"

Allen felt the flash kindle in his chest. He took a step into the living room. His hands cold and heavy. He stared down at DJ, who was grinning stupidly now, reaching for his beer.

"She does cook, huh? Yep." He sat up enough to swallow. "She sure can cook." He swung his legs over and lurched to a sitting sprawl, observing Allen over the swollen belly on which he'd placed his beer. The television jangled, throwing fractured panes of sick glitter on DJ's sallow cheek. "Bet you can't get enough."

He pressed the aluminum can to his puffy lips and sucked, belching, bubbles forming in the chapped corners of his mouth. Unable to look away, Allen watched the bubbles. They ran with yeast and mouth debris, slick and adorned with septic rainbows. As the corners of DJ's mouth deformed into a sneer, the bubbles escaped that hole, running in a stream down his cheek and perishing in the sofa cushion.

DJ's mouth opened for more witticisms, but his jaw froze. Something approaching a thoughtful expression crossed his face, replaced by doubt. As he looked at

Allen, the doubt melted into fear and then stark-staring terror.

Allen saw the change. He wanted to look behind him, to see what was making DJ gape and wither, but as he shrank into the couch Allen knew that DJ's eyes were fastened solely on him. He trembled, mouth working noiselessly. The beer capsized on his shaking belly, soaking his shirt and pants, exposing patch of pasty skin where the dampness spread. His hands gripped the couch. His head shook with a loathsome tremor.

Something like praying came out of DJ's mouth, but it was mingled with belching and a low whimper. His whole body shook so violently that Allen could feel the floor vibrate under his feet and the couch shivered like a live thing under DJ's quivering frame. He raised a hand, pointing, but his stricken arm could not hold still and the index finger looked as if it were writing invisible words in the air. He repeated something over and over, wordless and despairing.

Then Allen was struck, as if by a blow from behind, and he was blinded. There was no pain, no sensation at all, except a sort of pressure relief, like a diver ascending. But he was rising through himself, swimming out of his skin. Slowly, as his vision returned, he saw not through his own eyes, but through DJ's. In front of him there stood a Man on Fire, glaring with smoldering flints. In his huge hands were two hammers, glowing white. A steam of boiling iron rose, a blood smell, rich and piercing. His booted feet were wells of flame. He opened his mouth and burning creatures whooped out, scaled, winged, and shouting accusations. Smoke trailed from their silver feathers and they whirled around the room, filling it with fumes.

The man advanced towards the couch and as he approached his eyes merged into a single hole of fire that grew wider and deeper, glowing azure, then yellow, orange, red, argent milk, consuming his mouth, blotting out his entire face until only a searing sun filled the room.

What marched and flew now? Nations. Worlds. A galaxy marshaled its armies and besieged the nebulae, overwhelmed everything within its spiral arms, smothering infants and cracking the backs of the strong, the beautiful, the old and crippled. There was no mercy. All were to scatter and wither, all snuffed out, every sparkle and jot. All transgression was repaid tenfold. That which had never been came calling, and it laughed as it beat down the door. The song was done. The note was due.

A milling and a grinding spun and pulled and drew down all that fell within its reach, and its reach was wide and broad and deep. There was laughter, insensate TV chortles. There was beer, hissing on the hearth of the Eating Thing, disappearing with a smell like burned bread. A heavy shoe came down on a throat forever, the trachea crackled and collapsed and fell in pieces into the starless funnel. The bottomless bottom pulsed and drew and clucked like a devouring hen, calling its vicious chicks to roost burning under her wings.

There was a scream, from where and from whom could not be known. In that moment both Allen and DJ had ceased to be.

Chapter Seven

Morning came late to Allen's west-facing room. When he awoke at eight o'clock, the room was still indistinct, nothing in it having graduated much beyond varieties of gray. He looked around, not daring to move just yet, unsure if he could, or, if that was possible, what would come out from under the covers. But the body in the bed was his: long, thin and stinging with the pain that only his morning medication would ease. Getting up, he moved slowly to the desk. He swallowed down his pills with cold coffee as the room whirled around him.

It was half an hour before Allen felt safe to move again. He hunched over the desk, waiting for the world to stop. Eventually it did, and although still nauseated, he could stand and get to the bathroom.

In the shower he came fully to himself, diving back down through water into the familiar pressure of his body. It was only when this finally happened that he was certain he'd been away, out on some wandering rind of land, a lichen or a bit of garnet tucked into a mineral bosom, adrift on the mantle.

DJ had been there, too, or the thing that had been DJ. It didn't look like him or spit the same words. It spit nothing at all except some sulfate cloud, but it was the thing that he had been, or had become. All it needed was a stained clown trucker's hat.

There they had eddied, and Allen knew more of DJ's mind than he thought bearable. The more he knew, the less he knew. The DJ Thing was a subtraction, a reduction, pulling in oxygen and puking up beer-flavored crusty bits. There was no point at all to its being there and its only profundity was a pure and absolute absence of worth or purpose. It was a thing so stripped that, were it not for its miasma, it could have had a sort of charred doorstop dignity. As it was, it floated and stank and did nothing else.

Whatever it was that Allen had become thought, *what is it like to have as your only purpose the task of floating and stinking?* But he didn't have to guess. He knew. He could not escape the gravity of DJ's reek.

The Man on Fire was there, as much as anything could be there. In the endless stretching sky ocean cave that was their world, the Man on Fire stomped, waded, splashed fire waves that struck the sky and descended as sparks that streaked across their eyes. The Man on Fire bellowed and wallowed, clenched his fire-fists and beat the dead air. That which had been Allen watched and trembled on his stone raft, watched and listened to something. In another time it would have been called the radio.

The radio, bouncing off the Man's on Fire's thick hide. News sports and weather: a traffic pileup on the Bay Bridge. Cloudy with a chance of showers. His estranged wife found naked. The last plane out. Award-winning recipes. Trouble in Ukraine. A game-winning RBI in the ninth inning.

Then music. The Fabulous Super Hits of the Seventies, Eighties and Nineties. Transistors. Chrome and turquoise. Big bass notes disturbing the cloistered water. Doo Wop. KDIA Lucky Thirteen. KSAN, Jive Ninety-Five.

"Hey, kid, rock n' roll, rock on."

And then, great arms raised up, the Man on Fire opened his hands, fire-fingers splayed wide, a stock-still orant. The waters settled around his knees and the sky was still, mirroring those orange waters. Allen watched, mute, and the DJ Thing whimpered, its filthy begging noises crawling through Allen's ears so that he wanted to shake his head, but could not.

Beginning muted and low down, like a deep, distant horn, the Man on Fire began to intone his oratory. There were no words in it, but brass and wood, drum, hide and roots, dug deep. He spun the tone and it echoed in that great hall until Allen thought the reverberation would crush his skull. It roiled his guts. He wanted to be sick but couldn't. Slowly the tonal supplication rose in volume and deepened in pitch until it was no longer a sound but a rich, violent quaking that shook the foundations of heaven, rattled off the cloudless atmosphere and turned the waters to glass.

Reaching up, then crashing down, the Man on Fire shattered the sea and then there was no more, not a trace. He had consumed and been consumed. All former things had passed away.

Now in the waking world, in the shower, Allen wondered if that Man on Fire had come from his own body, or if he himself had been born in that fire.

"Neither," he said, and he knew that was true.

That man came from where there was no other. He came from where there was no there. That man burned, and the energy of the earth's core, the furnace that drove the engine that moved mountains and doomed entire sea beds was not even an afterthought to him. There was no relation between that man and Allen, not until Allen would finally walk out of the mineral world.

He dried off, renewed. Consciousness peeled away brain fog like skin off a tangerine. As the waking world brightened, and Allen along with it, the memory of the night crept back, not really as memory—nothing cannot be remembered—but as dream, dog thought, snake musing, a series of pixilated images in gray and sepia: hallways, couches, beer cans, windows, DJ recoiling, acrid smoke.

Then Maria. Speaking to him, to Allen. Not the Man on Fire. No underworld, over-sky vision, no hellish geology. Just Maria, wordless words, a cool hand, steering him gently and surely back down the hall, up the stairs, to his room.

Then nothing again, really nothing, an absence deeper than drugs, deeper than sleep, more silent than the vacuum of the radio-refusing thermosphere, where all that temperature in its upper reaches heated nothing. Rest and oblivion.

And here it was, day, and what lay outside his room, below him in the house or out in the world grown fully-awake, Allen didn't know. He was fairly certain he wouldn't want to know, not right now. He dressed quickly and, putting on his trench coat once more, left the room to its lonely self.

Ted presided over his tavern in the manner of all those tending bars, an expectant and philosophical patience radiating from his white-sleeved arms, his clean hands resting on the bar top exuding the confidence of all hands that know that those who drink will come to them and ask, and they will provide. Blessed assurance.

It was late morning when Allen came in, carrying something under his arm. He sat on a barstool across from Ted, who was already opening a coke bottle.

"Good morning," Allen said.

"Morning." Ted put the coke in front of him. "What do you have there?"

"This?" Allen produced a greenish, rusty rock. "This is some ophiolite."

"It looks like a rock."

"It is. It is a piece of ocean rock that traveled a long way to get here so I could pick it up, just now, on my way into town. There is an outcrop of the stuff below Jefferson Street, on the river side."

"Ophiolite."

"Yes. Snake rock." Allen drank his coke. "From long ago and far away. It isn't really a rock, but a sequence of rock that occurs where ocean plates are spreading away from each other."

"Not a thing, then," Ted said. "But a happening of things"

"Yeah. A series. And its story will go on when ours is over, by a long shot."

"Yes," Ted said. "Yes, it will."

"Do you know Maria?" Allen asked.

Ted said nothing. He took Allen's money and dropped it in the till, rolling the drawer shut with its usual solid thud. Picking up a towel, he wiped the already-glistening bar.

"She lives with DJ," Allen continued. "Or he lives with her. He lives on her." He drained his coke and declined another. "She keeps him around for some reason."

Ted returned to stand in front of him. "People don't need any reason to do what they do."

"No?"

"No. Reasons are just part of the clothing we put on events. They're part of the skin we make, so we can follow the bouncing ball."

"And where is the ball bouncing?"

"Nowhere. There is no ball."

"I like to think this rock came into my life for a reason," Allen said.

"Well, it gave us something to talk about."

"There you go."

Ted took Allen's empty bottle and threw it in the tub. Crossing his arms, he leaned against the back bar, looking out the window at the clear fall day. Allen cradled the rock in the crook of his arm, scratching it with a fingernail. Looking up, he watched Ted for a moment, then peered around the bar.

"I know what's missing here."

Ted smiled. "People?"

"Yeah, there's that." Allen gestured with his free hand. "But there's more, or less." He spun on his barstool, turning around to Ted. "There's no video poker."

"That is true."

"No jukebox. No DMX. No shuffleboard, no pictures of half-naked girls selling alcohol."

"No."

"There are no little neon beer signs. You have no hot links in a jar. And here's the deal, Ted." Allen jabbed a finger at him. "You got no *television*."

Ted held up his hands. "Busted."

"No wonder you have no customers."

"That's a valid consideration."

"I'm not objecting."

"Another coke?"

"No. Yeah, sure. Look—"

Ted opened another coke. "You need to be careful of DJ."

Allen accepted his coke and handed his money to Ted. "He might want to be careful of me."

"That's not how it works." Ted shook his head. "Things are moving that you can't control."

Allen smiled. "No kidding."

"No." Ted leaned forward and tapped Allen's rock. "More than you are aware of. Much more."

In the silence that followed Allen drank his coke while Ted deposited his money. Swiveling on the barstool Allen squinted at Ted. "Who are you?"

Ted flipped a towel and smiled. "I'm a bartender, man."

Allen resumed scratching his rock. "You ever see a lawyer in this town?"

Ted shook his head. "Never needed one. You?"

"I don't need one. But I'm trying to see one."

Ted laughed. "Yeah? Is that hard to do?"

Allen stood. "Apparently."

"Well," Ted said, resuming his patient stance, "be careful out there."

Allen headed for the door. "I have to be." He opened it. "I'm your only customer."

Leaving Ted's bar was like walking out of a secret room. It was safe in there. There was no need to explain anything, it wasn't necessary because Ted knew that nothing amounted to much. When one was in Allen's circumstances that was a comfort to be around. Now in the light of day, the burden of things making sense, the obligation of explanation, fell on him like another planet's gravity. Each day, each hour, every moment it became more difficult. Sometimes just walking was a complicated chore. Every face he passed reflected his longing to return to that safe and secret place, more secure and welcoming, at least for now, than his own rented room in Maria's house, where all hell might have broken loose. He shuddered, cradled his rock and walked on.

It was no surprise to see that the *For Lease* sign was removed from Liz's office door. Allen had figured the odds to be somewhere between fifty/fifty and *You may rely on it*. Now it was certain, and he crossed Main for a closer look.

Everything was as it had been before. (What "before" meant, Allen no longer knew. There was likely no way to know if there had been a "before" at all.) The lights were on, the place was open for business. The plump clerk was not at her desk, but the computer screen glowed. Allen opened the door and walked in.

The first thing he noticed was the smell. In peering through the glass all this time, it was one sense of the place he'd not been able to get, and now the impression was of hair conditioner. Strawberry. Some formaldehyde off the furniture, reasonably fresh paint, Chinese food, the sober, pleasant redolence of law book leather and rag paper. Under this there was another layer, older, much older, but also more recent. Today. Just having walked through the room. It was Liz's perfume, the kind she always wore, mingled with the memory of her skin.

Allen was dizzy with the smell. He could hear voices, one of them Liz's, coming from the inner office. Someone would be out eventually. He decided to sit in one of the comfortable chairs in the corner. That improved things considerably, but he was saddened to already lose Liz's perfumed skin scent.

"Nothing lasts," he said, "except those things that never were." Saying that cheered him immensely and he relaxed, listening to Liz's funny tomboy voice. He could only make out a word or two, principally "Wow" and "Way." But that didn't matter. It was Liz's voice, always sounding as if she had something in her mouth and was about to laugh, which she did, frequently. He wished he could sit and listen to her voice all afternoon, floating around this sad museum space as the sunlight through the glass washed him and he fell gently to sleep.

Before he could doze off, the inner office door opened and the clerk came out, shutting the door behind her, nose in a sheaf of papers, taking no notice of Allen in his corner chair. It occurred to him that she might not be able to see him at all, that this entire moment might not in fact be occurring or worse (or better), the very real possibility that he might no longer exist. He wished he had a Magic 8-Ball.

There being only one way to test his theories, he said, "Hello."

The plump clerk's reaction didn't entirely surprise him, but it was still disconcerting to see her leap from her ergonomic chair and clap her freckled hands over her mouth.

"Well," Allen said, "I guess that means that I am here, and so are you."

The clerk dropped her hands and cracked a nervous, plump sort of laugh. That was it. She remained standing by her chair and Allen was made aware of the rock in his lap, as the clerk was staring at it.

"Ophiolite."

"Excuse me?" Her voice was plump as well, and pleasant, unchallenging and secure. It was the voice of a good clerk, who made everything work.

"Ophiolite. That's what the rock is. It's a piece of the ophiolite. An ordinary bit of ocean bottom that gains notoriety and a title due to the company it keeps."

"Oh."

"Sort of a rocky social climber."

"Oh."

They said nothing else for quite some time and Allen could hear Liz's voice coming from the inner office. She was talking on the phone, he guessed, as there was no audible reply. She was laughing, something between a caw and a hiccup, the same laugh Allen had always loved and coaxed from her, easily, many years ago, when they were both young.

Regaining her composure, the clerk smiled and said, "Were you here to make an appointment with Ms. Terry?"

"Yes, if I might."

"Well sure, sure." She produced a clipboard from under her desk and brought it to Allen. "If you'd fill this out, we can set you up." She returned to her desk and tapped at her keyboard. "Ms. Terry only practices civil law."

"Best kind."

"'Scuse me? Oh, yes. Ha, so if you—"

"Yes, I'll fill it out. Listen, can I take this with me?"

The clerk looked at him. "Um, well."

"Not the clipboard, I mean, just the paper. Can I take it with me, bring it back when I come in?"

"Um, well, we usually—she has to know if there's a conflict right up front. She can't represent you if—"

"Oh, that's not going to be a concern."

"It's to save you time and money."

"Yes, I appreciate that, but it will be fine. When's your next open time?"

"Well"—she tapped at her keyboard—"We have a ten o'clock tomorrow morning."

Allen stood and brought her the clipboard. "That would be good, yes." He reached out his hand. "Al. Al Gabbro."

She took his hand. It seemed as if she didn't want to. "Nice to meet you, Mister, um, Gabbro. I'm Jasmine." She handed him a card with Liz's name on it. "Any questions, or if you need to change the time, just call me."

"No, that will work fine. No time-changing needed. Thanks so much."

"Sure, yeah, no problem." She was still wary. She wasn't warming up to the guy with the rock.

At the door, Allen stopped. "Say, this office wasn't for lease any time recently, was it?"

Jasmine was still standing. "For lease?"

"Yes. This office. Has it been up for lease recently?"

"You mean, like—"

"Rented out. Put on the market. Prospective tenants sought. Will build to suit."

"For lease. This office."

"Exactly."

She shook her head. "No. Not for years. It hasn't been, well, for years"

"Okay, thanks." Allen left quickly, rock under his arm, heading north on Main.

Chapter Eight

"Al Gabbro." Allen opened the desk drawer and checked his pill bottles. There was nothing out of place. "Al Gabbro." He shook his head. He wanted to laugh. "Mister Ophiolite would have been better." The rock sat on his desk, a tiny piece of wayward sea trough, spinning through unimaginable distances from unknown origins to an unknowable future. Allen tapped it. "Mister Ophiolite, you now have legal representation."

He removed his trench coat and stood a moment in the middle of his room. There was nothing for it. He had to go down and see what the damage was. New lodgings might be in order when the dust settled, but not knowing was worse than facing the music.

Maria's kitchen was especially welcoming. The sun came through the clean windows as it traveled low across the southern horizon, the last glowing drops filling bottles along the windowsills. Soon, Allen knew, the light would be brief and cheerless. He went to the sink, leaning into the afternoon's comfort. He was alone, but he knew the house was not empty. It watched and listened. There was a wounded air, but not hostile. Somewhere in the walls, along the baseboards, swirling in the corners like dust, there was a faint, expectant hope. It might have found its way in by accident, and could this very moment be looking for a way out, but for now there was undeniably a lightening of the air and something fresh and new stirred in the rooms. Allen inhaled it, sniffed, and blinked. It was probably the most surprising breath he'd taken in years. Where all was corruption and violence, now there was a spring day plucked from the grip of autumn and a new morning in bleak afternoon. He tried to catch what it was, but it would not be caught. It danced away from him and he let it go. One word came to him before he started thinking about other things: "Deliverance."

He heard the front door open and footsteps in the hall. Looking away from the window, he watched the hall doorway and waited. The footsteps approached the doorway, slowed, then moved on. Allen caught a glimpse of DJ slouching by, and in that brief look he saw the rooster was gone, replaced by something beaten, hangdog, and far more troubling to him: the visage of an empty thing, forced to look at itself and see nothing. It was a creature from a dangerous void that dogged DJ's trudging shoes.

Far down the hall a door opened and closed. The door to their bedroom, Allen knew. Almost immediately the door opened and shut again and new footsteps came up the hall. Maria appeared in the kitchen. She saw Allen and paused. He could not read her expression. She was far away, on her star, stirring mysteries.

"Your kitchen is nice," he said.

She went to the refrigerator and pulled out pots and dishes. "Are you coming to dinner?"

"Well I, ah."

"You ate in town."

"You know, the truth is, I don't eat much, Maria. I'm sorry."

She began putting dishes in the oven. Allen watched her move and his spirit stilled. Coming over with a head of lettuce, she waited for him to move away from the sink. He obliged, and she began rinsing and tearing the lettuce, patting it dry with a towel. He wanted to help, but knew she would refuse.

"If you don't eat," she said, "you don't live." She stopped rinsing and looked at him, cold water running over her hands. "Is that what you want?"

He shook his head. "No. No. I want to live."

She shook handfuls of lettuce. "Then eat."

Allen went and sat at the table, chin in his clasped hands. "I'll try."

Maria came and sat next to him. "I like you." She put her hand on his arm. "Don't go dying in one of my rooms."

Allen shut his eyes and smiled. Her hand was cool from the water. He put his hand over hers. "I'm doing my best." The stillness was good. In that stillness something rose, from his belly to his chest. He didn't dare think what it might be.

"Would you like to tell me what happened last night?"

Allen opened his eyes. Her face was close to his. "Um, let's see—I don't know?"

"Try again."

He swallowed. "But I don't. The nearest I can come to it is that these two landforms, an ocean apart, they collided. The resulting pressure created magmatic intrusion, lava everywhere."

"Come on, Allen." She pulled her hand away. "Come on. Be straight with me."

"I'm just guessing. It was your basic tectonic clash of North Despair and Dumbistan."

Maria threw up her hands and returned to the lettuce. "Whatever. Just—whatever."

"I'm trying my best. I—"

"Look!" Maria almost shouted it. "Look, I guess it doesn't matter, not to you. It might not even matter to me. But whatever went on in that living room, it got to DJ. You said something to him, you showed him something, something was done that knocked everything out of him. He's just been dragging around. He won't say anything. Something just—got to him."

Allen stood, wobbling slightly, steadying himself with the table. After a moment he went to Maria and, standing next to her, started tearing up lettuce. "Nothing got to him, Maria."

"Nothing."

"Absolutely nothing."

They stopped working and looked out the window at the traveling sun. It was a sweet pause. Finally Maria said, "Was there anyone else in the room?"

"Why?"

"Because DJ, he said—it seemed like there was, I don't know, from the way he was talking after, in his sleep, especially. He talked about something else. Someone else."

"Yes. There was a man on fire."

"A man. On fire."

"Didn't you see him when you came in? Sort of a thickset fellow."

"When I came in? I didn't come in."

"You came and got me."

"No. I didn't. I wasn't there."

A chill crept over him despite the warmth radiating off the glass. "But you came and—"

"I wasn't there. I was in my office."

"You helped me to my room. You helped me get into bed."

"I didn't, Allen. DJ came back to my office. He looked like he wasn't even alive. He was a mess. He'd—he'd made a mess of himself. I had to help him clean up and go to bed."

"You helped him."

"Yes."

"But it was me." Allen held on to the counter. He could break off pieces of it, he knew. Pull the sink out, plumbing and all. For a moment Allen's hands disappeared. His sleeves were empty. Events were sliding past moments, moments past minutes. With a snap and a jolt, the conveyor belt dragging the days down to be burned had stopped and now things refused to be. Nothing was possible.

"DJ, it's like he had a stroke. He goes out, he comes in. He goes out again." Maria started tearing lettuce again. Allen had stopped. She took a leaf from under his frozen hand. "He doesn't say anything. He's almost—"

"Human?"

"He's broken. Something broke him last night."

"Something needed to be broken, Maria."

"Easy for you to say." Her voice hardened. "Easy to say that, yes. And who decides that, Allen? Who decides what gets broken, who gets broken? Do you?"

"No."

"Well, that's a relief."

"Yes, it is."

Maria stopped working again. Her fingers knitted together, and Allen saw white surface in the brown skin on the backs of her hands. She bit her lower lip, then her lips parted. She looked out the window. "So many things get broken."

"Everything gets broken."

"Yeah. Yeah, I guess that's true." She resumed tearing the lettuce. "We don't have to go out of our way, you know? To wreck things. We don't have to try to break things even more."

"How was the living room?"

"It was a mess."

"And the television. Was it working?"

"The television."

"Yes. Was the TV working?"

"Um, it wasn't on." Maria stopped tearing lettuce again and looked at him. "Allen, what happened?"

"Nothing. Nothing happened."

She folded her hands across her stomach. "Nothing is something, is that what you are saying? The nothing is what happened?"

"Things," Allen said, "are not what they seem."

"And you think I don't know that?"

Maria shook her head and Allen saw her move worlds away. He wanted to run after her. In this moment, with the walls growing cold and anything like hope escaping with the drafts, he wanted to run, to stop her from leaving, walking down that cold hall to that office with the computer and the medical billing codes. He wanted more than anything to put his arms around her, to feel the heart and breath of another against his chest. That would have been so much more than enough.

Instead he only looked at her and was shocked to find that she had not, in fact, moved an inch. She was right where he'd left her. She looked back at him. Waited.

"The man," he said. "The man."

"Yes. The man."

"There was a man, another man in the room last night."

"Who?"

"He—he was us. DJ and me. He was us, but he was more than us. He was from that place where I'll be go—he was from another place, or from no place. But he, um, he seemed familiar."

"Yes?"

"He had a familiar odor. A familiar tone of voice. His face rang a bell."

Maria laughed, but there was no humor in it. "Was it that man who turned the couch upside-down? Was it that man who made a mess on the floor?"

"Um, I am guessing not."

"Yeah, that's what I am guessing, too. I am guessing not."

"Check the TV. See if it works. I'll bet it doesn't."

"I don't care whether it works or not."

Maria took the salad bowl and put it in the refrigerator. She began cleaning up the counters, darting looks at Allen. "You okay?"

"Yeah. I'm okay." He rested against the kitchen counter. It was true. Whatever path he plowed in this last bit of earth was a clean furrow. He'd work from can to can't—from first light to last—and that was all he could do. There would be rest in the kitchen at the close of the day. And there was one other thing: now, coming along behind him, there was another. Maria was there, bare feet stirring the dust as she followed him. She was at a distance now, but she drew closer, pulled along in his earth wake. When he stepped, she stepped, and as long as he could step he wanted her to move along with him, if just for a short while. He wanted her to walk him home.

She said, "It will be evening soon."

"Gets dark early."

"Yes." She returned to Allen and touched his arm lightly. "Don't go out tonight."

"I like to, you know. When the mountains start singing."

"I hear them, too."

He faced her. "Do you?"

"Yes."

"Do they make you afraid?"

"No."

"They could tear our lungs out."

"They won't. But stay in. Wait until morning."

"All right," he said. "All right, I will."

"I'll bring dinner up to you."

He still felt the draining chill cover him. He was less a creature of nerves and hair than a thing of chalk, leaf mold and ruined water. "This machine runs on hours," Allen's mud voice grated out. "We must have hours."

Maria took a step back. "Hours?"

Allen turned away from her, relieved that his neck muscles worked. "We have to have things move. If it doesn't move, it all balls up. It all smooshes together. We go crashing into each other. I mean, I have little DJ lumps smeared all over me. Do you see?"

"No," Maria said. "I don't.

She pulled away. He saw it and could do nothing to stop it. Anything he said now would make the pulling away worse, but he couldn't stop. It was the making sense that was such a burden, when the senseless was so strong and when the dark matter swallowed the seeing world. He couldn't say anything good now, nothing that would draw her back. He continued on without her, because there was nothing else he knew to do.

"Everyone's entitled to an explanation," he said. "And the explanation is this: it isn't possible to get through unbroken. We're here to break. To crack the shell. That's all we get here."

"So," Maria said, her voice far away, "you just accept that?"

"Yeah. I think so."

"Do you think that's some sort of revelation, Allen?"

"No. But you might agree that we try to fool ourselves into thinking it isn't so."

"Only if you have that luxury." Maria looked at him now. "Many people don't have that luxury."

He looked back at her, now ashamed. "You're right."

"There are many people," she said, "who would be very satisfied with your leftover life."

"I don't doubt that." He felt he should whisper. "But wouldn't you agree that there are also many who throw away what they have? Just for spite, or because they don't know better?"

Maria hesitated. "That could be."

"Take DJ. He's only half a DJ, or less, and there wasn't much of him to begin with. That's why he can't strut around anymore. There's just enough left of him to drag his ass up and down the hall and drink beer. Maybe he can't even drink beer anymore."

"He doesn't." Maria dried her hands and turned to leave. "He doesn't drink beer now."

"See? It's begun." Allen watched her as she walked to the hall doorway. "The unbecoming has begun." She disappeared through the doorway. "The wheels come off," he said to himself, going to the table. "We remain in fall. The leaf pauses halfway to the ground."

The town lodged in the spine of the West. Everything stopped here. Allen would look this evening to see if the moon had gained on them at all. If not, he imagined they would all eventually go flying out to join it. He put his head in his hands. "Even gravity will not be obeyed."

Allen's mind floated away again, and he didn't try to stop it. With each passing day the departing became easier, the wandering farther, to stranger lands. The kitchen walls disappeared, and Allen sat in the field that had been before this house was built. Only the table remained, in a late fall late afternoon. He looked around and there was no other sign of humankind or the works of human hands. There were only pin oaks, half-naked maple and bare cottonwood, bunch grass, taciturn boulders, and dry thistle. To the west, at the mountains' feet, elk fed. Looking east and south, Allen saw no town, just the high prairie funneling into steep canyon, river shining dull silver and tanned leather in the angling light.

Walking up the hill, a woman came toward him. Allen could not yet see what she looked like, but she was singing, the sort of song he heard on the edge of sleep, murmuring and full of reassurance. There was nothing in the words he understood, it was simply the fact that the song existed which comforted him. She carried something, and Allen knew that what she carried was good. She drew near, near enough to see her eyes. She didn't look at him, but Allen knew that what she sang was meant for him, and that it was good, too.

In some ways this woman was like Ted: aware of this place, listening and watching, taking note, and interested in the proceedings, but apart from them, moving before them, after them, or in a place where before and after did not cipher in. Allen listened to her evening song and it poured out a sudden gladness, like tears of joy and relief. He was only aware of one thing and that was simple gratitude for this kind, eternal song.

Sensing someone else's gaze on him, he looked up. The house had returned. Maria's kitchen was as he'd left it, except the sun, having rounded the corner, no longer shone directly in the windows. The pinched, wincing face of DJ blinked at him from the hallway. Maria stood behind him, her hands gripping his arm. She nudged him into the kitchen and walked behind him, full of dull duty. DJ's face was a sad clown mask, but, for the briefest flash as they approached the table, Allen perceived a sly glint in his hooded eyes.

Allen stood and walked past them on the way to the hall. "Have a nice dinner."

Seated at his desk, Allen watched the pearl crescent of the early evening moon move across his windowpane, a transit from corner to corner. It had grown from the previous night. The laws were working up there, for now. He had gone out to the deck earlier and looked down the hill to see if the woman might still be walking up, carrying her serene burden. All he had seen were old frame houses, backyards, and stray cats. Now as the night meds stole over him he followed the moon to no tomorrow.

The knocking came through years of water and bumped around in Allen's head. As he surfaced into his unlit room, he heard it again, a knocking at his door. He sat up, his neck stiff and his left arm numb where his head had rested on it. Slowly he rose, turned on the desk lamp and went to the hall door. He opened it and Maria stood, wreathed in light, holding a covered tray from which good smells rolled. He stared stupidly at her.

"Can I put this down in there?" she asked.

"Yes. Yes, come in." Allen let her in and watched as she put the tray on his desk. "Thank you."

"It's chicken," she said. "And rice." She gestured to the food. "Getting cold."

Allen sat and pondered the food. "Salad, too."

"You helped with that." Maria remained standing next to the desk. "Were you sleeping?"

Allen poked at the salad. "I guess so. I was watching the moon."

Maria lowered her head and looked out at the sky where stars were spreading in riot. "Gone now, yes?"

"But still growing." He ate a bite of chicken. "Thank you, this is good."

"Allen." Maria continued to look out the window. "Allen, everything is—"

"In an uproar."

"Pretty much, yes."

Allen put his fork down. "I should leave."

Maria closed her eyes. "I don't know what's going on."

Allen looked at her. Her slender body was strong, young and indomitable, but she was bowed, as if a weight pushed across her shoulders and she resisted it.

Pity rose in him, and something else, dull and inchoate, from which he turned away. He started to touch her hand and drew back. "It doesn't matter."

She looked at him. "It does. It matters. Are you, um, are you okay?"

"DJ got into my pills."

"I know. He told me."

"Did he tell you what they were?"

"Some of them."

"Yeah." Allen grinned humorlessly. "There are some he'd remember."

"He doesn't—I don't think he would take your pills."

"You know better than I do. But you're right, he didn't take any. Not his thing."

"You're very sick?" Maria asked. Allen was silent. "I'm sorry," she said. "You have a right to your privacy. I'm sorry." She looked at his plate. "And now you're not eating."

"I know. I just—I'm not hungry, that's all."

Maria sat on the edge of his bed and for a long time nothing else was said. As night deepened, the desk lamp lit their solitary pool and there they floated, cut off from all else.

At last Maria said, "I don't hear anything."

"No. there won't be any singing tonight."

"Is that what you call it?"

"Wild singing."

She nodded. "As I said, I hear it sometimes, too."

"And you really don't think—"

"I think that we'll be okay, Allen."

"Until we're not."

"That's right. And until then, there's no use worrying." She got up. "No use worrying, my friend."

"I should leave."

"DJ wants you to."

"I'm shocked. Shocked." He shook his head. "I wish he'd surprise me sometime. But he won't." He looked hard at her. "And you?"

"I want you to stay. I want you to stay here, Allen."

"You sure?"

Maria laughed. "You're the only customer I have."

Allen smiled. "That's my job, seems like."

Chapter Nine

Liz Terry's office was uncomfortably cool. Jasmine the clerk, bundled up, poked away at her keyboard with, it appeared to Allen, not much enthusiasm. After the submission of Allen's intake form and the perfunctory politenesses, no words were exchanged and Allen settled down inside his trench coat to wait. He'd been a few minutes early, and now the time sauntered by.

Allen's chief concern was remaining upright. The walk into town and down Main had been interrupted by bouts of vertigo that required him to pause, hold onto fences and lean against walls. He had wanted to stop in to rest at Ted's, but there had been no time and he only waved at Ted as he lurched by. Now he waited for Liz and hoped he would not fall on his face as he rose to greet her.

Ten o'clock came and went with no sign of Liz and no sound of her from her inner office. The frosted glass door was not lit from behind. At a quarter after ten, Allen started to inquire of Jasmine as to when Liz might make an appearance when the front door of the office opened and she burst through.

"So, I'm always late, such a bad habit." She talked as if continuing a conversation begun outside. "One of these days, Jas, one of these days." Juggling a coffee cup, brief case, and files, she walked past Allen and continued talking as she went into her office and closed the door. Allen heard, as the door closed, *"One of these days..."*

Jasmine continued typing. "She's always late. I should have told you that."

"She always was."

She paused in her tapping and looked at him. "Excuse me?"

Allen sat up. "I just—it's not unusual in this field, I guess."

Jasmine went back to typing. "I don't know. She's the only lawyer I've ever worked for."

Another ten minutes passed as Liz puttered and shuffled. File drawers slammed and a one-sided phone conversation ensued. Then the frosted glass door opened and Liz, Bluetooth in her ear, beckoned Allen in. He stood and followed her, relieved to discover his vertigo had not returned. She didn't look at him and concentrated on picking her thumbnail. Allen noticed her nails were chewed and remembered that she'd always had this habit. There were no rings on her fingers. Her nails were unpainted. Her clothes were the same as she had worn in the café.

"No," Liz said, sitting and indicating to Allen to do the same. "No, no." She chewed a nail. "No, we can't— we can't file yet. No he's—look, we, the judge will not approve that without—look, I can't. I gotta go. Yes? No! I said, we just..."

Allen looked around. Liz's inner office consisted of a desk with two chairs facing it, a computer, her framed Juris Doctor on the wall behind her, three filing cabinets and hundreds of expensive tomes on rows of shelves.

There were no pictures, no mementos, nothing to indicate that anyone other than a lawyer named Elizabeth Terry worked here. There was also no window. Allen and Liz were encapsulated in fluorescence, hemmed by walls of law books.

Liz finished her conversation and clicked off her Bluetooth, leaving it in her ear, where it wiggled as she spoke. She held out her hand. "Liz Terry, Mister, um, Gabbro. Nice to meet you, sorry for the delay, what can we get done for you today?"

The index finger of her right hand went to her mouth, then retreated. She had only briefly looked at him. Allen could think of nothing to say, and discovered that it was not necessary. Liz fumbled at a file folder, poking through it and talking to herself.

Allen smiled. "It's been a while."

Liz nodded, wiggling the Bluetooth, and making her blonde hair sway. "Yes, sorry."

Allen sat back, watching her. After all the years between, decades, a lifetime, Liz was still the same girl, now dressed up as an adult, impersonating a lawyer.

He said, "You probably haven't seen my intake form, the one you had me fill out?"

"Um, no." Liz kept thumbing the other file, some other client, on his dime. "But we don't have a conflict that I know of. Can you tell me briefly what you'd like us to do?"

"You could look at me."

Liz stopped thumbing and looked up. "Excuse me?"

"I have this sense of being alone."

Liz resumed perusing. "I know that one."

Allen let the time burn. The hour had Liz's fragrance, which was worth the wait. (Wait for what, he wondered, then forgot about it.) This was good, better than he'd hoped. It was like so many other hours in her company, and that was one good thing about being with Liz: one could be alone with her.

He said, "I missed you."

Liz stopped perusing. Her chewed index finger nail rested in the middle of some document. She raised her eyes again, this time really looking at Allen. But there was as yet no spark of recognition. "You what?"

"You, um, don't keep exactly regular hours."

"Oh," she closed the file and set it aside. "Well, there's just one of me, and Jas has to do a lot of the running. But here we are and, now, how can we help?" She was becoming slowly aware of him, now looking directly at him with her perplexed gaze, as if his face was a knotty math problem, an equation she had no hope of solving. It was this sober gaze that had first drawn Allen to her, when they were children. It had occurred to him then that if she wanted to solve his face that his face might have something to solve, it might be worth solving and that the one solving his face might be worth knowing. It was both unnerving and comforting, the first time he had felt the interest of and in another.

"Well," Allen said. She waited. "I am here—in Forester I mean—to, ah, put some matters to rest."

Liz chewed her finger. "Probate?"

"Probate. Yes, well, no."

Liz blinked. "Why don't you just tell me then what you are here to do."

As Allen opened his mouth to speak, there was a tap on the frosted glass and Jasmine poked her head in, beckoning to Liz.

With an apology, Liz got up and left, shutting the door behind her. Allen could hear them talking in hushed, urgent tones on the other side of the glass. Craning his neck, he could see Liz's shadow on the pane, arms and hands wheeling around each other. Then they moved away from the glass and their voices receded with them.

Allen wondered if his intake sheet had caused the commotion (under *Reason for Visit* he had written "Suspect terrane"), or if somehow Jasmine had found him out and was now warning Liz that she had a wacko in her office. He folded his hands and waited, as one who faces a barrage of bullets or an oncoming avalanche, content with the outcome of the matter, now that things were in motion.

After some time the door opened again. Allen didn't turn to see who it was and was only mildly surprised to see that it was Jasmine standing in front of his chair. She held a file folder under her arm.

"Mister Gabbro, I'm really sorry."

"Sorry about what?" This would be it, then.

"Ms. Terry had to go. She's had—she had to go out on an emergency with one of her cases and, uh, I'm really sorry, but I have to get down to the courthouse, also."

"Are you offering me a temporary receptionist position?"

Jasmine laughed, nervously. "No, but I—"

"I can answer phones."

"That won't be necessary."

"I was a postal clerk for many years. I can handle the stress."

"Well that is nice of you," Jasmine said. "But I have to close the office and—"

Allen stood, "I understand, got it."

"You absolutely won't be charged for the visit—or the next one." Jasmine followed him out of the inner office and to the front door. "We have your phone number and can reschedule."

Allen opened the door and squinted into the late morning sun. "Okay. Tell you what, I will call you tomorrow, if you'll be open."

"Oh, we will."

"Okay, not to worry. I'll ring you sometime then."

Having steeled himself for the mission and resigned himself to whatever result would come, Allen now felt dismasted and directionless. The reprieve brought less relief than it ought to have, in his opinion. Now it was not yet noon and his one task, unfulfilled, left an empty day. He didn't want to go back to Maria's and he didn't have the strength to hike to the mountains or the river. He decided to go visit Ted.

Walking, Allen was relieved to experience no revisiting of the earlier spins, and he navigated to Ted's easily. He almost hopped up the two cement steps, opened the door and entered his One Safe Place.

Ted was there, behind the bar. Allen wondered if he ever really left. There was no particular reason to. Everything one needed was right here. He opened a coke and handed it to Allen as he sat down near the cash register. "How you feeling?"

"Fine. Living on Coca Cola seems to agree with me. And you?"

"All is well, my friend. Having a productive day?"

Allen looked at Ted over his old-fashioned coke bottle. "Productive?"

Ted wiped the bar, his white-sleeved arms reflected in its surface. "You walked by earlier like a man on a mission." His stopped working and leaned on the bar. He looked at Allen. "Or just a man—"

"Trying to remain upright?"

Ted laughed. "You seem like a stand-up citizen to me."

"Yeah," Allen muttered. "Citizen of where."

"That's always changing, isn't it?"

"That depends," Allen said, "on what time it is." He continued to eye Ted, but there was no discernible reaction. "So," he said after a moment, "you didn't ever answer that question I had. The one about Maria."

"That's true."

"I'd like to know the answer."

"I have met Maria," Ted said. "I don't know her."

"Do you have any idea what she'd—-why she'd—"

"Stay with a guy like DJ?"

"Yeah. That."

"You talk about how one land form, instead of sinking down into the earth when it strikes another one, just gloms onto it?"

"Yeah. We're on one of those, I think. A suspect terrane."

Ted gestured in the general direction of Maria's. "I give you DJ and Maria."

Allen shook his head. "Not my lookout, I guess."

Ted squinted. "No?"

"I don't know why I do half the stuff I do. It's beyond me to figure out someone else's motives. Anyway, it's not my lookout."

Ted smiled. "That statement does not have the ring of authenticity."

"Excuse me?"

"Bullshit. I'm calling bullshit."

"Your perspicacity is exceeded only by your succinctness."

"That sounds like bullshit, too."

"I only meant—"

"Don't try to BS a bartender."

"Very well. Even though your bar doesn't need much tending, very well."

"People dream," Ted said. "People dream and they travel in their sleep. Sometimes the dreams continue while we're awake. Sometimes the waking world falls into our dreams. Sometimes those we dream about are dreaming about us, and we find them, and they find us."

"But are we dreaming about them, or are they dreaming about us?" Allen put his bottle down. "It could be we are only alive in someone's memory. We might have long since left, but they won't let us go. Or they might be living in our memory, but no place else."

"As long as there's memory, things will live," Ted said. "And as long as there's life, you won't be forgotten."

"I've forgotten," Allen said. "I've forgotten everything, it seems like. Except one or two things. Dumb, useless things. Zip codes. Movie scores. Not much, not after living a whole life, even a dull and unimportant one. Now all I seem to remember are other people's lives, and I'm hardly in them at all."

"I think you are in Maria's life," Ted said. "And she might be in yours."

"Such as it is."

Ted said nothing, but continued to squint at Allen.

"What?" Allen asked.

"Thinner."

Allen drank his coke and looked out the window. "Did Maria ever come here?"

Ted shook his head. "You must know she never goes anywhere."

"Then how would you—you didn't rent from her, did you?"

"No."

"But you know things, things about her, and about DJ. You have a line on a lot of goings-on, seems like."

"Bartenders and barbers. They know everything."

"When they have customers, yeah."

"I have customers."

"Small ones," Allen said. "Tiny. Or shy, or both."

"And thin," Ted replied. "Thin ones."

"Coke diets work wonders." Allen swigged from the bottle. "Very healthy." He drank again and leaned forward, close to Ted. "I'm pretty sure Maria has never been one of your customers."

"No. But you are one of hers. And it's more than that. Much more than that, now." Allen looked away, but Ted drew in close, so their noses almost touched. He tapped Allen on the arm. "It's not asking too much," he said softly, "to want kindness."

Allen wasn't expecting that. Ted might as well have taken a bat from under the bar and rapped him across the cheek. "I. She." But he could say no more.

Ted straightened. Allen thought he saw an expression in his face, for the briefest moment, either of great sadness or something else. Ted was looking closely at him, as if taking his measure. It seemed that he nodded slightly. It seemed that he said, but Allen could not be sure, "It will be as it should be."

"I wonder," Allen said, "when she sleeps. And I wonder, when she sleeps, I wonder what her dreams are like."

Ted walked back down the bar, leaving Allen alone with his questions.

Chapter Ten

The sitting room at Maria's was comfortable in the fall afternoon, although the day outside was chilly, with high, cold, skim milk clouds. Allen nested in a plump chair, drifting somewhere between the cushions and the washed sky. He was becoming accustomed to this away-going, used to the question that always posed itself: *Are you taking leave of your senses or are they taking leave of you?*

When his departure was assured, his absence firmly settled, Allen was at once lost in that thinnest of spaces between eye and sky, free to move about, unencumbered by the stiff, weak, creaky thing that had become his body, certain that if he chose to he could keep going. There was no place between skin and sky. He was nowhere.

"Allen?" It was Maria's voice.

"Yes, Maria."

"Are you just going to float around all afternoon?"

"You want me to eat something, don't you?"

"I don't think you can right now."

"Glad to know you're seeing things my way, Maria."

"No one except you can do that."

"I don't think I'm doing that, either. Not at the moment. You know, Maria, I came from a large family. Are you Catholic?"

"Recovering."

"We weren't Catholic. But there was a bunch of us. Just a whole gang. My poor mother. She always said, 'I figured with you kids that you were on your own. It was sink or swim.' And she was right. She just wanted to nap a lot. She napped every chance she got. And she was so quiet and we were so damned noisy."

"Are you close with your brothers and sisters?"

Allen hesitated. "Not especially, no. I was the youngest. Sort of an afterthought—or someone that might have been prevented with a little forethought, you know."

"Don't say that. All life is precious."

"Life is plentiful. I don't know how precious it is. Anyway, no, I hardly knew the brothers and sisters. They were more like cousins, distant ones. There were a couple brothers that were a little closer to my age. I didn't—anyway, there wasn't a lot there, between us. The rest, I just didn't know them very well. Big families have little sub-families, you know? Was your family big?"

"No, very small."

"Oh, well, in a big family, it's like a country, and there are all these little states in that country. Alliances. Feuds. I didn't have anyone to be allied with, so I was out of the whole deal. And so, it stayed that way. Plus, they all were pretty successful, made lots of money. I became a postal clerk, like my dad. I don't think that impressed them very much. Nothing I did mattered, so they didn't need to be around me."

"You should talk to them about that. I would bet you are wrong."

"Maybe. But I can't talk to them. They're all gone."

"All of them?"

"Yes. Everyone. My mom outlived half of them. Dad went when he was pretty young, so he didn't have to see that."

"I'm sorry, Allen."

"With Dad it was the War. The War killed him, in the end. Some of the others, just bad luck. But most, they had, um, we have, we had a..." He felt Maria's interest and wished he had said nothing about this. "There are some families that get dealt a bad hand," he said finally. "Anyway, they're gone and I watched them go. Then I saw them off. Carried the ones that needed to be carried."

"I have not had to do this," Maria said. "My parents, even my grandparents, they're still alive. I just can't imagine it. It would seem like a little piece of you would go with them."

Allen thought about that. He answered, "No. Nothing went with them. No one. I don't know. After so many, you forget. Whatever it was that they were, you forget it. Still, now, it seems like I remember things now and then, little things, more than I used to, more than I thought I knew."

"Like what?"

"Like, there are times when I'll be sitting in a room, and I'll think about one of them; my dad or mom, one of the kids—and then there they are, and they talk to me, or some event from forty year ago will come back to me like it was last night. But always one of them. One of their stories. I'm hardly there at all and I wonder if I ever was, sometimes."

"They all went on before you."

"They did."

"And now." She knew.

"And now I'm walking after them." He knew she knew, but they didn't say anything about that, about that thing they knew. "That's the deal with being the youngest. Very often, the youngest is the last, in everything. One of my brothers, when we were getting whittled down pretty thin, he said 'there's always one guy left, sitting in a room wondering what the hell happened.' I think he imagined that he might be that one, but he wasn't even the next-to-last."

"Things seldom turn out the way we expect."

"I'm taking little steps away, Maria."

"I know." She knew. That was all she said. That was all that was necessary to say. The rest would go without saying.

"I'm lucky. Little steps are easy." That was all he said. She knew. He knew. It was known, but not spoken aloud.

"It's good to do that, I suppose. Better than to go without any preparation."

"Still," Allen said, "In the end, it's the same."

"Yes."

It was agreed. That was it. Nothing else needed saying, and yet he wished that something else was said. It would ease some weight on his soul. Instead he said, "I wonder about God."

"What about God?"

"I think God might be dark matter."

"God might be no matter."

"Because it makes no matter what we think of Him?"

"Yes."

He watched Maria now, and saw her slip in and out of view. Whether his vision was failing or whether her presence was fading he didn't know, but after a while she was only the faintest impression against his eyes.

A wind from the west blew the clouds swiftly across the sky. The thin cerulean shifted to gunmetal. A storm lurked. High ice cut through him and sent him shivering back into his skin. This was not the day for him to leave.

He had been lying to Maria. His brothers and sisters were not such total strangers to him. The older ones, it was true, were citizens of another tribe, with their own customs and history, but there was a limited commerce between them and subsequent Wrangell strata. The younger brothers were close enough in age to recognize and dislike him, their occasional kindness sharpening the precise cruelty of their retribution. Their mother was there, quiet, her hands to her temples in an attitude of weighty dolor as the tumult of those she had brought into the world caterwauled around her. She tried to deaden the din with classical music on the radio, opus, key and mode announced by calm men, but Allen never knew if that worked for her.

At the center of the tribe, like some half-buried stone god, was their father.

Allen saw him now, leaning across from him, framed in the chilly sky window of Maria's sitting room. He looked just as he had in the last days of his life, not much older than Allen was now, but so gray, chewed and wasted by his ceaseless night patrols in the trackless jungles of the War that had never ended. As his days wound down, Allen wondered if he would more closely-resemble his father. It wouldn't matter. The tent would burn.

Allen raised a hand. His father raised his hand, too. Allen tried to speak, but couldn't.

His father came over and sat on the arm of Allen's chair. He rumpled his hair. "Hi, Son."

Allen opened his mouth. That was all.

"I've missed you."

Allen realized with a start that he missed his father, too. He missed the Sunday breakfasts, and his old shoes that he wore to nubbins. He missed his toolbox, and the oiled augers, the varnish worn off their round wooden heads and tapered handles, framing hammers with nail-etched claws. He missed the movies his father played on the old projector, Popeye and Mickey Mouse running around on a sheet tacked to the wall, the smell of popcorn and warm celluloid on Saturday night. He missed walking with him and getting lessons in geology, ornithology, and botany.

"I want you to know something." His father shifted on the chair so that he could look at Allen. "Those nights when you went out, I was awake. I heard you leave and go out in the street. I never slept at night, you know that, not very well. You heard me yelling, heard me running from the incoming shells, or pulling my foot from the guts of bodies in those blind jungles. You know I didn't sleep. I never talked about any of this with you. That's not what we did then. But I'm telling you now, because there is this one chance to do it. I knew. I watched. I heard you go out at night."

Allen nodded.

"So, I followed you. I watched you. I made sure you were okay. But I never interfered."

Allen wanted to ask why. He had many questions, but there was a gulf set between them which he could not cross. He could not ask anything.

"Son, there are many things we wish we could say, do over, take back. But you know that doesn't happen. Now I want you to know that I'm sorry. I had a disease, and you have it, too. It's not the disease you're thinking of—we have that too, sadly—but something else. It rots us from our souls out, and it can't be cured, not in this life. But it isn't forever, not if you don't want it to be. I just wanted you to know that."

Allen reached and touched his father's arm. He could do no more. The arm was strong, knotted with muscle and strung with tight wire. He thought of how those arms picked him up when he fell, how they carried boards and buckets of paint and swung a hammer when his father built their house, and how the hands attached to them had sorted letters and clasped injured birds and held the hands of his wife, Allen's mother.

He remembered too how those hands had struck his brothers, seized his brothers; those arms had lifted them, thrown them down stairs, broken them across the knee.

He remembered that, too. And how the father's sins had been visited on the sons. There was no escape. The thought of avoiding that bludgeoning never crossed anyone's mind, certainly not Allen's. It was. The half-buried stone god was. There was no gainsaying, no questioning, not even when the blood was up and the fist came down.

"Blackness took me over." His father spoke as if to himself. "It took me. It's no excuse, I know that. But when I woke up, sometimes there was blood on my hands. A broken child."

Allen remembered. Almost always the boys, the two brothers nearest him. He had heard of it happening to others, and not always the boys, the sisters as well, but he'd never seen it, just the two brothers in the stratum nearest.

"And I know that it was done to you, Allen. You didn't get what they got, not from me, but they gave you a sort of baptism of your own."

That was true. It was a cold baptism, unwitnessed and meaningless and it choked him. Later, when they were grown men, that baptism was a small bond, of low denomination.

"And when I died you were nearing that age. That age when you begin to question and to reason and to wonder why."

And the age when the fist came down.

"I was frail, son, frail and so afraid. I was alone, so alone, and I couldn't bear you children passing out of that world, that place I built for us. So, I tried to hold you, and you wouldn't be held. So, I tried to break you—not knowingly, but I did, nonetheless—and, even broken, each one of you left."

Allen remembered. The graduation of survivors, wounded and angry.

"They left. Everyone but you. Instead I left, and I know that your sorrow was balanced by relief, and I know you had guilt because that relief, and that you still do. I'm sorry, Son. I'm sorry that this thing was, and that it still is, and that you are the last to bear it. But you won't bear it long. Thank you for carrying it a little farther."

But he didn't want to. Not for another minute did Allen want this burden. He wanted instead the burden that was carried by that woman, the one who walked singing up the hill towards him from a time forgotten, before the wars of machine and detonation. Before fist and wail. That was the small, sweet burden he wished for.

"I need to go, Son. I wish it wasn't necessary. I wish I could tell you more, but I can't. I can tell you that I love you, if that means anything to you now. This is a truth when everything else is a lie."

That was all. He was alone in the sitting room. No father. No Maria. It was late afternoon. The sun had already slipped out of the valley and although the house was warm, he was chilled to the heart. In the darkening sky the crescent moon was smothered in cirrus, never to reappear. All out there was haste and worry, evening mothers clucking and nosing their broods along, seeking shelter. Here he was dry, but he would never be warm again.

Stretching his shrunken muscles Allen got up, holding onto the chair until the room quit revolving. He peeked into the silent, empty kitchen, where no evening meal cooked. Something held him back from entering and he took the hall door out of the sitting room instead. As he approached the stairs he paused. There were voices down the hall, coming from Maria's bedroom. He could discern no words but heard DJ wheedling away, alternately whining and blustering. Maria's replies were monosyllabic.

It seemed that DJ was regaining some of his old vigor.

Allen held on to the stair rail and waited. Soon the bedroom door opened and slammed shut. DJ, head lowered, steamed up the hall. When he was a few feet away Allen spoke.

"Hello, DJ."

DJ's head snapped up and for a moment he flexed and appeared ready to charge. Then his stance went lax. "Waiting on dinner or something?"

Allen shook his head.

"That's good, 'cause Maria ain't cooking tonight."

"Doesn't she feel well?"

"She's just not. She's not cooking."

Allen held DJ's eyes for a moment, until DJ flinched and looked away. "How are you feeling, DJ?"

DJ stabbed a look. "Why?"

"Can you remember what happened two nights ago?"

Something approaching a thoughtful expression crossed DJ's face. Then he said, "No."

"I can tell you, if you like."

"You weren't there."

Allen smiled. "If you can't remember, how do you know?"

"I just know you weren't. I drank too much. Saw some shit that wasn't real."

"It was real."

"You weren't—"

"A man on fire."

DJ's mouth froze open. After a long moment, he shuffled past Allen, heading to the front door.

Allen called after him, "Your whole world melting into his face. Then, just you. All your nothing self, with nothing else. Nothing. Yeah, I was there, DJ. Unfortunately. Too much there."

DJ stopped, his back turned to Allen. Something between a hiss and a sigh escaped him, then he laughed, a low unpleasant chuckle. He shook his head from side to side. "You were there."

"Yeah. Yeah, I was."

DJ laughed again, louder. "Naw. Don't think so. I checked out all those pills you take, mailman. Enough to kill a horse." He snorted. "You don't ever know where the fuck you are."

Allen thought about that. "You could be right."

"I am right. You know I'm right. You're so spun on that shit you don't even know what day it is." He looked at Allen over his shoulder. "Man on fire. What the fuck."

"You don't remember that?"

"No. You're fucking nuts. I don't. I don't remember that, or anything else you think you saw. No man on fire or burning birds or whatever the fuck you were talking about. No."

"The silver flying things, the scaly ones?"

"Yeah, whatever you said."

"I didn't, DJ. Didn't say anything about them."

"You did. Just now."

"No. Only you did. Because that's what you saw."

DJ continued to the front door and paused, hand on the doorknob. He looked back again. "I want you gone."

Allen laughed. "That will happen."

"Now!"

Allen considered him soberly. "Soon. When I decide to go."

DJ snarled and opened the door. He was through it and it slammed shut behind him with a gunshot bang. Allen stood a moment, then turned and, gripping the rail, climbed the stairs. From down the hall, he heard Maria's bedroom door click shut.

There was no returning. What days were left might be few or fewer. They might surprise him and hang around a little longer. But Allen was slipping down the well, or the well slipped past him as he passed through a rotation of the earth. He might swim through fire. He might remain in the white planet core, or bits of himself might spit back through the mantle and crust, to burn again in a steel forge or glitter in the red dust of Africa until some digging toiler plucked him out to quarrel over, water and breath clarified, placed on a privileged finger by the calloused hands of the hungry.

He turned over on his bed. His knee bones knocked together. It was easy to lie here. There was nothing left to do, except answer one question, and then he could go. The sheer luxury of this fact suffused his night bed, and something like joy or joy's sad cousin visited Allen, traveling with him as he stretched out and disappeared in the dark.

He thought about the way Ted had looked at him, in the bar, and what Ted might have said: "It will be as it should be."

Later, as the night song joined the wailing winds of storm, Maria came and stood by his bed, looking down on him, lost in black water. She swayed a little, lips forming silent words.

The storm broke that night, hurling rain, hail, and leaf wrack into the side of Maria's house. Naked trees gasped, loose boards thrummed and buzzed; the whole valley raised a voice, mingled with mountain cries, drunk and harsh with revenge. The blast barreled with locomotive percussions across hissing grass, through groves of locust, snapping limbs and bowling orphaned yard objects down cruelly-shining streets. A galvanized trashcan lid sailed, banged, rolled, and hopped past Maria's front yard, skittered right and took Jefferson Street all the way to town.

It was no night to be out, but DJ, hat blown off his lolling head, hand clutching a bottle, stumbled, and cursed through the town. He sneered past Pete's Bar, observed by Ted alone. He drained his bottle and hurled it at the bank on the corner of Jefferson and Main. The shards caught wind and sprayed Main with drunken gems. DJ seesawed between Jefferson and Main, finally looping his way back up the hill, leaning into the slanting ice sheets, the storm blowing his curses down his throat.

Chapter Eleven

Coffee and muffins were set out on the kitchen counter next to the sink. Allen spotted the carafe and tray and helped himself, taking a seat at the table. The storm had blown itself out overnight and a light like spring streamed through droplet prisms on the windows, gathering in dazzling pools on the kitchen floor.

He had an appetite. He would have eaten an egg had one been offered, but there was no one in the kitchen to ask and he didn't presume to fry one himself. He made do with the muffin.

He was halfway through his breakfast when his chest began to buzz. He slapped his hand up against his cellphone, registering an incoming call. It had been a very long time since the phone had done that, so long that he'd forgotten it was in his breast pocket, placed there out of habit born in slightly-less-lonesome seasons.

"Hello?"

"Hi, is this Al?"

"Al. Um. No. Yes. I mean, yes, it is. Al. Yes."

"Al, it's Liz Terry." Allen said nothing and the phone hissed for long seconds. "Hello?"

"Yes. Yes, hello."

"I, um, look, I feel bad about walking out on you yesterday."

"I'm sure it couldn't be helped."

"No, it really was pressing, but look, I have a pretty open morning and I was wondering if you'd like to have that consult today. Now, in fact, if you like. Free of charge."

Allen swallowed some coffee. "I can be there in about thirty or forty minutes."

"Thirty or forty—Um, you know, I am picking up some lunch stuff at a restaurant near my office and we could—"

"I know the one."

"You do?"

"I think I do. Is it on the corner, near your office?"

"Yes. The Main Street Grill." The phone hissed some more and Liz's voice resumed, changed. Quieter. "You know the one, then."

"Yes. Not many down there."

"I suppose not."

"Were you thinking of meeting there?" Allen asked quickly.

"Well."

"That would be fine."

"All right. About quarter to eleven then."

"Good." He let the call die and swallowed more coffee.

Looking up in mid-gulp he saw Maria standing in the hall doorway. "Hey. There you are. Thanks for the breakfast."

She came in and poured a cup of coffee. "Sure." She faced him, unsmiling. "Have you seen DJ?"

"Not since last night, in the hall."

She sat across from him. "He went out. In the storm."

Allen looked closely at her. She hadn't slept much. "I know. That wasn't a smart thing to do."

She shook her head. "I just wondered if you'd seen him."

"Nope. Not since he said he wanted me gone and then took off. I can't imagine him staying out all night. Not last night."

Maria sipped her coffee slowly. "He isn't doing very well."

"He doesn't seem like someone who ever does very well," Allen said. Maria's eyes sharpened. She started to speak, then stopped and drank more coffee. Allen touched her hand. "I'm sorry."

"No, it's true." She shot him a look over her coffee cup. "You had a call?"

"Yeah. Yeah. The lawyer."

"The lawyer."

"Liz Terry. She wants to see me, like, now."

"Do you want to take the bike?"

Allen considered the offer. "Thanks, but I can make it on foot."

Maria looked long at him. "This lawyer."

"Yes."

"She's the reason. The reason you're here."

"Yes."

"Did you know her? Is she—" Maria stopped and looked out the window.

"I knew her. Yes, a long time ago."

She looked back at him. "Did you love her?"

"I don't know if I did."

"Do you think you might have?"

Allen saw her skin, sallow and drawn with insomnia. Her hair was tied back, but struggling loose, tattering about her neck. Maria was being worn down. He avoided her eyes. "There isn't much point to it now."

"Not much point to what?"

"I'm—look, I have to go." He stood, took his cup and plate to the sink.

"Don't bother washing." Maria also stood. "Just go."

Allen didn't hear her. He was rinsing his coffee cup when he saw something huddled under the bare locust tree in the side yard. DJ, half-covered in wet leaves.

It was surprisingly easy to tote the lump that was DJ into the house and deposit it on the couch. It didn't move much, but it off-gassed. Maria tended to it and Allen stood back, watching her. He wondered why she did it. He wondered why he'd fetched him out of the yard.

Because it was a human, of sorts, that was why. A bundled mass of biology. Things went into it. Things came out of it. It could speak and it had the requisite low cunning. It had a mother. It had a face. It dreamed, and if the dreams were full of beer and tits, crackers, television shows, bad acts with DJ heroes and filthy thoughts wearing buckets of chicken and methamphetamine underpants, what business was that of Allen's? The human required a human. Another with opposable thumbs and knees that bent the same way. No matter that the DJ thing would kick him to pieces if presented with the same opportunity. It was required that assistance be rendered, and so Allen did, as he had so often before, what was required: he carried another human to find safe rest.

Maria was looking at him. "Thank you," she said. She bent and wiped DJ's bloated face with a warm towel.

"Yeah, no problem." Allen looked at the clock on the living room wall. "I'll take you up on that that bicycle offer, though."

"Take it, yes, please. You don't have to ask."

Allen started for the hall. He stopped. "He'll live, I guess."

"Yes. He will, although he might not want to."

"It beats the alternative." Allen wondered if he meant that. He waved and left Maria to care for DJ, who had started to groan.

Streets still wet, Forester shone newly-bathed and sharp-edged as Allen wheeled along Main. The night storm's debris had already been swept up, gutters cleared, every surface deep with dew, shining like objects on the bed of a clear lake. The town's colors shouted and jostled for attention as Allen spun by them, trench coat flapping in his wake.

The café on the corner wasn't busy. The same bewildered waitress waited. She rang up tickets, for what appeared to be the same people, ordering the same meals as when Allen was last here. Paper was hardly necessary. The request could fly from mind to bewildered mind; eggs could fly out of cartons and hamburgers leap frozen from waxed paper sarcophagi to glistening grill, a warm and generous unction suffusing the close diner air. Breakfasts and lunches could chew themselves, slide down throats and self-digest, unaided by peristalsis. The tab could be paid with generous thoughts.

Liz was in the last booth, fronting the side street, all the way in the back. There was a file open in front of her and she jotted things in it, chewing the smallest nail on her left hand. She was drinking coffee.

Gently waving off the waitress, Allen approached her. "Hello."

She looked up, pulling the finger from her mouth. "Oh, hi, please sit down." Allen sat. Liz jotted a few more words then looked at him. "How goes?"

"It's going fine. Have you resolved your crises?"

Liz's expression clouded in momentary puzzlement, then cleared. She smiled her slightly crooked smile. "Yes!" (A matter of astonishment and wonder.) "All resolved. Now"—she swept aside the file and, folding her hands together, leaned forward—"what are your issues, Mister Gabbro, and how can we resolve them?"

"I don't expect a resolution."

Liz smiled. She looked a little tired and pallid. "That's always a good place to start." Her finger went to her mouth and she pulled it away. "Always a good beginning."

"Ends that way, too. Often."

She considered that, looking past him. "That might be true. So, we can do our best to see that it ends well."

"That would be good, thanks." The waitress brought a menu and Allen pretended to look at it. "Anything you recommend?"

Liz laughed her short laugh. "Get something fried." She laughed again. "It's all fried. I think you can get a fried salad if you like."

Allen looked at her over the top of the menu. Her eyes twinkled in the old way. "Fried salad."

"Doesn't that sound good?"

"I'll probably have—"

"Get a burger."

"Are they good?"

"It's hard to mess up hamburger." She smiled. "But not impossible. Still your least-risky option, Mister Gabbro."

"I like to avoid risk."

"Do you?" She looked out the window and her eyes became instantly bluer. A pale blue. "And how's that working out for you."

"Honestly, not all that well."

"It shouldn't surprise you that this doesn't surprise me."

"I guess not, no."

"People don't need lawyers, usually, when things are going along just fine."

Allen heard something in her voice—a sort of resignation or weariness that pulled at him. He wondered what had created that sad voice in her. She still looked young, but her voice was old. His throat ached a little. He said, "Everything is fine."

She continued to look out the window. "Good." She turned back to him and leaned forward once more. "So, let's get to it. Why are we here today, Mister Gabbro?"

Allen leaned forward slightly, also. He said nothing, but looked back into Liz's blue eyes, eyes that smiled. He squinted. An old game, the staring. They would stare and squint, leaning toward each other until their noses touched.

They were leaning closer now. Liz's nose was two feet away. Now one. About five inches. His eyes were crossing, as they always had. Now her nose was two inches away, and her eyes too were crossed, still squinting, still smiling.

Now not.

The squint stopped playing, became interrogatory. She pulled back. "What—who—"

There was nothing for it. It wasn't supposed to be like this. He might have had several conversations with her before she ever found out. She might never have found out. But the staring game did it. The smell of her did it, her milk skin, strawberries and cotton driving back the diner grease winds. Her crooked smile, like a silly joke, that did it. Her every moment catastrophes and her flinging through rooms will-o'-the-wisp to nest in corner booths, chewing nails and scratching notes on legal documents, for all he knew drawing pictures as she always had (and he still had some of them), paying no attention until her attention was now full on him and she knew, she *knew*.

That did it.

"Allen. It's Allen."

"Allen." She looked down at the Formica. It was revealed in the Formica. She knew. She looked back up. "Allen."

"Yes."

"Allen Wrangell."

"Yes."

Her finger went into her mouth, her fingernail went between her teeth. "Allen. Allen. Allen Wrangell." He nodded. She nodded—she always repeated his nods, it made him aware of how much he did that—and she said, "Allen. Al. Damn. Wow. You look like shit. I'm gonna buy you that burger."

Time came and went. Minutes flamed out faster than they could be lit. An hour was filled with Liz's face, lips slightly chapped, moving, receiving fingernails, emitting staccato laughs, forming the word "Wow." More than an hour. A half hour more, then more. Allen's hamburger went uneaten. He asked for a box, buried the burger in it, drank a coke, chewed a French fry the way Liz chewed her nails, and on the same impulse. He poured words out. She poured words out. They danced between them, these words, then wandered off together through the café glass, into the already-fading autumn day. Then wandered back, into the warm.

Allen said, "I didn't think you'd remember me."

"I didn't." Liz laughed in short bursts. "I didn't at all. I still don't, Allen, criminy, you're fifty years old."

"No, I'm—"

"Okay, you're forty-nine or something."

"I remembered you."

"You knew what you were looking for," Liz replied. "Besides, I'm younger than you."

"Two years."

"Two years, yes. And I'm in better shape. Anyway, I was a girl, you were a boy."

"And now we're adults."

Liz looked sideways at him. "Yes." She nodded slowly. "Yes, we are." She looked at her cellphone. "Oh shit, Allen, do you know what time it is?"

"No idea."

"Past time. That's what time it is." She stuffed her file in a carry bag and stood. "I'm always late."

Allen stood and waited for her to walk ahead. "You always were."

Liz turned and frown-smiled. "Not always. Once I was right on time."

Allen looked at his feet. "Were you?"

Allen insisted on paying the permanently bewildered waitress, who handed Liz a raft of Styrofoam boxes. Hardly pausing, she made for the door, juggling her items. Allen got ahead of her and opened it. "Can I help you with those?"

"No, no, got it. Just some stuff for a meeting—for which I am now late."

"My fault."

Liz shook her head. On the sidewalk she turned and looked up at Allen. Her default puzzled expression returned. "How?"

"Hmm?"

"Your fault how."

"The time," Allen shrugged. "Just the time."

"Nothing you can do about that, big boy."

Allen grabbed his bike. "You going to your office?"

"The other way."

"Oh, all right." He wondered if he should offer to accompany her, and as he wondered, she walked away.

"See you, Allen."

"Hmm? Oh, yes. I'll, uh, see you."

Then she was gone.

Afternoon stood on the cusp of evening as Allen stretched out on his bed, medicine coursing through him. He didn't sleep, but wandered in the shadowland, listening to the silence. The talk with Liz intruded and he examined it, word, tone and gesture, for clues and signs.

She wasn't curious about where the years had taken him, and that was good: they hadn't taken him far. There was only mild interest in why he was contacting her now, and when he said that he'd just wanted to see how she'd been, that satisfied her. From her he learned that she'd been married and divorced, no kids. She'd gone into law because her father was a lawyer (Allen knew that of course) and—well, her father had been one. Allen said he understood. She'd moved to Forester because, why not? Allen agreed. She had a cat. She owned a little house outside of town. A couple of dozen pieces of information flew by him and Allen caught them, filed them, nodded and listened, happy to see Liz's tomboy face and hear her hoarse, busy voice. They had even done the staring game.

Then it was over.

He'd ridden around aimlessly on the bike for a while afterward, still clutching his Styrofoam box with the cold burger inside. Eventually he'd wandered back to Maria's house (silent as frost), put the bike away and retreated to his room. The minutes that had burned hot and quick were numb now, crawling. The burger box on his desk cast an ever-longer shadow until it hit the edge and fell into the great nothing that was Allen's room. Allen too came to the brink of things and fell off, became susurrus. He drifted in the gloaming, with the crescent moon, waiting for the stars.

It was almost completely dark when his chest buzzed. He reached in and swiped open his phone. Before he could say hello, Liz's voice, rapid-fire, said, "So I was in that meeting, the one I went to after I saw you, and I was thinking about you, and I thought, 'Shit, almost thirty years, it's been damned near thirty years and here's old Allen Wrangell. Old Al, just popping up in Forester to see how it's going. What's up with that?' And so that's what I'm wondering right now."

Allen's eyes cleared in the half light, but there was nothing on which to focus. "What?"

"Yes."

"What?"

"Yes, what's up with that, Allen. Why did you really want to see me?" Allen didn't reply. Liz breathed for a while in the phone hiss, then repeated, "Why?"

Allen felt his dry tongue working. "I need water."

"Huh? You need what?"

"Just a minute." He got up, head spinning, and got a glass of water, drinking it in one long swallow. "Are you still there?"

"Where else would I be."

Allen sat on the bed, head bowed. "Liz, I—"

"You what."

"I just wanted to see you."

Seconds passed and the hissing between them marked each one. Finally Liz said. "Okay."

The hissing stopped. Allen sat with the dead phone to his ear, head hanging lower, playing the staring game with his feet. In a few minutes the phone buzzed against his head. "Yes. Hello, Liz."

"Where are you?"

"Excuse me?"

"Where are you? Hello?"

"I'm—you mean—"

"I mean, where are you staying while visiting our little town. Are you in a motel?"

"A bed and breakfast off Jefferson. Maria's."

"Don't know it."

"It's good. It's good here."

"Good. So, did you ever become a geologist?"

"No. No, I didn't."

"Why not? You always liked rocks."

"Rocks, yes. I still am interested in geology."

"Why?"

"Why?" He grew careful. "I just am."

"You just are." Liz whispered now, conspiratorially. "And why are you just?"

Allen wanted to change the subject. With Liz, he knew, it would be impossible. Not until she had her answer. He took a deep breath. "Rocks are beautiful. They are beautiful and their beauty doesn't change."

There was silence. Then Liz said, "Okay."

It wasn't okay. Allen knew that. "Their time," he said, "is different than ours. They move, thousands of miles sometimes, but we never see it. We can only see where they've been." The words came out of their own accord. He would have stopped them if he could. "Say some creature stepped in the sand a few million years ago. Or even one of us, one of our ancestors, a million years, a few hundred thousand years ago, walking in the tidal flats, you know, or along a river, a riverbed or a tidal flat that no longer exists."

"Yes, Al."

"Well, that creature, that human ancestor, they're gone, long gone. But their footprints are turned to stone. They're still with us." The words rushed out. "Just as if they took that step yesterday, maybe the morning of this same day. They don't—"

"They don't what?"

"They're still here."

"The impression they left is still here, Al. Those cavemen, or those dinosaurs, they're gone. Only their impression is left, just where their feet were, a long time ago."

"That's all we get to do, Liz. It's all we get to leave."

"Some impression, huh?"

"Yeah. Yes. That. Or say some ancient creature, some huge dinosaur on a continent that no longer exists, say she falls into a cave. Her body turns to limestone."

"I get it, Allen.

"Her bones. Her eggs. We can dig them up. The strata of earth are like pages in a book. We can read the history there."

"Yes. I think I get that."

Now that the subject had been broached, it struggled out of him and he wanted to keep talking about it. "It's a story in rock. And the story is the rock, Liz. Such a beautiful story. It's told in the shape of the stone, how it deforms or spreads out, how it moves, the minerals it's made up of, all that."

"Okay, Allen. Thanks. Thanks for that." Her tone was mocking, but gentle enough. "I think I got the answer I wanted."

Allen stopped and breathed. He was warm. He was a little angry, but he also wanted to laugh. "Or," he said, "the answer you didn't want."

"No, that's fine. I asked and you answered." She moved the phone against her cheek. He heard it scrape and heard her sigh. "What did you end up doing, for a living I mean?"

"I became a postal clerk."

"Oh, do you like it?"

"I've retired. Retired early. It—I, it was okay. It paid the bills."

"Well that's good. You can be a geologist now, if you want."

"Yeah, that would be good, I guess."

"You always wanted that, right?"

"I suppose."

She laughed. "You're funny, Allen." There was a long pause, then, "I'm not working tomorrow. If the weather's okay, we could ride bikes."

After the phone went dead again, Allen had expected it to buzz once more, but it remained quiet. He lay with it against his chest, as if this would accomplish some miraculous restoration, but nothing else happened. It troubled him how much he wanted something to happen, and he had to remind himself that he was not to ever want this. He was to remain the specimen he had become, was to live the remainder of his days as such.

"So-noted."

But it had not always been entirely-so, he knew. The curtain had lifted once for a season and for a season he could climb out of the dish, feel the air on his face, put his arms around a girl, lie with her, watch the bits of sky falling, count each one and remember each unique trajectory across the mesosphere. (She would laugh at him when he said "mesosphere" and slug him hard in the shoulder.)

This was his season with her, and he wished he had never had it. It would have been far better never to have known that such seasons existed, and now it was imperative that he do his best to forget, not that it existed, but what it was like to have lived there with her. With Liz in the fields of their youth.

Chapter Twelve

Maria made coffee. Allen watched her from the hall doorway. Her back and shoulder muscles pulled against her navy t-shirt as she drew water, filled the coffee maker, got cups and laid them out. She moved with precision, swiftly and with no wasted effort. Her hair, bound tight against her scalp, was achingly immovable. Not one strand was free.

He wanted to keep watching her, but it was wrong, he knew, a taking of something to which he was not entitled. He stepped into the kitchen. "Hi."

Her movement slackened imperceptibly, then resumed its pace: from sink to cupboard, from cupboard to refrigerator, from refrigerator to counter, from counter to stove. Once only she broke her routine to silently gesture Allen to the table.

Allen sat, and she brought him a muffin. He thanked her. She nodded and resumed the breakfast waltz. Allen munched and stared at his plate. He had no right to do other than that.

Maria brought him coffee. He accepted it and looked up at her, standing with half-shuttered gaze. He said, "It's a beautiful morning." She nodded, shutting off her gaze entirely. He said, "Not too cold. Outside." She opened her eyes. They were tired but full of reserved, inscrutable will. He said, "How was your night."

"The same," she said, returning to her stove. "I worked, doing billing." She cooked eggs.

Allen swiveled slightly in his chair. He decided. Wrong or not, he wanted to watch Maria cook. "And what will you be doing today?" he asked.

She paused and leveled a long look at him. "Cleaning." She cracked an egg. "Is there anything you need upstairs?"

Allen shook his head. Fried egg and sharp coffee fume jangled. "No. I have everything I need."

"That's good." After what seemed only seconds, Maria brought him eggs. "More coffee?"

Allen said yes, and Maria reached for his cup. He caught her hand and placed his other hand over it. She didn't pull away. He didn't do anything else. He didn't look at her. Slowly her fingers laced into his. Her skin was firm and warm, and her fingers were strong. Her arm muscles translated into tendons, pulling shut the fingers. Allen responded to a silent catechist: *Abductor digiti minimi brevis; flexor digiti minimi brevis; flexor pollicis brevis; abductor pollicis brevis; adductor pollicis.* Now the heat of her hand suffused his, gathering at the wrist, warming him to the elbows. He bowed his head, lips moving in silent litany, thoughts and petitions arranged in instant, obdurate order, precisely marching toward some final joy, a festal bequest. He had never known such a certain and serene holding of hands. Nothing could go wrong in this moment.

"Coffee?" Her voice echoed across the bleak end of everything.

"Yes, thanks." He released her and went cold.

Allen was able to eat the eggs. It surprised him. For the longest time he had lived primarily on Coca Cola and a drawer full of pills and now here was an appetite to match the vital day.

Maria took his plate before he could clear it himself and brought him coffee before he could refuse. Just once she smiled a little, but he could read nothing in it. She was where he could not be. One of them had moved outside the circle and Allen had no way of knowing whom. It was possible that they both had: solitary creatures, panthers, shapes in the forest that crossed, re-crossed and melted away, taking their own private paths. But Allen was an old cat, game and hoary, yellow eyes full of rheum. He limped when he walked the trails and he had quit the hunt. Maria was young, and her limbs were taut and full of spring. Her movement had the confident nobility of the young. Even if she was shy and elusive, she could leap yet, and bring down life to continue living. She would go on long after Allen had slipped away. She would stalk the twilight paths and call in her cat tongue. Allen wondered if she would ever call for him.

Maria took his cup, breaking his meditation. "More coffee?"

"No. No thanks."

He insisted on washing the dishes and she relented. "I'll need the bike today," he said, scrubbing the frying pan.

She wiped the stovetop. "Yes, just take it, I told you, you don't have to ask." He watched her reflection in the window. Something in her movement changed, stiffened. She turned and looked at him. "Going any place in particular?"

"I'm going to meet Liz."

"The lawyer." Her voice was dry. She resumed her cleaning.

"Yeah." He wiped the pan. "The lawyer."

Without pausing in her task, Maria said, "Do you know how to touch someone, Allen?"

He let his hands rest on the counter. He focused on a rake, left in the yard by DJ days before. Her words became the rake. The rake, almost buried in leaves, become her words. He said, "I suppose I don't."

"What were you saying as you held my hand? Was it Latin?"

"I didn't know I was saying anything."

"You were."

"I was thinking about the muscles in the hand. Everything that makes it move, open and close. That."

"Why."

"What do you mean?"

"Why were you doing that."

"I don't know. I always liked anatomy drawings. The red and blue muscles and veins. The bones. Organs. My dad had studied to be a doctor, before the War, and he was a competent artist, so he did a lot of anatomical drawing. We had lots of his old work, all piled in the basement, and it was fascinating to look through those pictures. I learned a lot of the names for muscles and things. I guess I was saying the names of our hand muscles. I didn't know it was out loud."

Maria sighed. "Possibly it wasn't. You might not have said it out loud."

The rake in the yard became Maria's sigh. Her sigh become the rake. He wanted to go put the rake away, or use it, tidy up the yard. The desire grew until he was about to act on it, when he looked up into the window glass.

Maria was behind him. Her hands, warm from her work, fell lightly on his shoulders. Their faces were together in the glass, hers behind and below his, as if looking in from another room. Her window eyes looked into his glass gaze. She squeezed, and his shoulders loosened. He breathed in deeply the soap and metal of their chores.

"It isn't too complicated, Allen."

"It's very complicated."

She sighed again. "If you want it to be."

"I don't think I have a choice."

She squeezed again. Harder. "You know better."

"I suppose I do."

She released him and left the window glass. Immediately his eye fell on the rake. He now wanted to grab it and throw it into the road. "It takes millions of years for continents to collide," he said.

She said, from somewhere outside the glass, "You don't have millions of years. And I don't, either."

Allen remained at the window. "I want to ask you something, Maria."

"There's no guarantee I will answer you."

"That's all right. But I want to ask you anyway."

"Then ask."

"Does he—"

"You shouldn't ask."

"Does he hurt you?"

There was no reply. Allen stood with eyes shut, listening to Maria's breathing. His own had stopped. Finally, he heard her sigh. "There are many ways to hurt people, Allen."

"You know what I mean."

"I got what I came here for."

"And that hurts."

"Yes."

"And now? Now what."

"I couldn't. I can't."

"You can't leave. Not even—"

"If I wanted to."

Allen grew dizzy. Tides moved inside him, flooding the dry spaces. "Do you want to?"

She was still in the room, but her voice came from underground, a whisper. "Yes."

With that, something like a ragged little hope wandered by. It peeped in the window and kept walking.

"You do?"

He waited, but she said nothing else and he knew that he was alone.

Chapter Thirteen

Liz and Allen rode their bikes south, leaving town the way he'd come in, days before. The day remained clear and crackling. They were warm in the sunny spots and would have been chilled in the shady spots were it not for the heat produced by pedaling. Allen had noted with some shame that she had come dressed in riding gear and helmet, while he was bare-headed, in jeans and a sweater, which he was beginning to regret having worn. He also noted that Liz looked splendid in her riding gear. They took the highway to where it started to climb out of the valley, then swerved left onto the road that went down to the river, skirting the meadows south of town.

Pausing at a sunlit wayside, they rested and drank water and ate fruit that Liz produced from a saddle bag.

"So, Allen," she said between bites of apple, "you never got married, huh?"

"No."

"No live-in, no sweethearts?"

"Not really, no."

"You gay?"

He laughed. "No." He drank more water. "Just not very sociable."

"Well heck, aren't you at least horny?"

His face grew hot and he looked away, down to where the river ran, quietly in the flat valley land, resting between its tumble from the mountains and its crashing through the canyon.

Liz patted his arm. "Sorry, Al." She was the only one who ever called him that. "You know, I think it and out it comes. Anyway, you were my first and I was your first—I was, wasn't I—and so anyway, I was just wondering. Now that we're buddies again—we are, aren't we?"

Allen said, "Yes. Yes, we're buddies."

"That's good. Wow, that's good. I'm not buddies with anyone here. Jasmine, I guess, but I pay her. If I quit paying her, would she be my buddy? I wonder."

"You could try not paying her."

Liz spit out a piece of apple and a short, coughing laugh. "Hah!" She slugged Allen almost hard in the shoulder. "Hah. Hah hah. See what happens, right? Wow. What a good idea." She frowned. "No wait. No. It's a shitty idea."

"It wasn't a serious one."

She looked at him, as if surprised to see him there. "Huh? Oh, I know." She reached back and put her water bottle away, then reached for his. "Don't drink it all. Save some for lunch."

Allen handed her his bottle. "You always liked packing a lunch. That's how we got acquainted, remember?"

Liz slapped his handlebars. "That's right! You were at college already. I thought you were hot."

"I was still in high school, really."

"Yeah, but you were taking those geology classes at JC. Wow, you were always a rock nerd, huh. Anyway, I wanted you. So, I packed you a lunch."

"And we ate it on the lawn."

Liz mirrored Allen's nods. "In front of the student union. Man, I thought you were hot."

Allen looked at his feet. "You still look good."

"Yeah?" Liz said. "Yeah! I do, huh. But you really look shitty, Al."

"Thank you."

"No, you look okay, but—are you getting enough to eat?"

"Why don't we go to the river and see what you packed?"

"Good way to avoid answering."

"You can see for yourself how much I eat."

The road ran close to the base of the mountains for a mile, then crossed the river on a rusty trestle bridge. They paused on the bridge and Liz threw a stone into the rushing water.

"What kinda rock, Allen?"

"Jasper."

"Hah! Nerd."

They finished crossing the bridge then followed the river downstream, on the sunny side. Where the land widened out, Allen could see the jade and cobalt water off to their left, through the willows. He heard water running, briskly but not hurrying down the slope. The road became gravel and Liz, riding ahead of him, slowed. She stopped by a shady path that he would never have noticed.

"This is the place," she said. They got off their bikes and she led the way to a sandy willow copse by the water, full sun beaming in through yellowing leaves. They laid the bikes down in a little bay of coarse salt and pepper boulders that faced the water. They had climbed a short way out of the valley and the water ran more steeply in the rocks. Both warmth and noise were amplified in the boulder cove. Hidden from the road, it might have been some distant mountain retreat, made to shelter and rest in.

Liz laid out a checked table cloth between them and produced sandwiches, fruit, chips, and wine. She filled a paper plate and handed it to Allen. "Here, now eat something. Want some wine?"

"I'll just drink water, thanks."

"More for me."

"That's fine." Allen, surprised at his renewed appetite, ate and watched as Liz uncorked the wine. She drank it straight from the bottle and he laughed at her. "You always drink that way?"

Liz wiped her mouth. "When I don't have to share." She slugged again. "Pinot. Goes great with baloney."

"These are smoked turkey."

"I meant you, buster. What's your game?"

"What do you mean?"

Liz took a bite of sandwich and mumbled through the food. "You some weirdo or something? Here have some chips."

Allen took a bag of chips and rattled some onto his plate. "If I was, this would be an unfortunate time and place to find that out."

"Hah! Yeah, huh. Probably shoulda checked that out sooner. Wow. And me the lawyer."

"Well I'm not. A weirdo, I mean. Not dangerous, anyway. But you knew that." Allen chewed the chips, listening to the crunch in his mouth.

"Yeah, Al. I knew that." Liz drew a finger in the gravely sand. "So"—her voice was quieter—"why did you come here? What do you want?"

Allen knew the question was going to come up again. He was surprised it had taken so long to return. "Um. It. Um."

Liz laughed and threw a pebble at him. "Allen Wrangell, master of the monosyllable."

"No, I just—look, why not. I never forgot about you, Liz."

She slugged the pinot. "Aw."

"Not like there's some obsessive thing going on."

"Sure there is."

"Okay, fair enough. But you know, we both lived a life for thirty years. You got married—"

"You didn't."

"And—sure I know—and anyway, we both worked. And we met people."

"You didn't."

"I met people, Liz. I did. But I never—"

"Did 'em."

"No, now no, it's not—there wasn't, I don't know."

"A connection."

"Yes." Allen breathed a deep sigh. He watched the sun on the water. "That's right."

They sat, feet pointed toward the river, and said nothing for a long time. The sun radiated off the clean andesite, warming the little beach. They ate, and when the food was gone they still sat.

Liz shaded her eyes and looked at Allen. "So you wanted to see if there was still a connection. With us."

Allen let his head fall back, let the sun burn his throat. "No. No, not really."

"I'm hurt." She didn't sound hurt.

"You said I was your first," Allen said. "And you said you were my first." He rolled his head over and looked at her, eyes still shaded. "But you weren't just my first. You were my only."

Liz looked grave. Then she smiled. Then she looked grave again. "Aw."

Allen looked away again. "That's just a fact."

"I like facts," Liz said. "They're easy."

"Sometimes."

"I mean, you don't have to think about them. They just are."

"You might want to think about if they are true or not."

"Well they are. Once you decide they are, they are, then you don't think about them anymore. You knew I was your only. That is your fact. And now what about it? Is that fact why we are sitting here by this river, right now?" She yawned. "All sleepy?"

Allen rolled his head back and watched the water. The sun flashed in the current and made him squint. "I don't know."

"What don't you know?" She kicked some coarse sand at him.

"Facts seem sort of lazy. Like, that's it. Move on."

"You're the one who brought them up."

He laughed. "Well I'm sorry I did." He continued to squint at the flashing river, until it seemed the splinters of light came from his own eyes. "I don't know why we're here. I don't think there's any reason for it just, here we are."

"You sure?"

He thought for a while. "No."

"Me, neither. But I liked remembering, about, you know, us." She stretched. "Damn, it's warm." She stuck her bare feet down into the damp under-layer of sand. "Better."

Allen leaned forward and took his shoes off. He pressed his feet into the sand, then raised them and looked at the twin footprints, outlined with shadow. "You didn't have to be a lawyer. You could have been anything you liked."

"Yeah?" She was irritated. "A postal clerk, huh?" In the silence the water rushed louder. "Sorry."

"No, that's all right. It all follows along in its own groove, I guess."

"Or rut. It follows its own rut."

"And we get carried along in it."

"And carried away, Allen Wrangell." She closed her eyes. "Carried away."

Standing, he walked to the water, rolled his pant legs up and waded in. Liz watched him, then she, too, came and waded in the water. Slipping on a rock, she reached to Allen, who steadied her. They stood then, holding hands.

"This is why you came, huh," Liz said.

"Yes."

"I'm gonna kiss you, Al."

"Okay."

The ride back to town was leisurely. They stopped often and Allen pointed out roadside geological features, which Liz ignored.

"You see here," Allen said, kneeling by the road cut where they had stopped. "Look, it's a small shear zone. See how the rock is foliated? All that pressure, all that tension, bending, breaking, reshaping the rock. There are quartz veins in it. These places often have lots of hydrothermal activity, squishing out all kinds of valuable minerals. This Gold Country started because of it. Some people think life started at hydrothermal vents."

Liz stood astride her bike, shaking her head. "Shut up, Allen."

"But it's great stuff, it's—it's everything we are. If you think about it."

"I don't."

"But—"

"Do I have to kiss you again?"

Allen looked up at her from the road cut. "You could."

Liz waved him off. "Come on, I gotta get back and do some work."

They started off again. "Should you work after drinking?" Allen asked.

"Hah! You're talking to a lawyer, Allen. Are you serious?"

"Not really."

"Good! Because booze is how we roll."

"That explains a lot."

Liz smiled, raised her middle finger, and sped off down the slope to town. Allen followed close behind. The sun was touching the tops of the western peaks as they reached Main Street, already slouching in shadow.

Not much was moving in Forester as they pedaled up Main. Some of the taverns showed smudges of activity as smokers gathered near their doors—the antithesis of the black smoker hydrothermal vents, the alleged origins of terrestrial life in which Allen had just tried to interest Liz—bringing a bit of the bar out to tar the day. The last of the Saturday shopping was winding down, weekend shifts were ending, the town drew its covers for an early evening.

Liz's office was closed. She dismounted at the door and retrieved keys from her riding pants. "This is where I get off, Al." She unlocked her door.

Allen remained astride his bike. He watched Liz shunt hers inside, wanting to say something before she disappeared after it. "So. Yeah."

Liz paused, half in, half out. "Yeah?"

"Um, yeah."

She reached out and pulled his chin. "Thanks, Allen. That was fun."

Then she was gone.

There was nothing else to do but go too, so he went. The bike creaked as he finished the last blocks of Main and Allen made a mental note to oil and tighten things later. He crossed Main and began the climb up Jefferson.

Looking left he saw actual customers in Ted's bar. Some stood outside and others were visible inside, lined up at the bar. Allen felt a momentary, irrational sense of betrayal, his sanctuary defiled. He paused and looked closer. A different man stood behind the bar, dispensing drinks and jokes. Ted was nowhere to be seen. Digging in for the climb up Jefferson, Allen puzzled over this disturbing change.

He was halfway up Jefferson and slowing down when he heard his name called. Looking back, he saw Liz, on her bike, approaching at a good clip. He stopped, dismounted and waited for her. It was getting cold.

"So yeah, I decided I wasn't gonna work." Liz drew up, breathing heavily. "Who wants to work on Saturday night?"

"Right." Allen could think of nothing else to say. He waited for Liz to say something else, but that was it. She just looked at him. "Saturday night in Forester," he said at last.

"What are you doing?" Liz asked. She looked at him a little sideways, as if examining something that might squirt. "Gonna get dinner from the boarding house lady? Maria?"

"Maybe, yeah."

"Well that sounds like a blast." Liz got off her bike. "Come on, I'll walk you home."

Moving warmed him again. The dizziness was coming back and walking helped that, too. He liked listening to Liz talk about work, her amusing client stories, her small-town life. It seemed that if she would only keep talking that he might never leave here, that he might join one of her stories and just flow along with the words: Allen the wannabe geologist who lived at Maria's and had no friends. That would be okay.

Actual evening was coming on as they drew up to Maria's. Lights were on in the living room. "This is the place," Allen said, looking for signs of life.

"Kinda tattered, huh? How's the grub."

"Good." Allen looked at Liz, wondering what he should do now. She leaned on her bike and looked back at him. After a moment he said, "Would you like to come in?"

"Hey, I'm gonna just fly down Jefferson," Liz said. "I'm gonna see if I can make the turn onto Main without touching the brakes."

"You're not."

"Well no. Of course I'm not."

"That's good."

She continued to look at him. Her blue eyes blinked. He was sorry, in a way, that he had told her the things he had. But he had. In any case, the consequences would not be significant, not for him. He would only be the fool a short while, and Liz would not care, one way or the other. Allen could not imagine that his profession of thirty-year-old devotion would affect Liz Terry much.

She was still looking at him. "So. Yeah."

"Hey, Liz, I meant to ask you something."

"What was that."

"Your office. Did you ever—did you put it up for lease recently?"

Liz cocked her head. "Hmm? No, why would I do that. I lease it myself."

"Oh."

"As far as I know they aren't kicking me out. It's not like commercial space is exactly at a premium in this town."

"Okay, well, I just—"

"Why'd you ask."

"I dunno. I thought I saw a for lease sign on it, but I guess not."

"Get your eyes checked, Al." Liz laughed and got on her bike. "Have a wild Saturday night at Maria's." And she was gone again, flying around the corner as if she'd make good on her brakeless boast.

Allen opened the gate and started up the walk. He looked up. Maria was standing in the living room window. As he approached, she disappeared into the house as if sinking in a pond.

Whatever rally that had roused him abandoned Allen on the back steps of Maria's. By the time he arrived at the top his leg bones had ripened into thin gelatin with nothing like muscle attached. The journey from the top of the stairs to the door of his room was a burning liquid agony. Some force other than his own will unlocked his door, got water, stuffed pills down his throat and laid him gently on the bed, where he knew no more.

Allen Wrangell met Liz Terry when they were both in grade school. He remembered the day, a Tuesday, and the place, which was on the monkey bars on the school playground.

Allen could never figure out the monkey bars. He couldn't swing. He grabbed and dangled until one of the other kids tickled him, or punched him, or he got tired and fell. Sometimes he'd let go with one hand while reaching with the other. Then he'd fall and the fingers of the hand holding the slick metal bars would hurt. So would his knees. But he tried to swing anyway and failed every time.

On this particular Tuesday, Liz was behind him on the ladder, waiting for her turn. As she was two grades below Allen, he had the luxury of ignoring her demands that he hurry the hell up. So, he grabbed and dangled while Liz Terry hollered at him to move it along. He didn't move it along. He dangled, feeling his armpits stretch and his lunch squash inside him.

Liz finally had enough, and she booted Allen in the rear. That didn't loosen his grip, it only made him swing enough to try to reach the next bar.

Which he did.

He reached the next bar, and the next one, his body's momentum carrying him forward, his hands seizing the bars and the rest of him coordinating in the right way, until he reached the end.

Never having reached the end before, Allen stopped. He dangled. The opposite ladder was near his feet, but he'd lost the momentum to get to it. So, he looked at it as his shoulders stung and his feet grew leaden.

Liz had been swinging along right behind him when she encountered Allen's rear once again blocking her way. She kicked him again, but this time Allen fell like an overripe plum into the redwood bark.

Liz kicked his head as she swung over him (later she insisted this was an accident) and Allen fell again, forward into the sharp-smelling bark, drawing hoots, jeers and creating general mirth at his expense from the children nearby.

It didn't matter. He'd swung. That girl from two grades down had made him swing and he'd flung his disjointed self all the way across the monkey bars. He watched her as she turned at the top of the ladder and looked at him. She was a bit sober and severe now. He liked it that she didn't laugh at him.

From that day forward, Allen noticed Liz. On the playground, walking to class, waiting for her mother to pick her up from school, Allen watched her. Sometimes when he ran out at night he thought of her running beside him, impressed by his speed and daring.

Once he had gone to her house, late at night. It was a big house with a huge yard, landscaped and beautiful, in a wealthy enclave full of other houses like it. He stood, concealed by a hedge, looking up at the lighted windows until they all were dimmed.

Chapter Fourteen

Allen woke up after what seemed only a few minutes and would have gone back to sleep were it not for the morning sun on his face. He lay and let it warm him, running down his neck to his chest, which was as far as it would go. But that was far enough. Not daring to try his legs, he flexed his hands. They seemed all right. Soon he appeared to have his full assemblage of self and he tried sitting up. That worked. It all worked. Despite his apparent regression the night before, Allen had rebounded and was, for the moment, in better shape than he'd been in weeks.

Maria had replenished his coffee and he brewed a motel-sized pot and ran a shower. Cleaned off, with caffeine and medicine coursing through him, Allen decided to ride the miraculous renascent wave to breakfast. It was Sunday.

Descending the stairs to the main hall, Allen had the sudden realization that he hadn't given much thought to DJ. He had become the Thing That Wasn't There, and that was all right. If Allen faced regression, DJ was in full retrogression: devolution from inertia to inert. The thought neither cheered nor depressed; it just was, or was not, and what Allen thought of it made no difference at all.

At the foot of the stairs Allen started to head for the kitchen but stopped in his tracks. Down the hall, in the front door foyer, Maria stood in soft light. The sun shone through her, as through a glass. She was looking through the window to the right of the door. Something moved on the porch. Someone approached the door—Allen could see a shadow across the thinly-curtained glass —and Maria moved to answer the bell.

He didn't want her to. He wanted to call down the long hall to stop her, but as in a dream no words came out of his mouth. He was stuck to the spot. Maria, a mile away, charged with corrosive sun, answered the door.

He couldn't hear what she said. He couldn't see who it was that stood outside the door or hear what that person said. From a sort of stiffness in her spine, Allen could tell that Maria wasn't comfortable: whomever it was standing on the other side of the door was either not someone Maria knew or was someone she knew and didn't like. The conversation was short, and Maria closed the door. A shade crossed the porch. Maria left the foyer and vanished into the sitting room.

Quickly, Allen ducked into the kitchen. He was pouring himself a cup of coffee when Maria came in from the sitting room. He took a sip of coffee and said, "Morning."

"Good morning, Allen." She tugged at her hair as she resumed the morning tasks her caller had interrupted.

"Someone at the door?"

"Yes. There was someone."

Allen prodded, but Maria stopped talking. He finished his breakfast—his appetite was still strong—

and left her in the kitchen, lost in whatever was brooding behind the walls of her eyes.

The cellphone buzzed as Allen got to his room. He answered.

"Hey, Al. Wow, was that Maria?"

"Liz."

"Who else calls you, Al? Yes. It's Liz. I was just at the front door and I think I met Maria."

"I saw there was someone there, yeah." Allen thought back to Maria's stiffened spine and mute presence. "So, it was you."

"Yep. You there at Maria's Home for Retired Postal Clerks?"

"I, uh. Um. Yeah."

"Yeah you are there, or, 'um yeah, I can't think of anything to say'?"

"I'm here."

"Well, by golly, so am I, out front. In my car. I left for a while, but I decided that, by golly, nobody's gonna tell me I can't see my old buddy Al."

"Is that what she told you?"

"She said you weren't feeling well. I said no shit and you aren't looking that great, either. That seemed to go over like a fart in a bathysphere."

"She's—"

"Protective," Liz interrupted. "She sweet on you, Al?"

"I don't—"

"Well, you wanna take a Sunday drive? It's a nice day and I'm sitting here with nothing to do."

"Sure."

Liz's car, a giant white familiar-looking sled, was parked a block away. Allen shut the gate behind him. Looking back, he saw a curtain in Maria's sitting room close. He paused, but seeing no further movement he made his way to the idling beast, opened the heavy door and settled into the passenger seat.

"What is this thing?" he asked as Liz threw it into drive.

"Buick Wildcat." She put her foot in it and the V8 shot the car forward, the seat pressing into Allen's back.

"Your dad had one. It was an old car even back then. You drove it all the time." Allen fumbled for a seat belt.

"This is the same car. I still drive it all the time. Dad never wanted to get rid of it." Liz wheeled the Buick around, doubling back past Maria's and on to Jefferson, tires squealing as she cut the turn tight. There was a momentary suspension of gravity, then the tires grabbed and they hurtled down into town, aimed straight for Main.

"You drive it the same way, too," Allen almost shouted. He pressed his foot into the floor mat. "Tell me you plan to use your brakes."

"Aw, you're no fun."

"Fun? This is fun?"

"Fine, fine." Liz applied the brakes and Allen put his hands on the dash.

By the time they were even with Ted's place the Buick had slowed enough for Allen to see Ted behind his customarily customer-free bar. He looked up as they went by.

"Where are we going?" Allen asked as the car wallowed to a halt at the intersection.

Liz spun the wheel left and drove toward the bridge north of town at a more sedate pace. "Where do you want to go?"

"I don't know. I don't know this area at all."

"There isn't much to know." Liz accelerated as they neared the bridge. "We could just cruise Main like the kids do."

"They do?"

"Oh hell, I don't know. When I'm not working I stay out of this place."

"Oh. Well."

"So where do you want to go?"

"How about slow?" They were crossing the bridge at a rate that approached precipitous.

Liz laughed but didn't slow the car at all. "Let's drive to Gold Flat."

"Has a Bret Harte ring. Is it far?"

"It doesn't matter, does it."

"No."

"Damned straight." Liz yanked right onto a narrow road that joined the highway just past the bridge, then rose east, up the left bank of a tributary creek. Allen noted the road cuts on the left were striated with layers of slate, quartz sandstone and glistening serpentine. Liz looked sidelong at him. "Why do you like rocks so much?"

Allen pulled his gaze away from the road cuts. "Um. It's not that." He stopped.

"Spit it out, Al."

"I don't like them. I need them. If I wasn't able to, to look at them, dig them up, look at their granular structure, see what province they might have come from, think about where their roots go—hold them, you know—I wouldn't be able to make sense of anything."

"You aren't making sense of anything now, Al." Liz grinned and pushed his shoulder. "No sense at all."

"We're out here on the edge, Liz. Here in the West. We're the prow of a ship, cutting through the ocean, but the ocean isn't water, it's rock. And here you are with a piece of that ocean all around you."

"Allen, you need a different hobby."

"It's not a hobby."

"Yeah. Right. It's more of a, I dunno, a cry for help."

"It's necessary," Allen said. "For survival. For anything to last, at all. If I don't get this right, it all gets lost forever. I have to get what's going on down there, and what went on down there before, and what's going to go on down there. It's all the same. It is, was and will be. The proof is in the rocks. They follow us. They move faster than we can imagine, although we can't see it, because we're so, I don't know, limited. They last a lot longer than we do."

Liz looked at Allen and the car drifted to the road's edge. "Al, you make me sad."

Allen pointed to the gully to their right. "You're going to make us dead."

Liz corrected and hunkered over the big wheel. "How are you so sure, Allen?"

"Sure? About what?"

"How are you so sure we aren't dead already."

Allen said nothing. He had a reply, but he sat on it. Instead, he pointed out the window. "Those trees there, they thrive on poor soils. They can live in dirt that's low in calcium and other things plants need. They grow here in these barren spots, the old ocean rock that is full of nickel and heavy metals that most plants don't like. That's why they grow up here with not much else around."

Liz piloted the Wildcat around twisting, sharply rising road. "You're a nut, Al. Why the hell am I out in the woods with a nut like you?"

Allen resumed staring at road cuts. "Because I'm that fun to be around?"

Liz laughed. "Yeah. That must be it." She drove in silence a long while as the road climbed higher into ever-deepening canyonland, a shady water and moss world, nearly-naked streamside trees clotting the swift waters with rafts of leaf and twig. After some miles she slowed the car, pulling onto a narrow wayside overlooking a deep pool. "Look down there, Al."

He looked. Leaves swirled in frigid waters, overhung with fern. Ringed with knife-thin ice, pierced here and there with shafts of light that drowned in its snowmelt, the deep pool magnified glittering stones on its floor, hiding more treasure in its deep bank recesses.

Allen cranked the window down. "It's colder here."

"We're a lot higher up."

"I like it."

"Yeah. Me, too, Al." Liz opened her window. "Smell that." She batted Allen on the arm. "Smell that, Al."

"It smells like—"

"Like good medicine. Like sweet, green medicine, Allen."

"Yeah. Sort of. Sage. Quinine."

She cut the motor and rushing water sounds overlaid with the weight of canyon silence poured through the windows. She laid her head back over the seat and breathed. "There is nothing else. There is this river and nothing else." She twisted her neck and looked at Allen. "But you're somewhere under it all, aren't you?"

He rested his chin on his hand, peering. There were fish moving in the cold water, scales like thousands of mica flakes, like stars. "They're no more aware of the water than we are the air."

"I'm very aware of the air," Liz replied. "My lungs love it. I'm eating up the air."

"This river," Allen said, "is new. The slope that makes it run is pretty new, in geologic time."

"Rocks are old," Liz said. "And Old Man River just keeps rolling along."

"Some of the rocks are old, the way the Earth reckons. They came from out west."

"We are out West, as you just pointed out."

"West-er." Allen leaned out the window and looked up at the towering stone above the pool. He said nothing for a long time. He listened to Liz breathing. "Some of this is dolomite, like whale flukes, swimming in our world. Some of it is the iron ocean floor, shoved up by swollen mantle. Magnesium rock. Mud rock. Sand rock. Hot granite just blasting up through old islands and flood plains. There's shale folded in, maybe from some extinct delta." He stopped and looked over at Liz. She slept. Quietly he opened the door, got out and scrambled down the shale bank to the pool.

Sliding to a stop on a rough little beach, he squatted, leaned forward, and trailed his hand in the pool. The cold penetrated as if the water itself intruded right into his marrow. The sun approaching noon dove straight down through the canyon, through shivering branches, into the pool, igniting gems, revealing the smooth backs of fish. They felt it. Allen's neck felt the sun, also. He lay back against the shale and leaf bank and let the sun cover him up.

He closed his eyes.

A crow spoke.

Although Allen frequently thought about Liz Terry after the incident on the monkey bars, and knew her name, he never spoke to her after that day. She occupied a place two grades and two worlds apart from his and remained just a girl whose impatience had booted him into swinging over the world for a few seconds. He never went on the monkey bars again and Liz never again crossed his path. She remained a sober look and a kick in the pants.

It wasn't until his last year in high school that Liz Terry reappeared in Allen's life, and he hardly recognized her when she did. She had grown into a slim, quick girl who talked rings around him one day in the library, then invited him to a picnic lunch. It was she, then, who brought up that day on the playground, and they both laughed about it.

That was an odd thing. That laughing thing. Allen seldom laughed and when he did it never made him feel like he was kissing a girl. Or holding a girl against his chest. Or touching a girl's impossibly-smooth fuzzy sweater with the palms of his hands, afraid to let his fingers touch her, afraid that this would be a too greedy, too undeservedly good thing to do. But laughing with Liz made him feel that way, and it made him know a place in his chest that was cracking open and such an utterly new and unknowable pain and pleasure was so terrifying and full of uncharted delights that he knew he wanted more of it, just like that, without any question whatsoever.

And so he laughed with her, and laughing made him laugh more. And they were, without saying much about it, mated to each other that day, without the faintest idea, yet, of what that was, what that would be.

"Isn't napping just the best?" Liz's voice floated in over the water. "Isn't it the best?"

Allen opened his eyes. Liz squatted next to him, looking up at the sky. The sun was already leaving the canyon. It was cooler. "Yes," Allen said. "It's the best."

Liz looked down at him. "You bored me right to sleep, Allen."

He sat up. "Glad to be of service."

Liz laughed and splashed water at him. "Oh, wow, you're just, um, the same old Allen Wrangell, aren't you."

"For now."

She squinted at him. "What's that supposed to mean."

"Just that." He stretched and stood. "How far is that town?"

Liz got up. "Not far." She put her hand through the crook of his arm. "Tell me something, Allen."

"All right. What would you like to know?"

"Tell me why you left."

"Why I left?"

"You left. You left one day, and you never came back. No one ever knew where you went."

"You mean—"

"Thirty years ago, or whatever. You left. Where did you go?"

Allen started up the bank, pulling Liz along with him. "What we're walking on, what we're climbing up, you know, it goes down a long way. It might go down for over a hundred miles. Things that happen in the core of the planet, they affect what goes on up here." He struggled to the road bed, panting. "There's a sun inside the earth." He held Liz's hand. "It's an engine, moving these great stone ships around on a molten sea."

Liz withdrew her hand. "Shut up, Allen," she said gently.

They got back in the Buick and she started the motor. Allen looked down on the pool, already opaque in its early evening. "You said this river was all there is, Liz."

"It's all there was." She gassed the V8. It bubbled and mumbled, and they crunched back on to the road. "Now it's not."

"That's your answer then," Allen said. He resumed looking at road cuts and stream banks. "That's all that was."

Liz shook her head. "No. You had a reason for leaving. You must have. You couldn't just, I don't know, drive away. For no reason. You couldn't."

Allen's eyes ached. His hands found each other and knitted together, white-knuckled. "Reason." He blinked. "Reason. No, there's not much reason in what we do."

Liz smacked the steering wheel and the Buick's massive iron stuttered slightly. "I'm not talking about what we do, Allen. I'm talking about what you did. Why did you leave? One day you just weren't there, and everyone who knew you—who loved you—everyone just woke up one day to no Allen Wrangell."

"Everyone"

"Yeah."

"There was no everyone." Allen looked over at Liz, her face pinched in sudden sorrow. "There was just you."

"Well, thanks, Al. It's special to know that you uniquely and especially left just solely me and actually I don't give a shit if that was even remotely grammatically correct."

Allen's spine dug into the seatback as Liz drove the big coupe through canyon hairpins, up the rising road to cooler climes. He looked at his hands. "I didn't know what to do."

"With what? With me?"

"I didn't know how."

"You didn't know how to what?"

"I don't know, it's been so long."

"Not in geological time, Al." Her voice bit. "In the span of the ages, your departure is but a crumb of dust, the dry edge of a popcorn fart, fading slowly into the west." At that she laughed, not unlike the sound he'd heard in the library all those years ago. She poked his arm. "Aw, Al, it's okay." She stepped on the gas. "I got over it."

Allen hung his head out the open window, letting cold air pull his face around, filling his sinuses. He waved a hand against the rush. "That's good."

"What Al? Hey, you'll lose an arm you know."

He withdrew from the window. "I said, that's good."

"I loved you, Al." Liz looked straight ahead, addressing the windshield.

Allen blinked rapidly. He was dizzy. "I—"

"Don't say anything, Al." Liz accelerated on the straight shot out of the canyon and onto wider, level ground. "Don't say anything at all."

The Buick nosed due east as the road cut through wide-spaced pines and barrens of red and charcoal soil.

The understory was manzanita, twisted oxblood and leaves the color of storm ocean. Something had erupted here not long ago, Allen knew. "Not long ago. Not in geologic time."

"Hmmm?" Liz said absently. "You making fun of me, Al?"

"No. No, I was thinking about what put this rough soil down."

"Yes, Al. Of course you were. Well anyway."

"Yes."

"Anyway, Gold Flat is just a couple of miles." Liz's statement was verified by a sign whizzing by. "We can eat lunch."

"On me," Allen said. The sun had returned, and the air was warmer here. He felt life rejoin his inward parts. "This is high country."

"It's beautiful country," Liz said.

Gold Flat nested at the western end of a long valley, the watershed of the creek they had followed. The road they took was its main street, like Forester, but the town was much smaller. The houses too were smaller, with the requisite metal roofs. Many of them were log or timbered structures, plain and strong, showing the grain of the trees from which they were cut. South of the town rose bare peaks, and to the north was a large, eroded volcano, already frosted with recent snow. Allen now knew where the lava had come from. It was a magnificent peak in its dormant years, and it dominated the valley like a lord.

They idled down Main, Allen looking around at the few businesses: a barbershop, small grocery, a miniature bank, everything tidy, modest and earthy, smelling of balsam and wood smoke. This was not a town in opposition to its environment. It knew its place. It was a guest of the mountains and their mountain lord, and seemed content with that. None of the few people Allen could see were hurrying in the slightest.

"This is where I like to go," Liz said, pulling into a small, cedar-shaded parking lot by a little brown diner. The sign over the front porch roof read, *Lottie's.* "I just like it. Don't know why."

Allen opened his door and got out. "Looks like it's about the only place in town."

"No," Liz said, slamming her door. "There are a couple more, but Lottie's has a porch, and a jukebox, a real one. Where ya gonna find that anymore, Al?"

Allen thought about Ted's place. "Not too many places, I guess." He followed Liz in.

The jukebox in question sat at the end of a long counter, in the back, by the entrance to the bathrooms. It did not look functional. No titles showed under its slanted window. Besides the jukebox and the counter, there were the unsurprising glass cases with unsurprising pastries, wooden tables and chairs, blackboards with menu items and a cat clock that wagged its tail over the cash register. Only a few customers sat, waited on by a substantial woman (Lottie, Allen guessed) and casting mildly curious glances at Liz and Allen as they chewed. Comforting sizzling noises came from the kitchen beyond the counter.

"Sit anywhere," the solid woman directed with an equally ample voice. "Anything besides water?" She disappeared into the kitchen before getting an answer.

Liz and Allen picked a table near the front window. Allen noticed that it was very clean and smelled of oil soap. These two facts made him like Lottie's diner and Lottie—or whomever the substantial lady was—and predisposed him to think well of whatever he would be offered to eat.

He needed to eat. The room was beginning to spin. He thought of the pills in the inside pocket of his trench coat, how he'd get them out and swallow them without too much fuss.

Liz stared at him. "What's the matter, Al? You look bad."

"Throat's dry," he said.

"You look like an old bird. I hate to say it, but it's true. A middle-aged bird." She leaned forward to inspect him more closely. "But a bird. Definitely."

He was at a loss as to how to reply and was spared the effort by the lady of substance, arriving with menus and water. She smiled at them and Allen felt his face smile back. His face muscles knew before the rest of him did that this woman was good and could be trusted. Her water was good water. Her food would be good food. This must be Lottie.

She patted his shoulder. "I'll bet you want a coke."

"Yes," he replied, hardly feeling it necessary. "Thank you, Lottie."

She smiled and pointed to a picture behind the counter, near the tail-wagging cat, of a large lady much like her. "That was my mom."

"Oh."

"I'm Katie."

"Katie," he repeated. He drank the water. "Good water."

"There's a spring. Feeds the river."

"Ah. Great. Great."

Liz watched them. She frown-smiled. "I gotta use the ladies' room."

Katie and Liz both left and Allen quickly dug in his trench coat pocket. By the time Liz returned, he'd finished swallowing the pills and was also finishing her water.

"I mighta wanted some of that," Liz protested. "I hear its great water."

"It is." Allen set the glass down. "Very good."

They ordered hamburgers and, when Katie brought them, they ate quickly and with few words. When they were finished Liz sat back and sighed. "Now ain't that a grand burger, Al?"

"Yes. Yes, very good."

"You ate your fries, too."

"They were wonderful. Something more than fries, don't you think?"

Liz nodded vigorously. "Oh, yes. They are fried in ambrosia."

"Something like, yes." Katie arrived, and Allen gave his plate to her. "Thank you, thank you."

"Sure! Dessert?" They both declined. "More coke?"

"Yes," Allen said. "Thank you."

Katie brought the coke, smiled, and left them. Allen watched her. "She's good."

"Hmm? Oh, yeah. She's the girl," Liz looked at Allen. "You sweet on her, now, Al?"

"Yes."

Liz laughed and hit the table, so hard the other diners noticed. "Ha! I knew it. You are such a nerd, nerd, nerdy nerd, Allen. You really are."

Warm women always surprised Allen. He wondered how it was they became that way. They drew him into their safe circle. He wanted to watch them, to be near their orbits, to ask them questions. His mother had not been warm, nor was she cold. She was cool, friendly, gentle, but not warm; listening to Mozart and Villa Lobos, reading, sunning her legs, performing the endless chores required of her by her enormous, noisy family. Allen admired her. He wished he could help her when her headaches came on and when she surrendered to the weight of too much everything. When his father raged, and his implacable mother tried to hold back the candle-snuffing storm, Allen sometimes stood between them, trying to calm things. On occasion quiet did come, but there was nothing he could do for his mother in the long run, and there was very little he wanted from her. She was a mystery and Allen accepted that. It was one reason they got along: they let each other be.

Warm women, though, were something else. A different species. They valued and nurtured things that Allen had never heard of. They operated using different mechanics. There were customs and contracts and frames of reference which were foreign languages to Allen, and he wished to interpret them and understand what they meant. He never could, but he enjoyed the attempt immensely.

Katie was such a woman. Her mother had been such a woman, Allen knew, because she had made Katie. There was no more or less to it than that. If he had told Katie all this she would have listened to him. Then she would have asked him if he needed anything else. Allen was grateful for that.

They lingered and shadows were getting long when they finally left, thanking Katie so often she blushed. On the porch Allen stretched and breathed in the cool mountain sweetness. He felt young and strong.

Liz grabbed his shoulder and squeezed. "There, now. That put some starch in ya, Al. You even look better."

"Not so birdlike?"

"A younger bird. A healthier bird." She started walking and Allen followed her. "Let's see what the town has to offer, huh?"

"We've seen it, I think."

As afternoon deepened they ambled through Gold Flat, seeing the places they had passed earlier. Little differentiated the town from other villages up and down the hills and valleys, except that here the forest was not held at bay. The town was in the forest and the forest was in the town. Allen saw this not only in the large number of evergreens shading the streets and the humble hues and dimensions of the buildings, but in the people. They smiled more easily, walked more loose-jointed and less heavily. Whatever their destinations, they did not seem pressed to arrive quickly. Doors opened and closed more slowly, and people paused to talk, holding the doors half-open, allowing sharp air pine-scented ingress. It seemed to Allen a place that took pleasure in being a place, and its inhabitants those who relished the minutes one by one.

He didn't want to leave.

Stopping in front of the little grocery store, he peered in. A teenaged boy stocking shelves waved at him, as if he'd expected the visit. Allen waved back. "These are friendly people."

"Mountain people," Liz said. She seemed distracted and resumed walking.

"Good people." Allen followed. They headed due west, the sun in their faces.

"They're slow," Liz replied, walking more quickly.

Allen was irritated, both by her reply and her haste. She might have only made an observation about what he had also seen, but she might have meant something else, something pejorative. He hurried to keep up. "Relaxed, I'd say."

"Yeah." She slowed a little as he caught up to her. "Yeah. Could be, yeah. Nothing wrong with it, if you can afford it."

"It's free."

Liz stopped. "Is it?"

"Well. Yeah. Yeah, it is."

"I suppose."

Allen saw that they had reached the western edge of town. To their left a small park sloped down to the river. There was no lawn, but glossy wooden tables were scattered on granite soil under huge fir trees. Near the river a weathered gazebo sat alone, its shingles covered with leaf and needle, spandrels cobwebbed, benches and rails dusty in the east-running sunbeams. Of one accord they walked to the gazebo, sitting close together on a bench. They watched the water carrying away the last leaves of fall.

"I was thinking," Allen said.

"Not again!" Liz laughed. "What, Al. What were you thinking."

"I was thinking about being on the inside of my skin."

"You just keep thinking that way, buddy. It's the only place to be."

"But what if I wasn't me? What if I could somehow peel off the thing that I am from the machine that I'm in? And what if I was still stuck in here"—he pointed to where his throat met his chest—"just rattling around, hanging onto my tonsils?"

"You wouldn't want to let go," Liz said. She pitched a twig into the water. "It's mostly hydrochloric acid when you hit bottom."

"Well that's it. If we weren't who we are, we could easily fall inside ourselves and drown. Or suffocate. Or be crushed or, if who we are is small enough, we'd get eaten by our own immune system, or get chewed up by a nematode. They're crawling all around inside us, you know. We're only about ten percent us, anyway. The rest of us is bacteria, parasites, that kind of thing."

"Really Al, shouldn't you take up a retirement hobby? I mean, really. How about model boats. You need a hobby Al."

He looked at her and looked away. "Maybe this is it."

'What? Goofing about drowning in your own bodily fluids?"

"Goofing—if that's what you want to call it—about all sorts of things. I like it. When you're sorting mail all day, you get in the habit."

Liz rubbed her forehead. "Well. That's what happens anyway, I think."

"What."

"We eat ourselves. We fail ourselves. We just chew ourselves up. It's not enough to gnaw each other to bits, we gotta get inside and just rip and tear. Ya know, Al? Ya know?" She looked at him from under her hand.

Allen nodded. "Yes. Yes, I do."

He watched as she picked her cuticles. She got up and walked around inside the gazebo. Like a trapped thing, Allen thought. She could just step off the platform, go wherever she liked, but for the moment she would not. Could not. He pitied her. She was still young. She was beautiful in the same tomboy way she had always been beautiful. But a doom hung over her and Allen could not lift it. The deed was recorded. The paperwork had been signed long ago.

Liz leaned against a thickset upright. "Tell me something, Allen."

"What."

"Tell me if you loved me." He said nothing and she walked over, stood in front of him, looking him in the face. "Yes or no." She waited.

He put the knuckles of his right hand against his mouth, the small knuckle touching between his nostrils, the knuckle of the index finger resting between his lower lip and his chin. He opened his mouth. Closed it. "I—"

Liz straightened, rigid. "Wrong answer."

She walked away. He watched as she crossed the park, little puffs of silver dust rising and dying in her steps. She reached the street, turned right and disappeared.

Allen remained in the gazebo. It occurred to him to go after her, but he thought better of it. He watched the leaves floating west and listened to the wind rushing up from the canyon, blowing against the current of the little river, which answered with its own steady voice. "The wind will die, but the river will live until the earth dries up."

It wasn't long before a third voice joined the water and the wind. It was the steel hiss and roar of the Buick sucking air down Main, racing the leaves west. Allen saw her as she flew by, looking straight ahead, then lost her as she burned the last of Main and was gone, rolling towards the canyon. She echoed a long time and then even that faint reflection was gone.

He looked back at the river. Wind chilled the surface of the water and caused the trees to clap their knobby hands, shaking loose the very last leaves of the year to travel as far as they might. He was in no hurry, but stood anyway, and walked back to the road and into town again, passing the same little shops and the same contented townsfolk, not at all disturbed by the Wildcat that had roared through their forest village. He continued on, not too fast, until he reached Lottie's. He went in and Katie was there. She might have been waiting for him.

"I think," he said, "I'll have some dessert."

Chapter Fifteen

There was no hurry. There was nowhere to go and if there was he would have no reason to go there. There was a little apartment above the restaurant that Katie said he could use, free of charge. He said that would be nice, but insisted on paying her for it. She refused and he made up his mind to leave the money anyway. There was a bus coming in the morning. Until then, there was dinner, another walk, then rest as the stars came out and the waxing moon shed her light on the town, the forest and Lottie's mountain diner, alone at the top of the world.

The bus stopped at Lottie's at four in the morning. Allen was waiting for it and boarded in the silent chill. He slept all the way back to Forester.

It was still dark, although the eastern sky was relenting to dawn, when he got off the bus not far from Liz's office. No one and nothing moved on Main, except the departing bus, which had picked up no passengers and was already receding taillights when Allen crossed the street.

There was a *For Lease* sign in the window of Liz's empty office.

Allen had expected to see it, but that didn't blunt the cold invasion of his chest wall, the dizzy ache in his neckbones and along the back of his skull. He barely stopped to look and walked on, willing his feet forward.

He re-crossed the street at Jefferson and stopped in front of Ted's bar. The sign wasn't lit, but Ted was there, stocking the cooler. He looked up, then came to the door, unlocking it. Allen stepped inside, only then realizing how cold he was.

"Hey, Ted."

Ted resumed his station behind the bar. "Coke?"

Allen sat. "You have coffee?"

"Yeah, just made it." He put a white café mug of coffee in front of Allen, not asking if he wanted cream. "How ya been?"

"I've been better, and I've been worse."

"Kinda powering down the middle, huh?" He resumed stocking the cooler.

"I hope so." Allen drank the hot coffee, grateful for it. After a moment he leaned forward, addressing the back of Ted's head. "Look, I am gonna tell you something."

Ted paused for just a moment, then resumed putting beer bottles in the cooler. "Okay."

"I'm, uh, not well."

"Yeah?" Ted finished the last bottle and stood, facing Allen, his arms hanging loose. "How so?"

"I'm dying."

Ted nodded. "All right."

Allen liked two things: firstly that Ted didn't say he was sorry and secondly that he didn't get philosophical and say something like, 'We're all dying, just at different rates and at different places on the continuum,' etcetera. A bonus likeable thing was that Ted didn't recount any ordeals suffered by dying or now-dead relatives, friends and loved ones. Ted just stood there, waiting for Allen to say something else, which after a while was, "Thank you."

"Keep the change."

"I'm going to need an executor." (Allen almost forgot a fourth agreeable thing, which was that Ted didn't ask what was killing him. That might have been the best part of Ted's reaction so far.) "I could have the lawyer for my estate, but I don't know. Just need someone to sign the checks and stuff."

"The lawyer, that the one you were looking for?"

"Yeah, but not for the lawyer part."

"Okay."

"She'd do this, though, I think."

"So will I, if you need."

"Thank you. Thank you very much." It was becoming difficult to count all the likable and agreeable things about Ted, so Allen didn't try. "I, um."

Ted stood, waiting. When Allen said nothing else, Ted refilled his coffee cup and waited some more. When he still said nothing, Ted began wiping the bar.

Allen drank his coffee. "You bar smells like oil soap."

"Good for the wood," Ted replied.

"All good places smell like oil soap. Maria's, it smells like it in her sitting room."

"That doesn't surprise me."

"And there's a place in Gold Flat. Owned by a saintly woman named Katie."

"Lottie's Diner," Ted said.

Allen looked at him. "Yes."

"I know it well."

"I was just there," Allen said. "I just caught the bus back from there."

Ted stopped wiping the bar. He glanced at Allen, then away, out the window now streaked with dawn. He looked back at Allen. "The bus."

"Yes. The four A.M. bus out of Gold Flat." Allen had seen the pause. That pause got him thinking.

Ted resumed wiping the bar. "Nice little town."

"The best. It's—it's its own place. It has its own mountain."

"And Lottie's Diner."

Allen nodded. "She let me stay there. Katie did. When Liz left—Liz just left me there—and Katie, she had a place over the restaurant. She wouldn't take money, but I left some anyway. They have the best water there. The juke box, I don't think it works..." Allen trailed off. Ted continued to look at him, steadily, a question in his eyes, forming on his lips. Allen gulped his coffee. "What?"

"Liz?"

"Liz Terry."

"The lawyer."

"Yeah. The lawyer. She's an—we were—she was my—what's the matter?"

Ted shook his head. "Nothing's the matter, Allen. It's all good."

Allen looked at Ted over the rim of his coffee cup. "You're sure."

"Yes," Ted draped the bar towel over the stainless-steel sink. "All good."

They both looked out the window at the cold, empty dawn street. After a long silence, Allen said, "Her office is for lease."

"Liz Terry's."

"Yeah," Allen said. "The lawyer. It's for lease, her office." Ted nodded. Said nothing. "Sometimes it isn't," Allen said, "and sometimes it is."

Ted looked over at him. "Depends on the time."

Allen looked back at Ted. "That's right."

They resumed looking out the window. The right-hand frame cast a long, transparent shadow of a shadow across the pane, becoming a real shadow on the sill inside, slipping over and disappearing into the deeper and permanent shadow of Ted's bar, lost in the oiled oak floor that ran all the way back, through the storeroom, under the walls and over the old galvanized plumbing, to the puddled alleyway behind, still covered in leftover night.

The bit of sun on short loan was gone in a few minutes. The window cleared of light, revealing the still-deserted street, and the bar resumed its seasoned dusk. Ted's sole remaining task was to pour Allen's coffee and Allen's only obligation was to drink it. This was done with silent decorum until Allen cleared his throat.

"Ted?"

"Yeah."

"I'd like you to tell me something."

"What's that."

"Well. I've been thinking, and—just be straight with me, all right?"

"Sure."

"Something just crossed my mind, and I want an answer. Just a yes or no, if you would."

"Yeah, all right."

"All right now, listen."

"I'm listening."

Allen leaned forward, looking closely at Ted.

"There is no four A.M. bus out of Gold Flat. Is there."

Chapter Sixteen

There was something awful about the gate.

It hung on tired hinges screwed to a wooden post that anchored the picket fence surrounding Maria's yard. It hung and it bled, its galvanized wire dermis pocked and abraded by the extremes of seasons, draining russet into the washed-out concrete of the path beneath it.

An invisible spark leaped between Allen's hand and the gate's looped top as he reached for the latch. He pulled and a juddering complaint filled the air. The gate gave admittance grudgingly and closed behind him with its terrible snap.

Allen had never liked that gate, but it now appeared to have invited in demons. He fled it like he would a bad dog: not too quickly, not looking back.

Maria's house showed few signs of life as he made his way around to the back. He was aware nonetheless of a watching and listening presence, angry and alert. There was something of the beast hunkered down over its prey, a growling in the joists, a quivering in splayed and creaking joints. Something had crept between the cracks and a hateful mortar extruded, glowing with decay, smelling of ammonia and bitter earth.

Allen's footsteps clocked telltale disclosure, rapping loud between house wall and dormant fields. He tried to walk more quietly, but it didn't work.

As he approached a yellowing quince that grew beside the kitchen door, he saw DJ standing, half-hidden, hands in his pockets, watching Allen with a predator's mechanical indifference. Allen could see the tautness in his shoulders and arms and he knew that DJ's hands would come flying from the pockets of his dirty jeans soon. There were only a few pro forma remarks before the proceedings.

"DJ." Allen raised three fingers in greeting as he passed.

"Hey." DJ's studied slouch straightened and, predictably, his hand shot out, tapping Allen roughly on the shoulder. "Hey, where ya been."

Allen stopped, still facing away. "Where have I been."

"That's what I said." There was morning beer in the chill draft of his breath. "Maria, she worries, you know."

"Oh, well, where I have been depends on the time."

DJ paused, thrown off his rhythm, but only for a mote of a second. "You know, we don't like our guests just sneaking in and out. We don't like that at all."

"You don't." Allen watched DJ out of the angle of his eye.

"Gives us a sketchy rep."

Allen laughed. "Does it."

"Why're you laughing." DJ stepped away from the quince, hands balled, advancing on Allen. "What's so funny."

"Nothing," Allen said. "Nothing at all." He started for the back stairs, but DJ followed.

"I want you gone, freak boy." He reached and shoved Allen's shoulder. "Gone."

Allen stopped. "Don't do that."

"What. This?" DJ shoved his shoulder harder.

Allen stopped and faced DJ squarely. "Yeah. Yeah, that."

DJ grinned. Poking his finger in Allen's chest he said, "Don't like it, rock man? Don't like it? Leave."

Allen needed his medication. He had missed a dose. "I'm going to my room, DJ." He started to turn but DJ grabbed his arm.

"Pack your shit and get out."

Allen let his head lop over and he looked down at DJ. He smiled. "You've been having a rough few days."

DJ licked his lips. "Not as rough as you're gonna have. Leave."

Allen shook his head. Then in a stuttered second a blue-white flare lit his left eye. It wasn't until he saw DJ grinning and rubbing his right hand that he realized he'd been struck savagely in the temple.

DJ pushed him again, hard enough to snap his head back a little. "Leave."

Allen's eyes went in and out of focus, as if a lever in his chest were twisting and untwisting a lens through well-oiled gears and pulleys. His left temple throbbed. "I'm not leaving just yet, DJ."

Blue jetted through the center of his vision. DJ had struck him, harder, in the same place. Still grinning, enjoying himself, DJ leaned into his work, striking, striking, advancing as Allen retreated toward the stairs. DJ was using his knuckles, working the spot a little, then throwing one-two punches into Allen's chest. The effect was alarming: fists tripping the invisible sternum lens lever until Allen's vision careened between nauseating panoramas and tight, sickening circus pinwheels, writhing and twisting in gaudy chartreuse, orange, purple and pink, outlined by a jet border that intruded deeper with each blow.

"I'm going blind." He was. Or rather, he was departing the machine, already joggled loose from his brain straps, surrendering the field to somber velvet. He could no longer feel his arms or legs. His head was abandoned to the meat-blows. Most of him had pulled into the small space between chest wall and throat, and that little bit was fading quickly, departing breath by breath.

Then it all stopped.

A remark went unremarked. A sentence ended with *and...*

Allen observed DJ's puffy face, grinning under its ridiculous sideways cap, squinty-eyed, sweaty, hurtful red effort surfacing under paste-dead skin. As Allen watched, the grin faded into a confusion of pain and disappointment, a child whose Christmas was cruelly and inexplicably revoked. DJ's eyes rolled right in their pulpy orbits. They rotated up, as if he were trying to observe his eyebrows.

Following DJ's gaze, Allen looked left. There, suspended in mid-blow, was DJ's blood-knuckled fist. It quivered at the end of a muscle-knotted arm. Wrapped around it was Allen's own left hand, pale and insensate, unrelenting, and frozen as ivory. It closed tighter on the wriggling fist, swollen crescents of DJ's blood orange flesh popping out between the fingers. It was astonishing how tightly a hand could close over another, particularly one as hammy as DJ's. They both stared as the thin corpse hand cinched down, then began to rotate on its wrist. The trapped hand moved with it until it could move no more.

A thin ululation scratched its way into Allen's head, distant at first, then rising steadily until it shrieked in his injuries, forcing itself down through the roots of bruises into the inward parts of his brain. As he awoke to the DJ shriek, Allen was still unable to feel his hand. It operated autonomously, twisting, wrenching, forcing the rest of DJ to follow his captive fist or lose it. Over and down he went, pulling Allen down with him until he knelt over DJ's buckled body. Their faces were inches apart. DJ's cap slid off his sweaty scalp and lay near him.

There they remained, both men in thrall to Allen's dead hand.

Now mute and shivering, eyes wide, DJ appealed silently for release, but Allen was unable to grant it. He shrugged, looked at his hand, then back to DJ. "There are," he said quietly, "things better left alone."

How long she had been standing there, silent in the kitchen doorway, Allen didn't know. She was dressed, incongruously, in a yellow print sun dress and her hair was down. She wore no shoes in the cold autumn air. It was as if she had arrived months too late and now wanted explanations.

"Hello." Allen could think of nothing else to say.

"Are you going to let him go?" Maria didn't wait for a reply, but came down the steps and walked toward them.

"I'd like to." Allen looked back down at DJ, who rolled his eyes back to watch Maria arrive.

Maria knelt by them. "He'd probably like that, too." Then she saw the side of Allen's head and made a little grimace. "That's not good, Allen. It doesn't look good at all"

"That's not surprising."

She touched his already swollen temple and the damaged area where DJ had concentrated his malice, above the ear. She looked at DJ. "Why did you do this."

DJ lay and said nothing. His eyes closed. A fume of beer and adrenaline escaped from between his lips. Opening his eyes again, he said, "Urdu."

Maria shook her head. "You need to leave. Will you?" He nodded. Maria reached out and her hand closed over Allen's. "Listen now, DJ. Just get up and go. I'll have your things sent to your brother's."

Allen's hand relaxed and DJ, released, rolled away. They stood and faced each other. Maria watched them. Allen knelt and picked up DJ's cap. He handed it to him. Grabbing it with his left hand, DJ turned and walked away.

Allen listened to the wire gate complain. He turned to Maria. "I don't think I hurt him much." She said nothing. She appeared to be looking over his shoulder. He couldn't read her expression. "There's a story here," he said, "but I don't know what it means."

Chapter Seventeen

It was an awkward interregnum.

There should have been something: an embrace, a conversation. Tears. But Maria didn't cry. She didn't say anything. She went inside, her yellow sun dress flashing as she disappeared through the kitchen door. Allen followed. They had coffee. He excused himself and went to his room. He medicated and pissed a river. He went back downstairs. The day passed with no other events, no recap, no questions or coming to terms. Maria didn't ask where he'd been and Allen didn't say. Maria made lunch; Allen ate it. Maria cleaned; Allen did dishes. As evening approached, the house became an island in the mountain mist. Maria started to cook dinner. Allen suggested they just have cereal, and they did. Maria gave Allen ice packs for his head. The swelling wasn't too bad.

He wondered if he should tell her.

The hand thing alarmed him. Even after he'd regained sense and control of his limbs he regarded his left hand with suspicion, glancing surreptitiously at it from time to time as if he could catch it in some sinister act. It had taken down a foe on its own volition. Allen wondered if it would it likewise strike a friend. He knew his disease, had known for a long time that one of his hands might do this, might get a mind of its own, start grabbing, pointing, waving. Hell, it might start playing the piano. The day might come when Allen and his hand would not recognize each other. What then.

"Get a job at Ted's," Allen said. (He was in the sitting room, looking at his hand.) "Playing piano." Maria looked in him from the kitchen, then went away. It was likely he did this talking more than he realized, and she was more accustomed to it than he knew.

Allen's hand had not behaved completely independently. It had responded to an inner command or request to put down the thing that was killing its possessor. And Allen had no doubt that, had he been unable to stop him, DJ would have killed him, blow by blow. He would not have quit pulping Allen. He was having too darned much fun. Allen's iron left hand had done the job he'd hired it to do. His disease had saved him, for the time-being. No, the hand might be an independent actor, but it would not harm a friend. His body would weaken and flicker out, but it would not betray.

Still, he should tell her.

The clear sky showed red in the west. It was cold. Allen stood in the field behind Maria's house, rubbing his hands together. He watched the sky where the sun had just been, leaving a deeper stain where it had slipped over the mountains. He thought Maria might be watching him from her bedroom window. He wondered what her bedroom was like, then pushed the thought away. If she were looking at him, what would she see? Just a long shape, sharp against the evening sky; a molting crow rubbing dry feathers together. But he wanted to be more. He wanted in some way to be beautiful to her, a man again, believed in and trusted, even as whatever man there was in him faded, became stony monster with a crushing fist. He was seized with the sudden wish to stop loathing himself, to be cherished by one other soul. He summoned every gentle impulse and every kind thought, wishing that in some way he could sweeten his profile, become something, if not desirable then not monstrous in Maria's eyes.

Then he laughed a little at that and the laughter had the same dry feather rasp of his two rubbing hands. The sound startled him. He looked around to see what creature might be snickering at him and he saw no one, nothing. The fields were empty and nothing flew in the cold sky. The house sat impassive under bare branches, no lights in the windows yet.

He looked up once more at the sky, now drained of color. He raised his hand to the mountains, then started back indoors.

To the left of the house he looked and saw her, Maria, wrapped against the chill in a long coat, her face in shadow. He walked over to her. "Hello."

She stepped close to him and touched his shoulders, brushing his trench coat almost absently. "Are you cold?"

He could see her now, eyes shining in the dusk, mouth pulled into a serious line. He liked her doing this little task, brushing off the cool, starry dust, and he wanted her to keep doing it. He said, "I'm okay."

She said, "You stand out here, in the cold. It will get under your skin."

"It has. But that's all right."

She shook her head. "I don't think so. Were you listening to something?"

"Not this time."

"All quiet?"

"Yes, everything is quiet."

She stopped brushing him. She put the back of her hand on his cheek. It was warm against the skin. She said, "Come inside."

"I will, in a minute." He hesitated. "I was thinking about you." He watched for her reaction.

"Were you?" She smiled. "What were you thinking."

"I was wishing I wasn't a crow."

"I like crows."

"You do? But we're—they're not gentle and they're rude."

"Very intelligent, these crows."

"They steal."

"Who doesn't?" Maria took his arm and led him around the house to the kitchen door. They stood in the light from the window. "Who doesn't sometimes take what doesn't belong to them, Allen?" She smoothed back some of his straw hair. "I think it's just borrowing, anyway." Then she laughed, and she was like a young girl again.

He knew there was no way to make himself desirable, but he didn't care. He had never been desirable. He was grateful now, thankful that it didn't matter; Maria looked at him and smiled and he didn't have to hide in the cold and the dark.

She put her face up to be kissed and he kissed her softly on the mouth, tasting cinnamon on her lips. He was hungry, then. He wanted to kiss her again. He could kiss her for a long time. But he didn't do it. He looked at her mouth and knew that he could look at that mouth for the rest of his life.

He said, "I don't belong to anyone."

"Don't be too sure of that."

He thought about that, but the thought flew away, and an immense weight went with it. He saw just Maria there, in the light from the kitchen window, young and alive. Looking at him.

It was more than enough to look back at her. It was more than enough to know that when she saw him it was not a beast in front of her, a ragged bird or a mountain thing, but a man. What kind of man, and how durable, for now, didn't matter.

"It's getting colder," she said. "Come in and I'll make you something warm to drink."

Evening slipped into night. Allen, sitting in Maria's kitchen, was suddenly swimming in sleep. It was time for his medicine, and he knew he would not want to make another trip upstairs.

Maria, sitting across from him, watched him with her alert, reserved expression. "You are tired."

"Yes."

"Go to bed."

"Sounds like the right idea."

The walk to his room took the last fumes. Maria had offered to go with him, but he'd declined. His door wavered at the end of the hall, radiating, blinking in and out. By the time he turned the handle, Allen could barely see it. Without switching on the light, he stumbled to the desk drawer, slammed pills down with tepid water, kicked off his shoes and fell on the bed.

There was not enough strength left to think. Images overpowered his shrinking mind, a mélange of childhood toys, ocean trips, pages from science books; snapshots from the post office, avalanches of mail, gray streets in empty cities, a black mountain that summoned and would not be denied.

At last a bluebird alighted and, full of kindness and joy, flew away with him to the halls of forgetting.

It was always the same: an empty room, walls that were no longer walls but were the inside of some forever space, a nothing so big that it could consume all the everything that ever was and not take the slightest notice; a certainty that all the everything that ever was had never been, and the only speck of it now permitted was the knowledge that he was not.

There was fluorescent lighting, always. Flexible conduit. Harsh laughter. An indecipherable manual. He was compelled by the wretched, invisible force that had been Allen Wrangell to read its every word. There was a row of empty bottles. There was a mile of burning road, a room full of dead letters. There was a place where he sank and could walk no farther and there was finally a suitcase that always needed packing, and he was always packing it and it was always needing packing.

Then again there was forgetting.

He didn't wake up when Maria lay down next to him. At some point his back became warmer. A breathing other than his own made him aware he was still breathing. He didn't know who she was and he didn't know who he was. They were breathing and that was all. The breath belonged to no one.

Her hand circled his sunken belly. His sinister hand, mollified, found hers and gently covered it. She pressed her cheek to the back of his neck and they lay like that.

Here then is my prayer:

There will be a rising and a falling. There will be an end to it, and you will be there with me. I will never know you and you will never know me and that is the last and least that we need to know.

I want to believe. I want to believe that we will live on in each other, you here and I in that place where I am going. But I go to No Place and here the Great Alluvial will bury what I was to you. Dust grains, shopping lists, lint, cares and phone numbers, layer after layer, until the touch of my skin and the smell of it and the look of it will be gone, and you, the last and only one to see me, will forget. I'll haunt you then as I haunt you now, but farther away and deeper down, silent as the clay. In turn I go to where there is no returning, where I am not I and you Maria, will not be there.

So this is the best of it, the one and only. My bones and yours, my breath and yours, my warmth and yours, they're ours, our small and infinite moment, all that we get, and which we can't have: the wake of the gesture, the silence between the words, the parting of the lips.

One last ring of the bell forever.

It was late morning when Allen woke up. Rolling over, he ran his hand over the place where Maria had lain, now cool, but with the impression of her body still rippling the bedcover.

He got up and medicated, then went downstairs to the kitchen. There was coffee in the carafe and bits of pastry on a plate, under a glass dome. He drank coffee and ate nothing. Then he returned to his room.

He had wanted to go to her, but didn't. He knew he would always want to go to her now, and that was dangerous, difficult to bear. Something stopped him. He didn't know what it was, but its presence was as cold and remorseless as his own crushing hand, attached to someone else's arm.

A shower revived him. The medication, in addition to quelling the riot in his insides, also eased the throbbing in his brain. It did not, however, make the side of his head look any better. The swelling was easing, but a bruised mess crawled out from under his scalp and covered much of his left cheek. (Somehow DJ had missed the ear.) It didn't really matter. Seeing the bruises reminded him that his left hand would crush a car for him, if needed. That was good.

Pocketing some extra meds, he went out to the back deck. The fog that had persisted all morning had given way and sun regained the day, first in the highlands, then clearing the valley and the town below. Light and chill air further lifted Allen's energies and he decided to walk to town.

The windows of Maria's house were a blank stare. Standing outside the gate—now shorn of menace, only a complaining gate again—Allen searched the place for a sign of something. But there was nothing, as nothing a nothing as could be devised in the empty hollows of the driest desert. Chill settled on him, the shiver of knowing he was absolutely and utterly alone. It disheartened him to realize how quickly unused to solitude he had become and how little he liked it. Maria—her touch, her warm and wary eyes, strong arms, her quiet and determined voice—Maria was a garden, a winter garden, alive and growing when everything else was shriveled, snapped off, exhausted tubers clawing the frozen ground. Now the garden was closed to him. He wasn't allowed a glimpse, a thin note of greeting or the honey bread scent of her skin. He wondered why.

Allen sighed and walked away, letting it pass. The evening before, the kiss, her cinnamon mouth, these were only a dream, and one he might never have again. As he rounded the corner, he looked back and thought he saw the edge of a curtain pull closed. He paused and looked, but it cost too much to hope. It cut him like a dull blade.

It was almost noon when he passed Ted's bar. It was open, and there were customers washing down coffee and shots on the sly, but Ted was nowhere to be seen. Someone else presided over the cups.

Allen walked on. Main was busy enough. A certain cakewalk was in progress, people exiting and entering cars, stores and offices. There was a rhythm that went *chit chit chit, chatter chatter chatter chatter—no, no no no no, no NO, have a ladder, have a ladder.* Then a curtsey and a pirouette, a brushing of hands. It made Allen want to call the dance. He laughed, too loudly, and the motion faltered for a flash, then resumed, with a counterpoint of suspicious *who who who, who who?*

He continued down Main.

The lights were on in Liz's office. He opened the door without pause and went in. There was Jasmine, looking up at him from her computer screen. She had been typing. She stopped.

"Good morning, Mister Gabbro." Her voice squeaked a little.

"My name isn't really Gabbro."

"Um, I—"

"It's Wrangell."

"Oh."

"Allen Wrangell. Liz Terry's childhood sweetheart."

Jasmine's lower lip fell away from the upper one. "Oh."

"Gabbro is a kind of coarse rock. It is plutonic, meaning that it comes from deep within the earth. You find it where oceans are splitting apart, and where islands pop up out of the ocean. It's quite dusky, has lots of pyroxene in it."

Her lip descended lower, revealing slightly crooked teeth. "Uh."

"There's a lot of it around here. It's part of that Ophiolite sequence I found just out of town up there." Allen gestured vaguely north. "Anyway, is Liz here?" Jasmine looked at him. He stepped closer. "Here? Liz? Is she?"

"Liz."

"Yes, Liz Terry. Whose name is on the door. Your boss."

The light was on in inner sanctum, but there was as yet no movement. Jasmine darted a glance that way then standing said, "We're not seeing clients today."

"You're not."

"No, we prepare trial briefs today. It takes a lot of time."

Allen crossed his arms and smiled. "Only in your profession does brief mean time-consuming."

"I've heard that. Are you okay? It looks like someone's been beating on you."

"Someone has."

"Oh."

They faced each other for a moment, then Allen clapped his hands. Jasmine blinked. Allen turned to go, then paused. "The sign."

"Sign?"

The *For Lease* sign on your office door. The red and white sign. It's not there anymore."

Jasmine's head rotated so that she looked at him sidelong. "There was no—"

"Yes. Right. Do you smell something burning?"

"Something—"

"Burning. Something burning. Do you smell that?"

"No."

"Like burning rope."

"No, I don't. I don't smell anything."

"Right. Okay, then. Have a—brief day."

She was still standing when he closed the door and walked away.

The Forester courthouse sat next to a small park containing a few tables, metal benches and old trees, leafless now. Instead of a statue, the pitted remains of a giant riveted water cannon sat in the middle of the park, aiming its nozzle at the courthouse. Once used to wash away mountains in search of ore, accelerating the endless process of water and gravity, it had become rusty, staining its cement pedestal. From the bench where Allen sat he could see the courthouse steps. They were marble, veined with pale gray-blue, like a dowager's ankles. They led to a deep colonnaded porch, over which rose two floors of stone that needed washing, topped with a cornice that sagged at disturbing angles. It was a building of faded despots, haunted by the souls denied justice and souls for whom justice had been too-liberally supplied.

Allen saw them. Some leaned against the sagging cornice, shading their faces from the sun. Some lounged in the porch. A few had broken necks. They smoked cigarettes and waited for Resurrection.

The sun was in Allen's face. It warmed and dazed him and he allowed himself a few moments to sit. There was, after all, nothing to do. So he did nothing.

He waited and considered this going, entirely unrelated to gone. There was a gulf, a place of sighs, across which no soul living or dead could pass. There would be no names in the Valley of Black Moths. There would be no skin and no sun to warm it. No rising up, no going down, no walking to and fro. Allen was in no hurry to see the place and in fact wished to remain in the sun as long as possible. He thought about Maria's mouth, and how it tasted when he kissed her.

He watched the lounging souls of the courthouse. Some of them looked back at him, and the rest ignored him. There was no malice in them. There was nothing but a sort of sigh, high and far away. It wasn't unpleasant. He wondered if they had died bravely, or if they had clung, crying and pleading to the last satin edge of this world, begging for another mouthful of soup. Some heard his thoughts and shook their heads, but he couldn't know the meaning of that. A wraith in gingham shed an icy tear.

None of the spirits here hurried, either. They were neither cold nor warm. Sun or rain was the same to them. Absent from the body, but the more present because, they knew what Allen had denied: there is no time. There is no moment in the sun, no wealth, no flower, no pulse of blood. There is nothing here. There is only the barest spark and the coldest glimmer of farthest star.

Allen raised his hands to them. He said, "It's nothing that's forever. Empty that fills the void."

It seemed they nodded now, and smiled.

He said, "No one's in a hurry to face the unbecoming face of that which they are not: the sum of hammer blows to the heart, the tally of wounds."

It seemed they sighed, *Yes*.

"I see you," he said. "I understand."

With a last sigh the specters faded. The sun passed over the sagging cornice and the park immediately fell into cold shade. Allen stood alone, hands exhorting the air.

Another pair of hands clapped in one second intervals. Allen looked and saw Liz standing just outside the park, between him and the courthouse. A large briefcase was at her feet. Her hands fell together, an acerbic tolling. She smiled her crooked smile.

"Bravo, Allen."

He looked at her a moment, then walked away.

Chapter Eighteen

Maria's kitchen smelled of stew and bread. In spite of his shredded innards, Allen gained some appetite from the warm kettle on the stove and the baked rolls under the glass pastry dome.

He was alone in the kitchen at the end of the day. There was only Allen and the food. No note. No voice. No Maria. Only Maria's kitchen, Allen and the food. He sat and ate, washed up and then stood in the middle of the room. That was the trouble with having nothing to do: one stood around a lot. He listened for something, but there was no something. After a while he walked down the hall to Maria's room. He knocked on the door and waited. He knocked again, slowly, listening to the sound it made on the inside of Maria's room. He wished he was that sound. He wanted to be what Maria was hearing. He waited a while longer then walked away. He was getting dizzy. He needed to lie down.

The bed in Allen's room sailed, dipping, and swooping over onyx waves that broke soundlessly around him, cold and effortlessly powerful. He lay on his back and let the swinging and dropping pull his belly around. Despite all the medication, his head pounded and burned. It wasn't just the bruising. DJ's fists had knocked something loose, speeded up some physical or chemical processes in Allen's disease and now he roasted in his own blood.

He called out and no one answered.

He clutched the bedcover and grasped handfuls of splintered glass.

He swung and fell with the voyaging bed until they were taken by a wave that did not rise, but slid down, down into the groaning sea trench where stone contested with stone and protesting rock was swallowed by unrestrained continental appetite, roasting as he roasted, melted and ground by friction and boiled in its own flung atoms. Serpentine waters transformed magma, the sea and the stone became one and tossed spindrift onto the westward-creeping margins. Allen plummeted beneath, his bedship spiraling like a plunging lure, chasing that bit of ophiolite he'd found and had put on his desk. Now they dropped through eons into the searing mantle, invisible to all but the blazing nickel eyes of the planet's furnace wardens.

They fell and caught fire. The merest platinum arc streaked to the core and winked out.

It was a fair morning. Allen took his coffee and a dish of pastry to the front porch and sat in a wicker chair, letting the sun defy winter in his bones He was no worse for his night bed voyage. He'd known nothing, asleep in the deep. He'd bathed in fire and was clean. Now the day was new. There had been no Maria and he didn't go to her room. He accepted what she left for him and was grateful for this proof of life, ate and drank it, filled himself on that which her hands had prepared for him. It was a kind of devotion, the only one he'd get, and it was enough. It had to be enough.

He was finishing his coffee when he heard the Pentecost blast of Liz's Wildcat climbing Jefferson. The car itself appeared, rounding the corner with a warm rubber screech and quivering to a stop in front of Maria's gate. The motor choked off, the driver's door opened, and Liz got out. She slammed the door shut and stood, looking up at him.

He raised a hand. She crossed her arms. He thought she looked beautiful.

"Hello, Allen."

"Liz."

She came around the car and entered through the creaking gate. Allen watched her march up the old concrete walk until she stood at the foot of the stairs.

He said, "Beautiful day." She looked at him. He finished the last swallow of coffee. "Won't get over forty degrees, though."

"You scared my clerk."

"I'm sorry."

"What's wrong with your head?"

"Oh, I'm taking medication, you know, it causes problems."

"I mean the outside of it."

"Oh, that."

"You look like you caught your face in a wringer."

"They still have those?"

"Shut up, Allen." He did. She gave him an appraising look. "Actually, I know what happened.

Jasmine is the webmaster of the Forester grapevine. I guess you pissed off the landlady's boyfriend."

"It wasn't too tough. I just had to exist."

"That's tough enough now, isn't it."

"Tougher than you know."

Liz smiled. It wasn't her crooked smile. It was deliberately even. "Don't be so sure of that, Allen."

"I don't take anything for granted."

"That's good. Anyway, do you love her?"

"Who?"

"The landlady."

"Um."

"Do you get that little tingle in your chest? That warm spot in your belly?"

Allen looked at his empty coffee cup and wiped some pastry crumbs off the saucer. "I get breakfast."

"Is that it?"

"Lunch, and dinner if I want it." Liz scowled. Allen stretched. "It's not in the rental agreement, though."

"You're going to get yourself killed."

"Think?"

"Yeah."

"We're all going to get ourselves killed."

Liz started up the stairs, then retreated. She squinted at Allen. "I'm sorry I left you. In Gold Flat, I mean."

"Oh. That's okay."

"It's not, really."

"I'm sorry I left you, Liz. Back when. I didn't think I had. I didn't think—"

"It was a long time ago, Allen."

"It was. Yes. A long time." He started to speak, then checked himself.

"What?" Liz looked at him, eyes narrowed. "What were you going to say?"

"You told me, up there in Gold Flat I think it was, you told me something."

"I told you a lot of things."

"You said—"

"Spit it out, Allen."

"You said that, once, you were right on time. Do you remember saying that?"

"Of course I do. And I remember that time."

"When you—"

"When I was there. Right on time."

"And I?"

"And you never showed up."

"You."

"I had the car, Allen." Liz jerked her thumb over her shoulder. "That one."

"The very same."

"The very same."

"Yes, I remember."

Liz laughed. "You can't remember. You weren't there."

"You waited for me. You sat in that Buick, that very same Buick, and you waited for me."

"You can't know that, you weren't—"

"Yes. I was there. I watched you. You waited in the car, you listened to the radio and you waited."

"I did, yes. I waited. "

"I was there, Liz. I was there the whole time. I remember that. I had forgotten it, but I remember now. I watched you the whole time, until you left. But I couldn't go to you. I couldn't."

Liz shook her head. "Why not?"

"You know why not. Your dad hated me. He was a lawyer and he hated me. He was a lawyer, my dad was a postal clerk, and I was—I was a son of a postal clerk."

"You were my guy, Allen."

"And I was this guy who was going to be a postal clerk, like his dad, and that wasn't going to cut it."

"Woulda been fine with me, Allen." He said nothing. "So that's why you just sat there and watched me. Watched me shrivel up and fade away."

"No. That's not why. I remember it now like it just happened. That day we planned to go, the day we were going to pack up and leave, you and me, that day your dad came to my house."

"He did?"

"Yeah. He did. And he reminded me of something."

"What was that, Al."

"You know what it was. He let me know that he knew all about what we were planning to do—and he reminded me that you were seventeen years old."

"And that he was a lawyer."

"Yes. A lawyer. With a lot of lawyer friends. Judge friends, too."

Liz chewed her lip. "Yeah. I sorta get that."

"I sorta got that, too."

"So you left. Alone."

"Yes, I did."

Liz nodded. "And I lost you."

"You never lost me."

"Well I sure the hell never had you."

"But you still have the car."

Liz smiled, her crooked one. "It's a good car."

"With good memories."

"Yes. With good memories. I've had the engine rebuilt twice."

"Yeah? How about the tranny?"

"Three times."

"You aren't a gentle driver."

"That's no shit, Allen." She laughed. He laughed. She squinted at him again. "So."

"So yeah."

"So you love the landlady, Allen?"

He set his cup and saucer on the porch by his chair. He stood, looking down at Liz, who craned her neck to look at him. He smiled. "I came here to see you."

"Why."

"Because you still have the car."

"You want the car. That's it."

"Yep."

They laughed. He started down the stairs, then stepped back up to the porch. There would be no going down and there would be no coming up. He said, "When I left, Liz, part of me stayed with you."

Liz considered that a moment. "So you came to have a visit with yourself."

"I was just wondering how you were treating me."

"Kindly, Allen. I was treating you kindly."

"Thank you."

"You took part of me with you, Al."

"Yes. It sort of made up for what I left behind."

"And how have you been treating me."

"With great care. With kindness."

"Thank you."

They stood in the sun. They both closed their eyes. When Allen opened his, Liz was gone. The big Buick roared to life, bolted up the street, spun and returned. As she passed, Liz waved her hand. Allen saw her crooked smile flash by, then the car screeched around the corner. He remained still, listening to the fading Buick rumble. When he could hear it no more, he turned.

The front door, which had been open a sliver, shut with a click.

CHAPTER NINETEEN

The last words of Vincent Van Gogh were, "The sadness will last forever."

Allen had read this in one of his father's books when he was a boy and it changed him. These words went into his heart and lodged there, hooked into the flesh, tolling every time his heart beat, growing in the chambers, staining every season until Allen was certain beyond any other certainty that these five words were the truest ever uttered. That knowledge was a canker in Allen Wrangell's bosom, growing as he grew, growing stronger as he diminished.

The words had been recorded by Van Gogh's brother on the day he died.

Allen thought about those words on this new morning as he lay on the bed in his room, looking at the Gauguin prints on the wall. He knew that Gauguin had been cruel to his friend. He often wondered why, and why such a man, who could summon up the soul of serenity could inflict harm on one already so distressed and beaten. How Gauguin could hurt a man whose pain had already drilled so deep that it struck the springs of despair and turned them sweet and full of enough hope to feed the world forever after.

And that was precisely why Gauguin had hurt his suffering friend.

Allen got up and looked out the window as the day woke up outside his room. It was clear and a false spring shone. Allen wanted it gone, but its relentless cheerfulness would not abate. He swallowed his pills with flat water and waited for them to work, getting the sense of what this day would bring.

"Very little, is my guess. This isn't the day I die, and I have nothing else planned at the moment." The room answered with silence. "There might be something downstairs. This could be the morning Maria will appear." Allen knew this was not true, and the words rang hollow. "When my head stops spinning, we'll have a shower and just see what's going on."

Nothing was going on.

Coffee was in the carafe and muffins were on the counter in their glass-covered sanctum. Allen didn't disturb them. He poured a cup of coffee and went into the too-sunny sitting room to drink it. He could not bear sitting in the kitchen.

"I have managed it," he said after a few sips. "I have accomplished a life untouched by human hands." This was not entirely true, he knew, but it was truer than not, and there was no one to contradict him. "I'm sure it's not a singular feat, but it feels like an accomplishment, nonetheless."

He finished his coffee and was considering going into the kitchen for more when a voice stopped him.

"Is that all you have to say?"

Allen looked around and could see nothing. The Voice had been low, grinding, sonorous. If an earthquake could speak, that is the voice it would have, Allen thought.

"Is that all I have to say." He scratched his head. "I suppose not, as I am saying something else. Who are you?"

"We've met."

"Have we?" Allen detected something, he could not identify it. "Where have we met?"

"Where does not apply."

"When, then."

"No. That doesn't apply, either."

"I see." Something.

"Not yet."

"True, but I do smell a kind of—"

"You know me," the Voice interrupted. "We have spent time together."

"If you have it, you might as well spend it. You can't save it."

"Don't be so sure of that."

Allen thought about this. "Say, is that true? That thing about saving time? Is that true?"

"Not in the sense with which you are familiar."

"Thought not."

"Don't dismiss this. That would be a mistake."

"I'm speaking to a voice in the air. I'm living in a house with an invisible woman. I am not dismissing anything." He smelled something, an echo of a smell, a gunpowder whiff. "I'm listening to everything you say."

"The woman."

"Maria, yes."

"She's not invisible."

"No. Then I suppose I am."

"No."

"Well you sure the hell are."

"I'm right here." The Voice was jarringly close, right in front of him, the smell of sulphur in its words. "I can see you. Can't you see me?"

"No. No, I can't. I can only smell you."

The Voice said nothing for a moment. When it resumed there was something different in its tone: a note of concern. "You're going away."

"No kidding."

"It doesn't have to be, not like this."

"What do you mean?"

"You know as well as I."

"I don't know anything."

"Yes, you do, you've known it the whole time. The answer is underneath your feet."

"The answer." Now the smell was gone, whisked away on a draft of cool air. "The answer is underneath my feet."

The Voice said no more.

Allen knew what he had to do. He had no idea why he had to do it, but he knew it was time to be done. Returning to his room, he packed his bag. It didn't take very long to do it, and when it was packed he threw it on the bed and lay down beside it, folding his hands across his chest. He knew the party to whom the Voice belonged, had spent time with him, indeed. All the time in the world. Now it was time to go.

The bed took him quickly and he was soon sailing it through deep waters which shortly began to whirl, lazily at first, then rapidly, with a noise like a thousand dropped stoves. It deafened Allen, and the spume blinded him. Soon all was spinning motion, salt and ice, scale and drowning voices.

Allen opened his eyes in the familiar darkness of his room. He was cold. Patting himself, he was surprised to find dry garments, but his muscles were chilled past the point of feeling. It was a long time before he could move and longer before he could sit up. After that it was an eternity of opening his suitcase, swallowing his pills (dry, because he couldn't reach the water glass), standing and walking to the hall door.

He thought he'd heard knocking, that was what woke him up. He opened the door and there was no one there, nor did he expect to see anyone. He slowly made his way down the hall, down the stairs, holding fast to the railing. He went into the kitchen.

The pastries and coffee were gone. Food was on the stove, and it was still warm. Allen had no idea how long he'd been away, but it felt as if he'd missed several dinners.

Allen washed the dishes, wishing Maria was there, talking to him, her voice sure and hushed, hands brown against the china plates. He wondered why the Voice had assured him that she was not invisible. If she wasn't invisible then she was hiding, and doing a damned good job of it.

But no one could hide that well.

Some other force was in play. Some other hand moved the events. Allen could feel the earth's skin shiver, like a sleeping dog's; a worm gear twisted its helix ever-so-slowly against the planet's teeth. Fractured lands slid beneath them, carrying them past each other, Allen on his terrane, Maria on hers.

He would at least like to wave at her now and then as she went by.

It was still unbearable staying in the kitchen too long. Allen went to the hall door and listened in the downstairs hall. He heard nothing—no words, no music, no tapping keystrokes—nothing except the ticking and creaking of an old house on a cold night. He again restrained himself from going to Maria's door. It was not good to want this, and worse to act on the desire. He had enough volition and strength of mind to resist it, and he did.

Back in his room, he sat down heavily at the desk, trying to see something outside his window. It wasn't long before the eastern sky showed the first inkling of moonrise. Soon the moon was in view, captured sun shining silver off its peeping face. It shank as it rose into the cloudless sky, dimming the stars around it. As Allen watched the moon's transit he knew that his bed voyaging had carried him here, to this night, to this desk, to see that transit from this particular viewpoint. Watching her arc, Allen was filled with envy and longing. The moon's azimuth, no matter where he stood, would always be reliable, mathematically-determined, adjusting itself perfectly to his perspective. By contrast, Allen's trajectory was erratic, prone to bouncing and subject to friction, extremes of temperature and obstruction by unyielding objects.

This would no longer do. He didn't bounce as well as he used to, and he wasn't getting any younger. His gait faltered. A stalking thing pursued him. He was out of time.

Chapter Twenty

It was this night of the full moon, then, when Allen went out walking. He set off across the fields behind Maria's house, heading west, for the mountains. Only the moon went with him, silver in the cold sky. They found paths in the brittle grasses and sharp brush, made by marten, deer, fox and bear, but none of the pathfinders traveled this night. All was silent. The grass was already fragile with frost and it crushed forever under Allen's boots. After he cleared the fenced lands the world opened and rose. He followed the leaping andesitic spine, up to where it was colder, clearer, all tree and rock. When he looked back, the valley lay below in deepening fog, tinged gold and faded scarlet where the town intruded. He pulled his collars up and continued.

Under the deeper folds of the firs, where he'd expected the wild voices to be, there was nothing. Moon shadows fell in groves of first snow. As he went up the night wall the snow grew deeper and he waded in it, punching through the icy coat until he could go no farther. Then he sat in the snow, in a small cave of it, letting his head hang. Here he waited.

It might have been hours before he woke up. The moon was near its zenith. A liquid quartz light dripped through the snow, and in the alabaster hall his hands were pale gold, frozen in prayer. It surprised him when they moved, of their own will, and Allen thought the disease had taken them both over now, and that he might be subject to some violence at his own hands. But it was he who moved them.

It was the disease which woke him and saved his fingers, the unnatural warmth it imbued enabling his limbs to work, keeping extremities full of lifeblood. He clapped his hands together and they felt each other. He raised his face to the moon, then stood and walked, taking the path back through his earlier journey.

Deep beneath his feet the earth strained. Rock pulled against rock. A blind fault wished for release, to displace, to rend and to fly, to toss the dust above it into oblivion. To snap the spine of the West. But rock held rock. It would not hold for long, Allen knew. Not long now and the world would shift its ponderous weight and the falling down would begin. But that moment was not immediately at hand and for now only Allen moved, retracing his mountain steps until he had cleared the snow and once again wandered in mere frostlands. Turning south he moved along the face of the escarpment, picking his path among the sharply-etched detritus, his ankles feeling for the slope's angle of repose, where walking would not hurt them so much; where the boulders would stop their roaming.

So he went, southbound and down, until milder lands moved under him and the dry snap of grass again marked each step. He watched the moon as much as he was able, because after this night it would wane, go from him, taking its kitchen light.

"I might not see you again. Not like this." He stopped a minute, to look at the moon until he could see its spirit through shut lids. He let his arms hang loose and, warmed by the mantle of the killer inside, he said silent farewells. He resumed his walk, continuing his leave-taking as he went. It was surprising how many goodbyes there were to say, having said so many already. But he was diligent, matching the words with his steps until a cortege tramped along behind, a recessional of mornings and nights, a parade of moments lost and found, a second line of saints marching, angels of orphaned hours.

"I didn't do very well with what I was given," he told them, and none murmured dissent. "Sorry about that." He increased his pace and the retinue matched it. "I'm going to go back now. This is a town of visitations." He would have run if he could. "I'm not yet one of these apparitions, eating their crumbled biscuits and drinking their dry wine. There will be plenty of time later for that, when I'm finally out of it." There was general agreement from the Host of Days. "I can haunt where I like, at my leisure. For now, I'll just make my way out of this valley. I'll walk until I fall over. I'll go on grinning until I freeze that way."

Allen came to the highway, already rising through the trees, the town and valley to his left, the empty road to his right. He looked back down the valley. The mountain fog had pulled away, revealing Main Street's humble lamps glimmering. Maria might be sitting in her bedroom with the lights off, or at her keyboard, doing her billing. Liz drank gin and edited her briefs. Ted wiped the bar and served the spirits. That bewildered waitress would be dreaming her television dreams. The whole town slept or drank or made love or worried pointlessly. Someone felt a lump that meant the end of him, and he thought about missing next year's elk season. Someone else called out in her bed for a lover long since gone. Fingers plucked guitar strings. A baby drifted in amniotic memories. A night nurse smoked, a radio spoke, an old man forgot one more thing.

The mist curtain closed and the town faded, leaving Allen and the west-going moon. He stood a moment longer then turned and walked up the highway, back up the way he had come down those many days before, alone now, as he was then.

Ted opened the rear door of the bar and made his way to the cash register by the dim glow of the bar-back lamp. He rolled the heavy drawer open and counted the cash. When the drawer slammed home the concussion made the bar top vibrate.

Wringing out a towel, he wiped the shiny bar, working toward the front of the house. As he neared the window, he looked over at the door.

A mass of shadow pressed against the glass, like something dumped or forgotten in the doorway. He dropped the towel on the bar and went to the door. Unlocking it, he pulled and, pushed by the dead weight from the outside, the door swung inward.

Allen Wrangell reeled into the bar, and grabbed the door jamb, remaining barely upright. Grinning, he looked at Ted and said, "Hey. Why did the cowboy buy a daschund?"

"I don't know. Why."

"Because he wanted to get a long little doggie."

"You need to add that to your bartender repertoire." Allen hunched over his coke. "That's an exceptionally good one. Long little doggie."

Ted stood by the cash register, wiping a glass. "I will, thanks."

"Listen, let me ask you something." Allen pointed at him. "I want to know, how come the only time there are people in here is when you're not?"

Ted put the glass down. "You're here, aren't you?"

"Don't be so sure about that."

"So-noted."

"I'm not sure what's here and what's not."

"A reasonable doubt."

"Well what is here?"

"That depends."

"Yes. Yes, I know. Anyway, if you don't want to go bankrupt, let your partner bartend more often. He has them in here morning and night."

"Partner?"

"Yeah, Al or Pete or Joe or whomever."

"Ah."

"Because whatever you are, Ted, you're no bartender."

Ted studied his neatly-clipped fingernails. He looked up at Allen. "Another?"

"No. Yeah, yes, please. I've been walking all night."

"Shouldn't you be having breakfast?" Ted put a fresh coke down and removed the empty one.

"Too early for breakfast, or too late. I had dinner at some point and—I can't eat now anyway."

"Where have you been walking?"

"I've been walking—" Allen paused and drank. "Oh, I've been walking. You uh, you remember a ,long time ago, that psychic healer guy they said could cure people using Coca Cola?"

"Sort of."

"I was fascinated by him. Imagine that; heal people with Coca Cola."

"Yes. Something else."

"That could be an angle, Ted."

"How you feeling."

"Healed."

"My first patient."

"You'll be famous." Allen drank and belched quietly. "Excuse me. Anyway."

"So where have you been walking."

"Oh, up in the mountains. I've been in the snow."

"Kinda chilly with just a thin coat."

"I can't die, Ted. I am immortal."

"Yeah?"

"Well. I can't freeze. This thing inside, it's hot. I'm burning up half the time."

"Why were you up there?"

"Leaving. Leave or die, that's my goal. I didn't die, so I left. I walked south, back down the highway."

"Oh."

"I know. Yeah. I couldn't walk fast enough. This town, this valley, it's too quick for me."

"Caught up with you."

"It did. You're on a transverse fault here. It must have moved. Yanked me north while you moved south."

"That's some fast earth."

"It doesn't have to be all that fast. It has all the time in the world."

"And we don't."

"That's right. So here I am. What time is it?"

Ted checked a luminescent wristwatch. "It's four in the morning."

Allen whistled. "Say, you're an early riser."

"I don't sleep much."

"Listen. You all done with your bartender duties?"

Ted gestured around the room. "It looks pretty buttoned up."

"Listen, Ted. Would you do me a favor?"

"Ask."

"Would you take a walk with me?" Ted said nothing. "It's not like you're gonna get a customer this time of morning. Or ever." Ted's forehead wrinkled. Allen drained the coke. "It won't take long."

"How far you walking?"

"Not far."

Ted sighed, looked around the room and put down his bar towel. "All right. Let's go."

There was no sign of dawn outside the bar. It was cold and both men buttoned their coats as they walked. Nothing moved in the fog on Main Street. Buildings and streetlights looked like paintings from another century. The moon was obscured as it prepared to strike the western peaks. Ted was the only solid thing on the street and Allen drew next to him as they walked.

"Who was the Fourth Man, Ted?"

"What do you mean?"

"When Shadrach, Meshach and Abednego were thrown in the furnace at Babylon, there was a Fourth Man with them."

"Yes. I know the story."

"And when Ernest Shackleton was trying to cross South Georgia Island with two of his crew, trying to escape Antarctica after his ship was crushed in the ice. He felt the presence of a Fourth Man walking with them. Who was he?"

"Someone he needed," Ted said.

"Yes." Allen walked more quickly. "Sometimes it's a third man."

"I've heard that."

"Sometimes it's just one."

"Yes."

"Stay with me."

Ted kept pace. "I will."

A block before Liz's office they crossed the street. As they approached, Allen looked ahead through the mist. "It was there when I walked by earlier."

"What was there?"

"That." Allen stopped in front of Liz's office and pointed. "That."

The *For Lease* sign advertised vacant office space. There was no lettering on the glass and no furniture in the front office. Ted looked at the sign and peered in through the glass. "Yep. It's for lease. That it?"

"Yes."

They stood, saying nothing, Allen touching the glass, Ted with his hands in his coat pockets. He cleared his throat. "Um."

"Yes, yes." Allen touched Ted's shoulder. "You saw it."

"Yeah. Yeah, I did."

"Thank you."

"Sure."

"This, uh, this used to be a lawyer's office. Maybe still is."

"Your lawyer?"

"Yeah."

"I don't recall a lawyer here. Not recently."

"I do," Allen said. "Frequently." Ted's face had been momentarily troubled. The cloud passed quickly, but not before Allen noticed it.

They hastened back up Main, more quickly than they'd come down. Allen waited on the sidewalk outside the bar while Ted unlocked the door. "I appreciate it."

"No problem. You coming back in?"

"I'm going back to Maria's."

Ted looked at him. "Is all well?"

"I don't know." Allen looked up the hill, toward Maria's. "You didn't ask me what happened to my face."

"I guess if you'd wanted to tell me you would have."

"It doesn't matter." He looked back at Ted. "Maria. She's gone."

"Gone?"

"She's there, in the house. But I never see her. She won't answer her door. She leaves food out but I—she's not there."

Ted scratched his chin. "There but not there."

"She, she's like a—"

"Ghost?"

Allen smiled. "No."

"What, then."

"I'm the ghost. Maria, she's the one I left behind."

"And your lawyer?"

Allen looked back to Main. "I'm thinking I'm the one she left behind."

"Well." Ted opened the door and stepped in. He pointed at Allen. "If Maria's still cooking?"

"Yes?"

"Keep eating."

Dawn followed Allen up Jefferson Street, the slightest fraying of the hem of darkness as the fog parted. Allen sensed it on the back of his neck, a lessening of the chill, but it didn't comfort him. He did not want to see or be seen and the daylight offered only exposure. He walked faster. He had no desire to view the gray faces of the houses as they passed. Their worn-out parade made him want to shout, wake them up, break their windows. He saw them burning, shaking, falling into sparks of ruin and he wanted to weep and laugh. All along the street the mortgaged souls were stirring. Allen pitied and feared them, waking up to another rented day.

He didn't feel the blow. A sour bell rang behind his forehead and his optic nerves twisted off. A decaying reverberation brought him into silence, a cool slab, repose. Here was oblivion, calm and mild, without sting or stain.

It said, "Oh."

Chapter Twenty-One

He surfaced through amnesia to pain, his comforting friend and familiar. It wrapped a firm arm across his shoulders, pressed its palms against his ears, twisted, fingers tangled in his forlorn hair, yanking Allen Wrangell up from the abyss to resume the walk.

The back of his head pulsed hot against chilled concrete. He lay flat where he'd crumpled and rolled, spread to the leering dawn. As yet no one had found him. He was alone and oozing something, some iron and sugar into the calcium, lime and ash of a Forester sidewalk.

He said, "Oh."

Got to his knees.

Got to his feet.

Started walking.

It wasn't much farther to Maria's. There was a light on, spilling out over the porch. Allen hated the look of it. It had a cold gleam, answering the dawn in a mocking reply.

He approached the house warily and made his way around the side. The kitchen was unlit. He moved along to the stairs and began climbing, each step steeper than the one preceding. He reached the top as the first live fire of the sun ignited the eastern mountains. He looked and cursed. Then Gold Flat came to mind, over there east, where the sun was rising over the little café with the room above it. Where a kindly woman woke up to a day of waiting. Where the clear river ran with its rainbow fish floating over rainbow pebbles, beneath the sheltering rock walls of the ages. For a moment pain left him and the sun was still the sun, warming life awake even as it subsided day by day into winter.

Going to the door he pulled his room key from his pocket and slid it into the door lock.

It didn't turn.

The spring-loaded brass pins refused to acknowledge him. The plug would not revolve in its cylinder. He wiggled the key. He smacked the doorknob. He twisted, jiggled, twitched metal inside metal. The lock remained fast. Pulling out the key, Allen examined it. Nothing looked wrong, but it was nonetheless wrong. The key's particular lineage of scratches and oxidation did not comport with what he remembered his key to have. It was too old or a different caste, not at all the key Maria had handed him.

It was not his key. He was certain.

He beat on the door, calling for Maria. No one came. Cursing, he returned down the stairs he'd climbed with so much effort, seething with new anger-fueled vigor. He ran down the side path and to the front porch, taking the stairs two at a time. Pounding on the front door, he called again for Maria. His head throbbed from damages old and new. The more he pounded, the more it throbbed until the two were indistinguishable. The throbbing shouted out, the pounding pulsed Maria's name. He slammed the flat of his hand on the door molding and drew back a fist to break the glass.

Footsteps approached from within.

He paused, fist cocked, waiting.

The handle rattled and the door opened as far as the chain would allow.

DJ's face appeared in the gap. "What do you want?"

Reeling from shock, weariness and suddenly-arrested momentum, Allen steadied himself. He leaned forward to the crack in the door until he smelled DJ's rotten plum alcohol breath. "I want back in my room."

"What are you talking about?"

"I want back in my room, you little fuck."

"You're nuts."

"What have you done with Maria."

"What—look, get lost."

"I am coming in, you piece of shit. I am coming through that door." Allen seized the edge of the door before DJ could slam it shut. "You whacked me, didn't you." DJ pulled from within and for a moment the door pinched Allen's fingers. "No good, little man. Open the fucking door." Allen wrenched the door back open a crack.

"I ain't done shit to you, man, now let go."

"Yeah, you did. You whacked me back down there." Allen's breath burst out of him, hot and ragged. "You whacked me on the head and you took my key. You *switched keys on me.*"

"Dude." DJ's breath rasped in hoarse exertion. "Dude, I called the cops."

"Good, you punk. Good. Because I have some questions I want answered. Let me in, shit-wipe. I want back in my room. I want answers and I want my meds. I want to know what you did with Maria."

DJ jerked on the door and this time he caught Allen's fingers against the jamb. "Get *lost.*"

The pain galvanized. Allen gave the door a ferocious shove. The chain popped and the door flew back, striking DJ in the face. Yanking the door wide open, he tumbled out swinging, catching Allen with breath-stealing rib shots aiming to bruise and break. Allen circled his arms around DJ and squeezed. They spun on the porch in a tottering dance, crashing against wall, reeling, teetering along the steps until a foot slipped and they rolled to the concrete walk, beating, biting, butting skulls. They rolled across the leaf-spattered lawn, toward the front gate, neither one able to gain an advantage until, halfway across the yard, Allen's hand awoke and seized DJ by the throat.

It would have been over in a moment: a crushed trachea, a broken thing in the dirt. But the moment never came. Steel and polymer, the muzzle of a Glock 22, warmed by the thigh of a rookie Forester patrol officer, pressed into Allen's forehead. From somewhere between earth and sky a frantic voice wired by adrenalin to the hair trigger of the Glock shouted, *Let go, let go, let go, you sonofabitch.*

Allen's hand let go.

In the whirl that followed, as he was thrown, cuffed, yanked to his feet, marched through the shrieking gate, tossed against a patrol car, he watched bits of sharp-edged words float by like dust motes: *Out of his tree...tried to break in...not from here...said he wanted drugs...* DJ standing with the old cop, arms flailing while the young one, the one attached to the Glock, patted Allen down then thrust him into the back seat of the patrol car.

When the cruiser door slammed, thick silence covered his wounds. He rolled his head against the glass, watching DJ's monkey motions, the old cop writing in a little book, the rookie taking a dip of chew. Only the subtonic, deaf man rumble at the bottom of words made it through the glass. It was restful. It lulled him. It let him slide easily down until at last he passed beyond the place where senses vex, to drown in pools beyond the seeing world.

The knocking woke him, a steady thud-thud-thud, falling dead in space like someone hitting a carcass with a mallet. Allen lay on something stiff but yielding, sensing little but the thudding knock, increasing with each meat bat blow the blood fire between his ears. He tried to move, but there was nothing to move with and there was nowhere to go. If there had been eyelids he would have opened them. If there had been eyes he would have looked around.

Slowly, as something like consciousness crawled over him, Allen remembered that he was. What had happened to him, where and how he was were beyond recovering. The fragment of Allen that remained floated from gray to gray, scratching at the wooly end of things, the leftover bits. Eventually even this exhausted his Allen-sense and he went away again, for how long there was no way to know. Then there was a rusty squeak and someone else's breath.

"Allen."

"Yes."

"It's Liz."

"Yes, I know. Hello."

"How are you."

"I don't know. It's none of my business."

"I can't come in. They let me talk through the hatch."

"That's all right, I can't come in, either."

"Shit, Allen, you just look worse and worse."

"Yeah. "

"What are you doing, Allen."

"That's also none of my business, but whatever it is, it doesn't seem to be improving things."

"It's not improving your face."

"Do I have one of those?"

"Sort of. Look, you are in trouble."

"I know a lawyer."

"I don't really do criminal law."

"Oh. Well, I could use some estate planning."

"Quit it. Just—look, this is no joke."

"I wish I could see you. I'd like to touch you."

"I can't come in to touch you, either."

"I miss you, Liz. I'm sorry."

"You're sorry for what."

"When I left, all those years ago, you got up that morning. You put on your bedroom slippers. You watched TV."

"I hardly watch TV."

"Well this was a long time ago. Maybe you watched like, MTV."

"Might have."

"And some guy with hair wings played a guitar, and then you got in that Wildcat Buick and you drove around town. You went to the library, or the movies. You and your girlfriends. Went swimming. Then you got a coke at the Parkside Café. And then you called me, and the phone just rang."

"Pretty much, yeah."

"Every day I wondered what you did. Every morning I saw you get up and go downstairs. You had toast."

"Muffin."

"Well it was toast that I saw. And one day followed the next, each one made up of little moments. And those moments piled up and the weight drove the days and the days siphoned the years, like an anchor chain following its own pull, and then we got middle-aged and the days brought us here, Liz. And I'm here to tell you that I never forgot you."

"I never forgot you, either, Al."

"You have to be remembered to be forgotten."

"I remembered you."

"Keep remembering me, Liz."

"I will."

"Mountains, Liz. They're not just there, sitting there, you know. They move. They flip, flop and roll. Water wears them down, they move to the sea, they cook in the furnaces of the planet. They become other mountains and they die as rubble and they are reborn as mountains again."

"What are you talking about, Wrangell."

"I'm saying that nothing is ever destroyed, it never really goes away. We don't die, Liz. It's our life that can be a kind of death, and letting go of that can mean getting to live again."

"Come on, Allen. Say it. Just say it. I want to hear it. Tell me."

"I'm saying I'll see you again, Liz."

"Yeah. Yeah, you will."

"That's good, Liz."

"I think so, too. Yes. I do. But we won't be who we are now."

"What makes you think we are who we are now?"

"Because this is what we have, Allen. This is it. And when we're not here, it won't be this. It'll be something else."

"I believe that, too, yes."

"Do not—repeat, do not—repeat."

"It might not be much longer this time around, Liz."

"But you have it still. You have some of that good stuff. So, Allen buddy, enjoy what you have left of it."

"This isn't really my idea of enjoyment."

Liz laughed, a short laugh. It echoed down some unseen hall. "That's the first evidence you've shown of some good sense here, Allen. There might be hope for you yet."

"A fool's hope, and a slim one," Allen said.

"Well you're just the fool for it, buddy." Liz's voice was gentle enough and when she spoke again Allen could hear a different timbre, the bravado gone. "Was there any hope. Any hope left for me, Al?"

Allen heard the tonal shift. It perplexed him. "What do you mean?"

"Was there, Al?" He thought he heard something else there. "Was there some of that left over?" A catch. Something that wanted to—no, not Liz. "Was there, at one time, a little bit left for me?"

Cry.

"There's always hope. While we're breathing."

"Yeah." Liz's voice was back. "Yeah, while we're breathing."

"Hey, at our elementary school, every May we did the maypole. Remember that, Liz?"

"Yeah, I did the dance."

"I did, also. Only the sixth-graders were allowed. There were three poles, big white square ones, with thick cross bases. We'd grab those ribbons, boys and girls."

"Red and white on one pole, green and white, then blue and white."

"Yes. Around and around, in and out."

"The best weavers got a prize."

"Yeah. Did your pole win, Liz?"

"No. We sucked at doing that maypole dance."

"We didn't win, either. But it was fun."

"I guess."

"They're still doing it, Liz. They're still dancing, weaving in and out, green and white, red and white, blue and white, weaving down the pole, wrapping it in long diamonds of colored ribbon until the ribbons and the boys and the girls all meet."

"Pole dancing. The fertility rite implications are inescapable."

"But don't you see, it hasn't stopped. The kids are the same. They will always dance there, on May Day, around the maypole, weaving their colored ribbons."

"Um. Yeah."

"It doesn't stop, Liz."

"Allen, there are no children. They're all grown up, or they died. I don't think the school's even there anymore. It's over. Past is past. Move on."

"The past isn't past, Liz. It's there in its own terrane. It's only because we are stuck in this one that we don't see it. But I see it. It gets closer every day. The old school is there. I see the kids dancing, Liz, and you there dancing with them."

There was no reply. Rust and silence and nothing else.

Allen's eyelids peeled back to reveal a shiny expanse of gray: the ceiling of a room intersected by walls of a slightly different shade of gray, lit by a bare incandescent bulb. Someone had painted as much gray as could be painted on cement, then painted it again and again. Generations of painters had deepened the gloss, enriched the absence until the surface attained its own gravity, pulling color from all its walls enclosed.

The throbbing had stopped. Silence pressed out of the walls, pushed Allen down into the thin mattress, restraining all but his eyes. These moved around, recording the cell in which he lay. There was no pain. Allen suspected it was there, but he had nothing with which to sense it. *So is it there?*

"Is what there?" The voice came from the opening in the steel door of the cell. Allen was unaware that he had spoken aloud and was startled by the response. He stared at the opening but could see nothing. The voice repeated, "Is what there?"

"Who are you?"

After a long silence the voice replied, "You're waking up."

"I guess."

"Do you need anything?"

"I need my medication."

"You didn't come here with any."

"It's back at Maria's."

Another long pause and the voice replied, "I don't know who that is."

"Is Liz still here?"

"Who's Liz?'

"Liz Terry. She's—she's my attorney."

"Liz." The voice paused. "Liz Terry. Yes, I know who you mean. But she isn't here."

"But she was. She was here."

"She hasn't been here for a very long time."

"Well how the hell long have I been here?"

"Two days."

"Two—Look, I can't move. I can't feel anything. I need my medication. If you can't go to Maria's and get it, call Liz, she'll arrange for it."

"That can't be done."

"It has to be done, damn you."

"You don't understand. There is no one to call. No one has been here except the gentleman you are charged with assaulting. I don't know who this Maria is."

"She's—it's her house that 'gentleman' lives in. I rent a room there. That's where my medication is. You have to get it for me."

"You rent a room there?"

"Yes. From Maria."

Another long pause. "The gentleman said that you were found, bleeding and delirious, back up the highway. He stated to the officers that he aided you after a motor vehicle accident."

"That's not true."

"Was there a motor vehicle accident?"

"No. Yes, but that was days and days ago, and I wasn't injured."

"That's not what the gentleman told the officer."

"I don't give a damn what he told the cops, he is lying. My injuries are from that piece of shit assaulting me."

"The gentleman stated that you refused hospitalization and you were allowed to recover at his home. After you had done so, he stated that you became aggressive and irrational. When he asked you to leave, you assaulted him. He managed to remove you from the premises and call the police. You attempted to force re-entry, at which time the police arrived."

"That's bullshit. Look, at least call Maria."

"There was no one mentioned by that name."

"She's—"

"There was no one mentioned by that name."

"I can give you her number. You call her." Allen shouted Maria's number out and waited. He thought he could hear footsteps leaving, then returning a few minutes later.

"The number you gave me belongs to the gentleman you are accused of assaulting."

"They live together. Or they did. Did you talk to her?"

"No."

"Why the hell not?"

"There was no one mentioned—"

"Oh piss off."

"Is there anything else that you would like?"

"I would like for you to go away."

There was much Allen could have told the voice on the other side of the door. There were narratives of suffering and of wonder. There were other voices, speaking words unimagined by that jailer voice, and there were landscapes where extinct creatures still walked, drinking from cool rivers. But it would have done no good. He could have shouted and no one would have heard. It was a voice only, Allen knew that, and as cold and lonely as this cell world was, a lonesome land awaited that was far colder, a nation of solitude that would make that voice weep with shame and pity.

So he let it be. The last lines were being cut and he was unmoored, drifting down, one tiny shell casting, destined for the lime.

And then it was the abiding in the deep. It was forever Sunday and the scuttling things that swallow carrion and drink draughts of seawater snapped their claws and danced. The feast was from sun to sun, all dipping from the same pot of oil, smiling, and one of them a devil. It all came down to them, eventually. They plucked their meat from the gooey sands and stuffed it in their pincer jaws. If one should lose a limb, it just grew back. They were immortal, their hunger endless, endlessly feeding hunger.

And then there was the rising. Through gas chambers, over sheeted dykes, boiling pools saffron with the stink of life not lived. Spewed out on calcite shores, crawling, wriggling, dragging to the cool amnesiac snow under forests. A sputtering indigo thing, grabbing planet hide, hissing, muttering, cursing, praying to a god unborn. A blasphemer crying wolf, profane and full of envy.

And then there was the folding of hands, the repose of opaque eyelids, light sequestered from the hollows of his cheeks, brow unfurled like a flag of peace, the poor ragged quilt draped on its loom, weaving shuttle snapped in two. But the lips were parted and small breaths fogged the frozen air. Death was cheated and went away, biding his time. The sleeper only slept, and his dreams rolled through the countless hours like a wheel on fire.

And finally there was the waking up. From the vital recesses of the liver, a pulsing along the strands of wire, viaducts, canals, water gates sluicing buckets full of blood sugar and patented chemicals. The throttle fell, the flywheel spun, the piston rose and dropped, and a thrumming hymn rose steadily in the watchtower.

Now what had been pale music caught words in its chords and the captured verses jitterbugged behind the sleeper's eyes. His lips opened wider and he croaked, *Yes*. And the answer was more than enough. He had agreed, and that agreement was signed without further negotiation.

He trembled under the weight of one more day.

The ghost of daylight entered Allen's cell. The steel door had opened quietly on well-oiled hinges, but the barest change in the room's monotony found its way into his mind, like lost rainwater in a well. He lay on his back, head to the side, watching the door swing wider, its progress not entirely silent: there was a faint friction, a faraway slipping-across.

"Here" It was the voice from earlier. "He hasn't moved much."

The door opened and Ted came in. He stood in a wedge of sunlight, smiling down at Allen on his jail cot. "Here you are."

Allen raised a hand. "If you say so."

Ted stepped forward, stooped and put a hand on Allen's shoulder. "Didn't think you could get any thinner. You been eating anything?"

"I don't think so."

"He's only taken water," the voice said from behind the door.

Ted's eyes narrowed, the first hint of anger in him that Allen had ever noticed. He turned his head to address the doorway. "I'd like a few minutes to talk with my friend here." His voice was calm. "Please leave us."

There were no further sounds outside the cell, and Allen knew they were alone. "Thank you," he said. "Thank you."

"For what?"

"For not forgetting me."

It took an effort for Allen to sit up, but once he did his strength found him. Ted gave him water and helped him to his feet.

"How long have I been here?"

"Three days."

"Three. I must stink."

"You're okay. And you look sharp in that orange jumpsuit."

"Goes well with pallor."

"You look like a Creamsicle."

"Don't talk about food. Anyway. It's nice to stand up. Glad I can. When can I leave here, or can I?"

"You can come with me now."

"They're really letting me go, then."

"On bail."

"Bail? Ted, you didn't—"

"Don't worry about it."

Allen took two steps. "I can walk." He grabbed Ted's shoulder. "I can sort of walk. Hey, lead the way out. There's a bank next to your place, same one I bank at down in the Bay Area. I'll go and have funds transferred right away."

Ted took him by the arm and led him to the door. "Don't worry about that. What you need is food, if you can manage it."

"I could manage some soup." Allen remembered Maria's soups and stopped. "I wonder where she is."

Without replying, Ted led Allen through the door and out into a long hallway, painted the same glossy gray, skylights letting in the distant sun.

Allen blinked. "Hallelujah."

The hall led past more steel doors to a common area dominated by a sort of pod in the middle where a deputy in khaki stared at a computer screen. Allen wondered if that voice (it seemed from so long ago) belonged to him. There was no one else in the room.

Ted took Allen over to the deputy. "This man needs his clothes."

The deputy pointed to a door on the far side of the room. As they approached it a solenoid kicked the latch free and they entered a small cell with a cement bench and a steel-grated window, to the left of which was another door.

Allen looked at the window. "Confessions, Ted?"

Ted pushed a buzzer to the right of the window. After some time, the steel grate slid aside and Allen's former clothes tumbled through. Ted handed them to Allen and pushed another buzzer by the exit door. It clacked and he opened it. "I'll be in the lobby. Just push the buzzer when you're ready to leave. Then let's get the hell out of here."

Ted's car navigated the back streets from the old courthouse to his bar. He avoided Main, for which Allen was grateful. It was cold afternoon and the sky leaned close and sullen. They parked in the alley behind the bar. Allen was able to get out of the car and into the bar without assistance, and Ted led the way through the store room and a small kitchen stocked with jars and cans.

The bar was closed. Allen took his customary seat by the cash register. Ted resumed his station behind the bar and Allen barked a dry chuckle. "Got a coke?"

"Sure." Ted was already reaching for one. "Drink that and I'll make you some soup." He looked at Allen as if for the first time. "You need anything for that face?"

"Long past time for that, Ted." Ted smiled and Allen returned it weakly. "Maybe a couple aspirin."

"Be out in a minute."

It had been nearly four days since Allen had taken his medication. Enough time to be fatal, he had been led to believe, or paralyzed, crippled with respiratory failure, foaming at the mouth, deranged, in pain, barking like a dog. But none of that had happened. He was sore and tired. He was possibly withdrawing from some of the narcotics, although he'd been careful to calibrate them to the pain and avoid dependency as much as possible. Mostly though he was—he searched for a word—clearer. The glaze pealed back and something like being awake, willed or unwilled, crept up on him. Along with this new alertness came the certain knowledge of his disease and its plans for him. It fixed its gaze on him and he looked back at it, no shield between them. It should have terrified. He had been terrified of it terrifying him, but it did not. He looked at it and there was no fear at all. It simply was. He was there with it, and simply was as well. The disease would do its work, but that didn't matter. He'd lived with that certainty a long time and by now that was a dry fact, without much punch left in it. The days were short, and the shedding was near.

"I don't think I will miss you." Allen spoke to his reflection and his reflection spoke to him, from the smoky mercury of the back-bar mirror. "I don't think you will miss me, either, but that's none of my business." He thought a moment. "It's none of your business, either."

The mirror quivered, and Allen's battered face clouded. Something had moved, way down low. He waited for it to happen again. It did not, but Allen was now attuned to the regions under his barstool: the clatter of latches, the pulling of weights, the slithering of stone. His three days in the cell had led him down to the deep places. He had visited molten chambers, walked the groaning paths and splintered halls of the Nether Kingdom where mute nations contended with that for which millennia are bare ciphers, where stone giants wrestled and struck with heavy fists. He knew that a revolution brewed beneath his feet, and a great schism, long in the making, was about to break the bonds of friction and gravity, throw off the mantle, leap around naked and reckless, not caring a bit for the soft things it smashed or the high places it threw down. This power would not even notice those it destroyed. They did not speak its language and they did not figure in its grinding calculus.

The half-blind, tunnel-crawling hole-dwelling creatures knew. They read the warnings telegraphed through soil and stone and they chattered in terror and anticipation.

It was coming.

Allen looked away from the mirror just in time to see the Buick Wildcat flash by, headed down Jefferson to Main.

Liz could have had visited Maria, told her everything, such as there was there to tell. When they were young, they had rolled in the firmness of each other, arms and legs and thighs, wild hair, faces pressed in fever and wonder, astonished that bodies could do this. They went to the river and jumped in. They spread themselves on the emerald grass while the earth beneath them slouched toward Megiddo. They hadn't cared and the earth hadn't cared. There was no time for them and they were there still, jumbled in each other, tangled in each other, spirits endlessly summoned to meet at the place where long-forsaken shadows fall together.

He turned back from the window and Ted was there, holding a bowl of soup. Allen took it and began to eat. "Did you feel that?" he asked.

Ted handed him two aspirin. "What?'

"That little jolt, under us."

"Yes. I did."

"The bit of crust you're on is going north and another bit of crust is going south."

"Passing each other by."

"Yes. But not without some disagreement."

"About what?

"Who knows. But here we are and there we were. Going all directions at once."

"Could get confusing."

"It already has."

Ted smiled. "Anything you can do about it?"

Allen looked in the mirror at his pulverized face as he poured soup into it. He looked back at Ted. "No. There's nothing anyone can do about it."

"It will do what it wants to do."

"Yes. It doesn't even know we're here. If it knew, it wouldn't care."

"Well that's that, then."

Off the kitchen in the back of Ted's bar was a small apartment with a bed and a bathroom. After Allen finished his soup, Ted showed him to the quarters. "Stay here. As long as you like."

"Thank you. Thank you so much."

"If anyone asks for you, what should I say?"

"No one's going to ask for me."

"What makes you so sure."

"It's not possible now."

"If they should try the impossible, what would you like me to tell them?"

Allen took off his torn trench coat and threw it on the bed. "Tell them anything you like."

Ted left and Allen stood in the windowless room. "How do you do this," he said aloud. "How do you do this?" He sat on the bed and thought of his room at Maria's. That had been his home, and now this was. For a night in between his home had been above Lottie's Diner in Gold Flat. Then there had been the jail cell. "This part of the procedure, it seems, means taking rooms with others until you don't need to anymore."

That satisfied the question. He lay on the bed and stared at the pressed tin ceiling. He tried to summon up images, as he had always done, but the ceiling stayed where it was and no past came calling. A stillness hovered. Here in the back room behind Ted's bar it could be any time of day or night, and so it was: a place between and beyond, a space to continue for a little longer. Few other obligations came to mind, except the need to get to the bank on the corner to transfer funds. He would move all the money from the Bay Area here to Forester if he was able. Those would be the last little pieces of Allen Wrangell, and some good might come of that yet, some fragment of cheerful silver dust.

"The smaller I get, the happier I am." He detested the battered bird man that had his name. There was nothing to love in that tired sinew and frayed muscle, torn hair, ragged nails. His head was scabbed, striated with abrasions, mashed, punched, misshapen. Nothing in him didn't ache or burn. He was a horror show. A piece of pain. Letting himself go was the single greatest joy remaining and he was ready.

The iron-frame bed on which Allen lay hopped and wiggled. His dry hair waved like some undersea creature. He smiled and crossed his hands over his chest. "The earth is restless."

Chapter Twenty-Three

In his half century Allen had moved through the requisite stages—infancy and childhood, adolescence, young adulthood and middle age—leaving as little a mark as it is possible for one life to leave. As he lay drifting back to consciousness he knew now with an unexpected acuteness that he would not see old age. He lay in the semi-dark and wondered what being old would have been like, but it was no more possible to grasp a future Allen Wrangell than it was to view the Allen Wrangell that had been.

And yet back at Maria's he'd slowly become aware of a new possibility. Something in the way the land was moving, not forward or backward. Neither was it moving sideways, up or down. It was moving *through*. When Allen had gone voyaging he had traveled the same way the land was moving. There was no way—not from here or from anywhere—to know where it was moving.

"It's moving nowhere," Allen said aloud. "It's moving when, not where."

As far as he could tell, he'd slept the clock around and surfaced again in morning. He hadn't died. Quite the opposite, his energies had returned. When he stretched, there was less fire and stiffness in his joints. His muscles too had cooled, and the deep ache had diminished.

Sitting up, he saw a pitcher of water and a glass on the night stand. Ted had been in. Allen drank and came fully-awake.

He hadn't sat long when there was a tap on door. "Come in."

Ted entered with a cup of coffee and a plate of toast. "You take jam?"

"No, that's, um, that's great, thanks." Allen took the cup and plate, setting them on the night stand by the water pitcher. "What time is it?"

"It's morning."

"I slept a whole day."

"Two. Two days. You kept missing your meals."

Allen nibbled the toast. "Thanks, Ted. Thank you."

"No problem. How is it all going?"

"Not bad, considering the alternative."

"Stronger?"

"Think so. I need to be. I have some stuff to do before—I have some stuff to do."

"Okay. Do it when you're ready." He started to leave, then stopped. "You feel that shaking again, a couple days ago?"

"Yes."

"Things still moving down there. Getting more frequent."

"Yes."

He continued to the door. "All right. I'll let you wake up. If you need anything, I'm in the bar for a while, then I have to, um, go attend to a few things."

"A few things?"

"Business. Business is all."

"Okay. Ted, I—I just want to say—"

"You've said it. Just get better. Get as good as you can get. You might surprise yourself. You could get a few surprises before it's over."

The door closed and Allen took stock. With strength and life came obligation. He had to move. Observing himself, he found his outlines roughly the same as he had left them, just with the bony protrusions protruding more, skin stretched a bit thinner and more translucent. He could see more clearly. Everything in the plain room—worn asphalt tile, leathery papered walls, dull enamels and ancient tin—looked full of strange hues, new and without names. The still air was charged with fearless bright motion, something hurrying in between the places he could see, something afoot, something that wanted out and free.

He sighed. The burden of breathing grew easier. Whatever thrummed in the air rushed into his lungs, pushing out his chest walls, pulling out exhausted atoms. He drew courage. The bad airs were in turn drawn away, to trouble him no more this day. He was lighter. He was younger.

It was too late to be joyful, but not too late to laugh, and so he did; not the dry bark of two days ago, but something almost merry.

Allen tried standing. His legs were heavy. They were half-numb. But they worked. He walked, pacing the little space, gathering momentum. When he gained enough strength, he went to the bathroom, stripped and showered. He wanted to stay naked, in water, the rest of his days.

Ted had left a new toothbrush and a small tube of toothpaste on the bathroom sink. Brushing, Allen knew pleasure such as dental care had never before provided. He had to make himself stop scrubbing. The jail had washed his clothes and they were still reasonably fresh. The pants and shirt were nonetheless ripped and stained and Allen wished he had a change of clothes to go with his newly-washed self. With no other choice, he put the old rags back on. He would have to go about like a beggar, but he was now ready, ragged or not, to fulfill his final obligations. Pulling on his trench coat, he went to the door and opened it.

Maria stood in the hall, Allen's suitcase at her feet.

It wasn't necessary to say anything, which made everything they said especially good. The music of her voice was like spring, when insistent life pushes up from the grave of earth. His answers rang from the hollows of the mountains, and the wild night voices sang with them, laughed soundlessly with them, chorused together as Maria's hand fitted into his.

"I thought you forgot me."

"I thought you forgot me."

"I went to your room and knocked. You never answered."

"I also went to your room and knocked. You never opened the door."

She sat on the bed beside him and he kissed her with cracked lips. "I'm sorry," he said. "My face is a mess."

She stroked his broken cheek. "Thinner still."

"I'll try to eat more."

"I left you food every day."

"I found the food you left for me. I ate the food."

"I know. That's how I knew you were still with me. But I never saw you."

"I was there. But we went past each other."

She smiled. "Like your rocks. Your stone islands slipping past each other."

"And slipping under," he replied. "Going under."

"You are not going under yet."

"No. I still have things to do. I know that. I have to get things done before—"

She placed a finger on his mouth, gently. "You need to eat."

He covered her coffee milk hand with his bruised one. "You know."

"I know what?"

"Maria, I'm dying."

She frowned and looked down. After a moment she said, "You still see your reflection, in the glass."

"Yes."

"Then here you are still."

Allen looked at the suitcase, sitting by the door. "You brought it."

"Yes. Everything."

"I'd like to change clothes." Allen let go of her hand and went over to the suitcase. "Everything?"

"Your medication is in there, on top. I didn't poke around. Just put the bottles in."

"It wouldn't matter. There's nothing interesting in there." He hefted the suitcase. "Feels a little heavier."

"That rock you had in the room. It's in there."

"Oh, good." He laid the suitcase on the bed and opened it. The bit of seafloor lay there, still journeying. It would travel with him to the end of the earth. "Thanks." He reached first for the bottles of medicine.

Maria touched his arm. "Allen."

He looked at her. Her eyes were lowered. He said, "Yes?"

"I, um—" She looked away. "I did look at the medicine you take."

"That's all right. I don't care."

"You know, I looked it all up and there are—there are problems."

"What kind of problems."

"Have you seen a doctor recently?"

"No."

"Just from what little I've picked up doing the medical billing, I, I've learned a little bit, and as I said, I looked up your medicines. There are some you shouldn't be taking together."

"No?"

"No. It's not good. You have a lot of doctors."

"Had. I don't see them anymore."

"And that's part of the problem. A bunch of doctors writing prescriptions for lots of meds and it's possible they don't know about each other, and you are taking medicine for a condition that has—that has changed."

"Gotten worse."

"That could be, but no matter what is wrong with you, no matter how much it's doing to you, that stuff in the pill bottles is even worse."

Allen sat by her. "What do you suggest?"

"I suggest you see a doctor."

"I'm not going to do that."

"Then," she reached in the suitcase and pulled out three bottles, "just take these. And one kind of pain pill, not four."

Allen took the bottles. "Doctor Maria."

"You won't go to a real doctor. You get what you get." She looked at him sternly, but she smiled.

Allen got fresh clothes from the suitcase. "I'll be right back."

"Okay."

"Maria."

"Yes, Allen."

"What did you think of her?"

"What did I think of—"

"Of Liz. When she came. To the house, what did you think of her."

"I—I didn't see her. There wasn't—there hasn't been anyone at the house."

"But she was there. She was there and you were there. You saw her, you must have."

"I didn't see anyone."

"That day, that day when someone came to the door. I could tell that whomever it was, you weren't happy they were there. That was Liz, wasn't it? On that day?"

Maria thought a moment. "No," she said at last. "No, it was one of DJ's bar buddies. I remember now, if it's the day you were thinking of. He came to the door looking for DJ. Just one of his lousy bar buddies."

Allen looked into her eyes. "Tell me you are real. That you're really here."

Maria looked back, unwavering. "I'm real. I'm really here."

Allen knitted his fingers together. "Maria."

"Yes, Allen."

"I don't trust my hands."

"I do."

"I will see a doctor. Later. If."

"You have time."

"If."

"Change your clothes, huh?"

It didn't take long to get into the new clothes. His ruined old ones he placed in the bathroom waste basket. Looking in the mirror, Allen saw that he was in fact still looking back at himself. Somehow the face didn't seem as ruined as it felt. He took the pills Maria had suggested, straightened his shirt and tried to look chipper.

When he came back to her, Maria clapped her hands. "Much nicer. Do you feel better?"

"Yeah. Clothes make the man." He reached his hands to her and pulled her up. Holding her close, he smelled the sweet oat and lemon of her, embraced her thin, strong waist. He put his face in her hair. "Where I come from," he said, "In the late spring, there are bachelor buttons."

"What are they?"

"Flowers. Poor flowers, plain, that come along after most of the other flowers are done blooming, when the fields are turning brown."

"Lonely flowers."

"Yes. I imagined that they were called bachelor buttons because poor boys picked them, too late, and brought them to girls who didn't want them."

"And the poor boys went away."

"Yes, they went away."

"Allen..."

"I love you, Maria."

"I love you."

They sat on the bed, still holding each other. The plain metal bed frame sang a little under them, and they laughed. They clasped hands and they kissed and the kissing was so inebriating they had to stop. Then they started all over again. Then they had to stop once more.

"I'm panting," Maria said, and she laughed.

"I have that effect on women," Allen said.

Maria pulled back and looked at him. "Really. Have you had lots of women, Allen?"

He couldn't tell if the question was a serious one or not. Erring on the side of caution he answered with gravity, "No."

Maria smiled. "None of that matters."

"No. This is what matters."

"This has always been what matters. All that will ever matter."

Allen kissed her cheek. "This has always been."

"Yes."

They lay together and Allen was clumsy. He hated his hands and his bruised face. He hated his skeleton body.

But Maria held his hands to her belly and kissed his bruises. She kissed his scarecrow body and called him beautiful.

Allen could not believe that, but he knew that Maria was there and that she really was beautiful. She was the most beautiful human who had ever been and even though he was clumsy and deaf and mute and terrified he could trust her, trust the beauty in Maria, radiating out from her, her cinnamon hands and lotus belly. He could trust her eyes, like shining black seeds, searching out a place to plant in him, and when they planted they would root in him, and when they rooted they would grow in him and she would see his every inside secret and she would still love him, love him all the more. Her hips and legs were strong from journeys in the night places, where she walked, in the same places he had limped, under the moon.

Now he saw her mouth again. It might have been the first time he saw it, curved like an Arab knife, and she was like an Arab girl, from Al-Andalus, speaking in masonry arabesques, sweet knives like sharp flowers. She murmured her Andalusian prayers and he nodded, and she kissed him with her curved mouth and the kiss was a sweet cutting, without pain, only merciful with a sure and placid desire.

Allen remembered now. Ted had said, "It's not asking too much to want kindness."

He thought he had known what Ted meant, but Allen had no idea that this was it. This kindness was wise. It was fierce, and its language was desire, written across lips that curved and smiled, and the smile of that mouth was adamantine. Its kindness was strong and tough, unrelenting in its mercy. The breath of freedom was in its wordless words.

Steadily their arms drew each other tight, hip and thigh, feet entangled. Maria's breasts pressed against him and he started to pull away, but she held him the more insistently. Her lips found his once again, and this time they did not stop.

The bar was empty. Allen had hoped to see Ted still there, but found only a note, taped to the front door. He carefully untaped it and turned it around. It said, *Away on business.*

Maria, coming up behind him, read the note. "Nobody here."

"No. He's gone."

"Who is he?"

"Ted." Allen taped the note back to the glass. "Ted the bartender."

"Oh. Is he your friend?" Maria sat at the bar. "This Ted. Ted the Bartender. What's he like?"

"Well you've seen him. You must have talked with him. What's your impression."

"Seen him? I didn't see anyone."

Allen sat beside her. "Ted. The bartender. Didn't he come and get you, just now? Didn't he—"

"I drove here." Maria looked out at the morning cars going up and down Jefferson. "I took the truck. I got a note, that's all. The note said you were here."

"You didn't—"

"No, I saw no one." She leaned against him, he put his arms around her and they sat, the two of them, alone in the bar. "I parked in the alley."

"You drove here. You really did that."

She nodded. "It wasn't easy."

"No. No, I imagine not. Did you do that because you love me?"

"What do you think?"

"Um? Yes?"

She laughed. "Now, when do you think this Ted will come back? I would like to meet him."

Allen shook his head. "He won't be back. Not any time soon."

"He might come back. Is he a good man? He must be."

"He's a good man." He shook his head again. "A very good man. I owe him bail money."

"You owe him bail money?"

"You are in the arms of a criminal, Maria. One who plans to be a fugitive."

"The fight, you and DJ."

"Yeah. The DJ Thing and me. Didn't you hear that commotion?"

"No. I heard nothing. Later on, DJ said you attacked him and of course I knew he was lying. He wouldn't tell me where you'd gone. I waited for you to come back, but you never did."

"Well, while you were blissfully unaware at the back of the house, I was getting hauled out the front gate by some pimply cop with a wad of chew in his mouth."

"You?"

"Yeah. DJ spun a line of crap and they believed him."

"So, DJ is your victim? That's how it works?"

"Yeah. If your victim was born in this town and you weren't. But it won't matter. It's not going to matter at all. I'm going to leave here, too."

"So am I."

"Yeah? Good. I don't guess you'd want a criminal riding along with you."

"I would love a criminal riding along with me."

"A dangerous man."

Maria laughed. "You said you didn't have enough imagination to get into trouble, remember?"

"Yes. I remember."

"Well you were wrong."

"I've been wrong about many things."

"Sometimes that's okay." She touched his arm, stroked it. "I'll drive anywhere you like."

"I'll buy the gas. So. Speaking of DJ."

"He's back there. At the house."

"Is he, now."

"He was gone, for a while, but he came back. He always comes back."

"And you let him."

"He didn't—he didn't come to my room. He stayed in one of the guest rooms. I had to let him. It's his house."

"His!"

"His mother's. But she lives in town now, in a rest home. So he gets the house. He'll never leave. He'll never leave and he'll never grow up. He's there now, eating himself up."

"But he's not eating you up anymore."

"No." Maria stood. "I am free."

Allen stood and took her hand. They walked back down the bar. "That's all that counts. Come on, let's go."

"Where?"

"I don't think it matters, do you."

"No. No, it doesn't matter."

"There's a little town not far from here. Even smaller than this one. Have you been there?"

"No. When I came here I stayed here, in Forester. I've never been anywhere, not for years and years."

"Then let's go there. It's up in the mountains, the real mountains, high up, where the wild things go to be safe. There's a little place there, it's run by a very nice woman. I rented a room from her. It's over the restaurant. It's a great restaurant. I like this place a lot."

"Then I will like it, too."

"I hope so." They reached the kitchen door and Allen turned, giving the bar a final look. It reposed in amber light, smoky and far off, a scene viewed through evening air, through long years and lives of men, an axis on which turned matters small and great, wicked and good. Tonight, it would still be here and there might be customers and there might just be Ted, standing patient and expectant, waiting. It had been Allen's refuge and he already missed it. "I don't know how long I have."

"Yes. Yes, that's true."

"It could get very bad, near the end."

"I know."

"If I tell you that you have to go, will you promise to go?"

"No, Allen. I can't promise you that. I can't promise you anything more than you can promise me. It would probably be a lie."

"All right. No promises."

Chapter Twenty-Four

It took a while to do his banking business. Over Maria's protests Allen added her to his accounts, then took out enough cash to see them comfortably through the winter. After looking at his face, the bank officer had asked Maria to leave while she quizzed Allen about the whole business. He endured her concern with equanimity and, satisfied that Allen could make informed decisions and knew the nature, location and extent of his bounty, the officer conducted the transactions.

It was afternoon when they left the bank. Allen squinted at Main Street's thin, busy emptiness, his gaze pulled down and across the street to a far glint of office plate glass. "We're done here."

"I didn't want that."

"The account stuff? I had asked Ted to take care of this and he agreed. But he's gone and you're here. I'm sure he knows that. I have no one else, Maria. No family. A few nieces and nephews, at most, who don't even know I'm alive and won't know when I'm gone. When that happens, do what you want with the money, but keep enough to live where you like, be comfortable. There's enough there. I never spent much, when I was working. I had nothing much to spend it on."

"I don't want your money."

"It doesn't really matter what you want."

"Oh, really?" Maria's indignation was only partially in jest. "That's so, is it?"

Allen laughed and touched her arm. "It's only money. I'll live happier knowing you'll be okay. You know how much to give to Ted, if he ever comes back."

"Will he come back?"

"He felt the earth moving. Didn't you?"

"I did, yes. It's happened before."

"Oh, yes," Allen said. "Many times. And it's getting ready to move and shake and throw this whole valley around."

"When, do you think."

"In its time? Soon. In our time, who knows. In either time, it's a minute before midnight. How long that minute is, that's the question."

"But if you think it will be soon, shouldn't these people be warned?"

Allen looked back up Main, at the little procession of shopping, driving and gossip. He had sudden pity for this poor, thoughtless little place. "I guess we could stand in the middle of the street and proclaim the end is near."

Maria followed his gaze. "We could."

"And I'd be back in the slammer in no time. No, people a lot smarter than I am have been warning towns a lot bigger than this one that they're riding the tiger. No one notices until the tiger swallows them."

"There are all kinds of tigers."

"There are. Yes, there are."

"So, we can't do anything? Nothing at all?"

"Ted warned me that there were things moving that were far bigger than we are. I think I know now what he meant, Maria."

"That things are actually moving. That things are always moving like that." She took his arm and they started walking.

"Yes. Yes. And we're taken along, whether we like it or not. The mountains move around us. The land beneath the mountains moves, and there are lands beneath that land moving, turning, falling and rising. We see only the smallest bit of it and we think that this is all there is."

"And you? Do you see more?"

"I only guess at more."

"And what's your guess, Allen? Do you have one now?"

They rounded Main on to Jefferson. "I don't dare guess, Maria. And I don't dare hope."

"Then I'll hope. I will hope for both of us."

"You'll have to."

"I will."

"No matter how it turns out, Maria, I know this— our luck has changed."

"Yes, so put your hope in that."

He stopped. "Here we are."

The alley behind Ted's bar was a secret place, unpaved, shrouded with faded vines and boxwood hedges, creosote-stained, puddled, overlooked. Maria's truck huddled by the rusted steel back door, in the shadow of brick and dripping pipes. Their luggage was already in the jump seat. They got in, Maria started the truck and they sat, listening to the motor run.

Allen leaned over and kissed her cheek, honored by the privilege. "Thank you. Thank you for making me lucky. Thank you for loving me."

"Do you love me any less than I love you?"

"No." He put his arm across the back of her seat. "I could climb a mountain and fight a bear."

She laughed and threw the truck in gear. "Could you. Well, you should eat first."

"Let's wait. Let's wait until we're out of here. It isn't too far, to that little town."

"If you like." Maria's knuckles whitened. She gripped the wheel as the truck emerged from the alley on to Jefferson. "Oh."

"You okay?"

She stopped the truck halfway into the street. "No. No. I am afraid."

"I'm not. We are lucky now, Maria. Our luck has turned. You could climb a mountain and fight a bear, too."

She shook her head. "I'm afraid."

"You don't have to be. But if you are, eat the fear. Just eat it up."

"It was difficult enough to come this far. One street."

"Same street. It's the same damned street, wherever you go."

"Yes." She let her breath out, put her foot on the gas and the truck cleared the alley. "I wish you could drive."

"Oh, you don't really, no. I'm pretty tough on vehicles. But give me some time in those mountains. I'll drive again. I'll, I'll eat a tree and pick my teeth with its branches. I'll skin a cougar and drink a river."

Maria drove through the intersection, heading north on Main. "And I will take this one road with you. I'll go where it goes."

The road to Gold Flat traveled from fall to winter. As the truck climbed through the canyon, the trees lost their last color and bare limbs reached over cold water to a glacier sky. The falling waters pooled into mirrors of that sky and Allen looked into them as they passed. Looked in and looked up.

Soon the snow would fall. The eyes of the water would film and close. All around the land would lie swaddled and silent, crossed only by the sharp tracks of the mountain folk, those that remained awake, calling and crying, hunting in the sleeping season. He didn't know if he would be awake to hear them.

Maria's grip loosened on the wheel. The higher they rose, the more lightly she grasped, until she steered the truck easily through the turns. Looking over at Allen, she touched his shoulder. "How are you?"

He looked back at her. "You can see everything in that water."

"Can you? And what do you see?"

"I see" —he raised his hands— "Just everything."

"And how is everything."

"It's good. Everything's good."

"When I was a girl," she said, "back where I'm from, there was a river kind of like this one."

"You're from the mountains."

"Yes. The mountains. They could be cousins of these mountains, I don't know. You would know. But they weren't as cold. Anyway, yes, and there was a river, like this one, but not as cold. This one looks so cold."

"It is. Just a little warmer than ice and snow."

"Well, our river was warm, pretty warm. And we swam in it as soon as we learned how. When I was a girl I went there as often as I could."

Allen resumed looking out the window, at the river that was not warm, the river that ran with cold sky. He thought of the bathing girls in the Gauguin prints on the wall of his now-forlorn room at Maria's. "Very nice. Very nice."

"It was. And I would paddle out in the pool, and look up between the branches of the trees. These trees, they didn't lose their leaves, as these have. It was all a dream, the water and the sky and my little body, dissolving in it."

"You must have swum a long time, to dissolve like that."

"I swam forever. And falling into that pool was a waterfall, not very big. It came over the cliff from a pool higher up, just running over the moss and falling into my pool. And I would watch it, and see how it broke into drops, big and small, or held together in shiny ribbons that braided together until they fell into the water below."

"Like these pools here," Allen said. "And these little waterfalls."

"Yes, but I imagine these will freeze pretty soon."

"Probably, yes. I imagine so."

"These never froze. They just kept on going, the same waterfalls, the same river, coming from where I didn't know and going to where I didn't know."

"And you stayed."

"Yes. I stayed. And nothing changed, except that water was always new water. A waterfall for a while. Then a pool. Then a river. It started as snow, or rain, going into the rock, coming out of the rock, rolling past me, all around me, then gone, but always more. And, where I couldn't see it, it could have become a swamp or filled a ditch to irrigate melons or cotton. Or it kept going all the way to the sea."

"But where you were?"

"Where I was, it was waterfall and pool. It still is. It is that forever."

Allen wanted to tell Maria that it was not that, not forever. But of course she knew that. It wasn't necessary to say it. The patient water, river, falls, pool, rain and snow ate the rock and soil over which it ran. Stone by stone, pebble by pebble, grain by grain the water carried mountains away. River became canyon, canyon became valley, valley became plain and all were carried to the sea, spread out, washed and sorted, baked and glazed with the cast off armor of dead sea things, folded, pressed, uplifted again into mountains, carrying along with them islands, ocean floors, the burst-through hot planet blood, pouring in new stone rivers down the sides of new terrain.

But it wasn't necessary to say it. She already knew. She had learned it in that pool, that warm cousin of these cold pools, in her childhood long ago.

Soon they'd be in the mountain town, nested safe above the diner, warm, replenished, their bones young with good luck. They would lie together as long as their luck held out. Sometimes they would go out, mingling their tracks with the mountain hunter folk, and would return to soup and fire, skin alive with ice, lips as new as babies'.

Down in the foothills, someday, the earth would move again. The restless fragment of a long-gone island would rise up and strike the land that had caught it in its teeth. Streets would heave and buckle. Bridges would fall, gorges collapsing around them in a racket of crashing plates. Buildings would gallop until they died, falling like foundered beasts on their masters, shrieking windows, glass splintered into pitiless knives. The sagging courthouse would split in two and give up its dead. The condemned would have their redemption. The law would be fulfilled, every jot and tittle.

And somewhere in the ruin a white Buick would run, chasing from one broken street to the next, turning back at the outskirts of the burning town to disappear once again in its jealous smoke. It would go like that. The gear was thrown; wheels turned, the great ragged maw opened. There would come the fall and there would be no rising up. When it was satisfied, the earth would sleep.

Allen looked away from the window and watched Maria drive. She looked back at him and smiled. The canyon was coming to an end, the road leveling out into the high valley.

They were almost there.

ABOUT THE AUTHOR

Philip Newton is an author, poet and musician living in Oregon. He blogs at www.newtonword.com. His poems, articles and essays have recently appeared in Ink in Thirds, Here Comes Everyone, Coal Magazine, Ibis Head Review, Scriblerus Journal and others. His original music has been recorded on multiple studio albums and receives airplay worldwide. He is represented by Natalie Galustian at DHH Literary in London, UK.

ABOUT THE PRESS

UNSOLICITED PRESS is a small publishing house based in Portland, Oregon. Learn more at www.unsolicitedpress.com